FIC HAN
Hansen, Peggy, 1953-
War widow
2801386383   12.56

WAR WIDOW

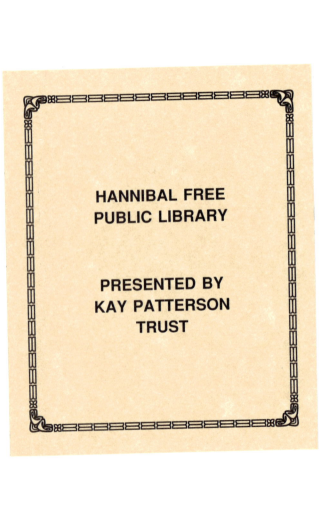

WAR WIDOW

•

Peggy Hansen

AVALON BOOKS
NEW YORK

© Copyright 2007 by Peggy Hansen
All rights reserved.
All the characters in the book are fictitious,
and any resemblance to actual persons,
living or dead, is purely coincidental.
Published by Thomas Bouregy & Co., Inc.
160 Madison Avenue, New York, NY 10016

Library of Congress Cataloging-in-Publication Data

Hansen, Peggy, 1953–
　War widow / Peggy Hansen.
　　p. cm.
　ISBN 978-0-8034-9827-3 (hardcover : acid-free paper)
　1. Authors—Fiction. 2. Widows—Fiction. 3. Veterans—Fiction. 4. London (England)—Fiction. I. Title.

PS3573.E87W37 2007
813'.6—dc22

2006101344

PRINTED IN THE UNITED STATES OF AMERICA
ON ACID-FREE PAPER
BY HADDON CRAFTSMEN, BLOOMSBURG, PENNSYLVANIA

For George, Shadow, and Bear, and
the summer days.

Chapter One

London, 1919

Allan Marchmont's seat on the windowsill gave him a good view of the pavement two stories below. It was the end of the luncheon hour, and clerks were hurrying back into the various business firms that clustered around the Covent Garden area.

He knew his attitude made him a throwback to Victorian times—his female cousins and even his mother often informed him of this—but he still couldn't get over the fact that so many of the office workers were women now. He remembered going on an errand to his bank in the City in what seemed like only yesterday, before the Great War, looking down from a window as he was looking down now, and seeing a moving herd of bowler hats broken only by the very rare flowered saucer of a pioneering typist or switchboard girl.

If he reached back even further into his past, to a time when he had been taken into the City by his father as a treat before the turn of the century, he didn't remember seeing any women at all, though of course even then a small number must have been there.

More women to look at! If he considered it that way, another attitude his female relations would deplore, this was one enjoyable change the war had made in the daily life of London. Allan's gaze lingered on one pleasing figure in particular, a young woman running across to his side of the congested roadway. He had a view of shapely leg and lacy petticoat as she narrowly missed being hit by a two-seater auto driven by someone in a large flat cap. The cap shook his fist at the young woman, and she laughed and waved in return, the picture of good humor and modern heedlessness. Her hair was gold under one of those droopy hats. Allan caught the merest glimpse of a most attractive face.

Then the girl made it to his side of the street and he had only a bird's-eye view of the top of her hat and her flashing heels as she ran up the steps directly below. She was in the building with him.

"Are there any offices here but your own, old boy?" he asked the other man in the room in a casual tone.

The room in question was a book-and-manuscript-strewn sanctum of the type often inhabited by up-and-coming young editors. Allan was rather crowded upon the wide windowsill; he and a foot-high stack of literary reviews, a cricket bat, and a potted palm probably introduced by some female for the purpose of making the place more homey. Allan wondered as he batted at its fronds if the palm was the work of Michael's brand new wife or one of the endless stream of motherly secretaries the company boasted.

Michael Parkington himself was enthroned behind a massive mahogany desk that looked much too big for him. He readjusted pince-nez on his round and cheerful face. "Why do you want to know?"

"Oh, no reason. I had a short look at an absolute stunner, and I wondered if she would work here or not. She came into this house."

"You and your absolute stunners! She must work for us. Borderfield's is the only company here." Michael puffed out his chest. "We're big, you know. You've signed on with a good firm, captain—my good fellow."

"I would've signed with any firm you worked for, Michael, you know that. And I like to think you'd have published me no matter what rot I'd tried to push at you. Loyalties of war and all that."

"Even though it was I who wheedled you into giving me the said 'rot.' Sporting of you." Michael grinned. Allan smiled back at the sanguine and prosperous-looking young businessman who had insisted on publishing Allan's book of war photographs. Allan had labored over the book while the war raged around him, but he had been thinking of saving his work for a later time; say ten years later. The Great War was too raw a wound to probe not even a year after the armistice. He had been more surprised than anyone except Parkington that his book, just out, was selling extremely well and being reviewed in the important journals.

"War guilt," was Michael's explanation of the praise heaped on *Pictures of a Year,* as Allan called his slim volume of photographs taken back in 1914. "Also, it's good."

Michael was a natural-born editor if he could make such a good call so early in his career. Allan studied the young man behind the desk: The cashmere vest, the foulard tie, the scholarly looking spectacles. Yes, he was the image already of the successful man who knew his business.

Very far from the khaki-clad fellow, crusted with dirt and with his arm in a sling, limping shyly in to visit Allan at the field hospital near Ghent. Which was the truer image? Allan wasn't sure. The war might someday recede in his memory but it was early days to tell. At any rate, the real-life picture of a recovered Michael was more cheerful than some others which lined one's brain.

"I'll read through this text for the sequel another time," said Michael now, tossing the slender manuscript Allan had delivered onto one of the piles of his desk, where it teetered, fell off, and landed on the carpet. He scooped it up casually and settled it under a pipe-rack. "The photos are the thing, and they're top-hole. Now what say we go to the Aero Club for lunch? If the toilers are back, it's time for us gentlemen of leisure to take our turn."

"Capital." Allan eased himself off the windowsill.

The two took up hats and canes and emerged from Parkington's office into a small outer room, where Michael's middle-aged female secretary was just settling back at her desk, and thence to the corridor of Borderfield's Publishing Firm, electrically lighted and lined with other massive office doors, hung with nondescript etchings, and carpeted with something good but long-wearing.

An ill-tempered and wrinkled male face topped by a shock of white hair looked out of one of the doors and barked, "Parkington!"

"I say, it's old Beaky. Pardon me a minute, Allan," Michael murmured. He approached the glaring face with his good-humored, bouncing walk only slightly impaired by a limp that was a souvenir of his time on the Somme, then disappeared behind the door with the choleric gentleman.

Allan loitered about, not knowing whether to go back into Michael's office or continue to the reception room. He decided upon the latter course, having a vague idea that there in the common area he would be more likely to encounter that young woman he had glimpsed in the street below.

Then, all at once, there she was.

She was approaching him from afar, from where the corridor turned out of sight. She wore a simple white blouse with a velvet bow at the neck and a black skirt which did

War Widow 5

more than silks and satins would have to set off a shapely form. Golden hair in a soft bob waved gently about her face; and that face!

The beauty's eyes were lowered to the paper she held in her hand and read silently as she walked along. Suddenly those eyes looked up. They were brilliant and blue. Allan looked into them and smiled. He had been told he had a devastating smile.

She gave him a brisk nod and stepped around him to pass. He was blocking the middle of the corridor.

He sidestepped and stopped her. "I say, miss, did anyone ever tell you"—he hesitated, pondering what should come next—"to be more careful of autos?"

"What?" She looked at him as though he was a lunatic.

He was. She was making him crazier by the minute. "I saw you coming into the office just now. Chap in a two-seater nearly ran you down. I thought if you would come out with me this evening, I might protect you from such perils."

"Of all the cheek," she murmured, raised a pair of finely shaped eyebrows, and stepped to the other side. "Pardon me, sir, I'm in a hurry."

He stepped with her and put an arm about her waist. "You're practicing for tonight, I see. I plan to take you dancing at the finest place in town."

She stepped on his foot, hard, though he didn't much feel the slim court shoe. A love tap, no more. "You're impossible, sir. Let me pass at once."

Oddly enough, his vaunted charm, which never failed to work on females of whatever class, didn't seem to be operating at full tilt with this office girl. Who was she to resist him when they were so obviously meant to be together? Time to bring up the big guns. "Let me tell you the truth. I've been struck by your beauty, and I want to get to know you better. Much, much better. You must feel it too."

"Unfortunate you weren't struck *dumb*," said the vision,

jabbed an elbow into his ribs, and made a dash for it just as Michael emerged from Old Beaky's office.

She had to pass Michael on her way down the corridor, and that young man cocked an eyebrow. "I say, what did you do to Mrs. Westwood, Allan? She looks like thunder."

"She stepped on my foot and caught me in the ribs," Allan said in a dreamy tone. "Just the beginning, I trust, of ever more intimate physical contact between us. What did you say her name was?"

"Westwood. She's a typist here."

"Mighty high-nosed for a typewriter girl. Spoke well too. I would have thought, 'Oh, thank you, sir, I'd be ever so glad,' in consciously refined tones would be more representative of that class than the maidenly refusal—" Allan cut off his rambling abruptly. His eyes suddenly lost their faraway look and riveted on his friend. "What did you say her name was?" he repeated.

Michael told him. "And I don't think she was amused by your man-about-town act, old boy. Can't say I blame her. What I do say is, you've got to stop playing about and settle down."

"Oh, no." Allan groaned, ignoring the fatherly advice of the newly married man. "You're certain the name is Westwood?"

"Why shouldn't her name be Westwood? She's a war widow, I believe, come down in the world, so that's why you find a 'Mrs.' in a job like this." Michael laughed. "You wouldn't find my Mary grubbing away in an office, not by a long shot."

The young Parkingtons were a shining example of a happy love story brought to fruition, a rare post-war tale. Michael was unbearable right now on the issue of family happiness; and though Allan hadn't yet got to know Mary well, he was reluctant to because she might be as smug as

Michael. Next they would be having babies, and they would become even harder to take.

He was quite happy for his young friends; deliriously happy, make no mistake. But Michael didn't have to lord it over one because he, rather than Allan, was cozily paired with his true love, while Allan in his own romantic life seemed destined to wander in an aimless fog.

Allan was fumbling in his breast pocket. A widow, and named Westwood. That, added to the face . . . surely nobody had ever had such dreadful luck as his blighted self. He took out a gold pocket watch and opened it.

Opposite the watch was a photograph, much faded but still distinguishable: An image of a woman with light hair and the most beautiful, gentle face he had ever seen. "I've muffed this so badly I don't think there's a way out," he said, putting the watch back into his pocket before his friend could get a proper look at the photograph. "Might as well shoot myself."

"Or go to lunch?" Michael suggested with determined cheeriness. "Perhaps you'll be more chatty over a bottle of some good vintage. This has the sound of an interesting intrigue. Can it be that there exists someone on the planet who has said no to you? And as a matter of fact, we have other business, so lunch will be on the firm. Old Beaky wanted me to speak to you on a delicate subject. A matter of lion-hunting."

Allan shook his head over his own stupidity in the case of the blond. He was not even curious about what Old Beaky—presumably a leading light of Borderfield's—should wish young Parkington to say to him, but he let himself be carried off to the Aero Club for the promised lunch on the firm.

Hours later, Elaine Westwood was still stewing over that horrible moment in the corridor at Borderfield's when yet another male had proved himself unworthy of the title of gentleman.

This happened from time to time. Put a girl into any sort of a questionable situation—and, sad to say, a working girl was still in a questionable situation nowadays despite all that the war had done—and some wolves would pounce. Why should it hurt so much more when a man so apparently cultivated, so well-spoken, so downright handsome disappointed you?

Whoever that fellow had been, he ought to have been a gentleman. Every social expectation Elaine had been raised with demanded that he show her the proper deference; and he had shattered all of them with his hideous maneuvers to "get to know her better."

If only he had bowed as she passed by and perhaps given her an admiring glance from those attractive gray eyes. She had no objection to admiring glances from handsome men. She could have emerged from the encounter feeling flattered rather than soiled. Instead, she would be stuck with those horrid words of his, "You must feel it too," echoing in her brain until she could somehow manage to erase the whole embarrassing incident from her memory.

How could anyone have been so presumptuous? No, she had not "felt it too." She was not one to be overcome by the feelings of which the fellow spoke.

Then why was she thinking about him so much? Elaine shifted on the hard wooden bench on the City and South London Railway carriage that was rattling its way from Elephant and Castle to Clapham. Such a seat was a rare find right after working hours in London. She had stood for the first leg of the journey, on the Bakerloo line from Leicester Square to Elephant and Castle.

Now she was wedged in next to a large, comfortable woman who wore a dowdy pre-war hat and carried a shopping bag. Two similar women sat across from her. She wouldn't have taken the seat if any of the three had been men; not on this day. Elaine was usually modern enough to ignore such concerns, but assaults on her respectability tended to turn her into a mid-Victorian.

Actually she didn't like being in a train at all and was missing her normal dose of open air. She usually walked the moderate distance from her office to the Women's Hostel near Euston Station even in nasty weather, but on days when she was to visit her mother-in-law she couldn't afford to lose the time a walk all the way from Covent Garden to Clapham would cost her. As for the return journey, she would tell the elder Mrs. Westwood she was taking a cab whether she did or not.

Elaine looked out the window at her own reflection and sighed. Being blond and not repulsive had been all very well in her young days—she was twenty-five and thought of her young days as far distant—but such attributes as she possessed were doing her no good at all in the world of business. And she liked the world of business. She enjoyed being an efficient typewriter and sometimes being allowed to do a reader's report of a manuscript for Borderfield's.

Thanks to the war women had finagled their way into many offices, and some of them were not giving up the footholds so perilously won. Elaine was one of those women. Yet what had happened to her today—being mauled about by another encroaching male—left her with a sinking feeling that nobody would respect her, let alone promote her, for a very long time indeed, even if she remembered to wear the unbecoming spectacles her female relatives recommended as an aid to an intellectual, forbidding appearance. She had forgotten the glasses today. They must be on the bureau in her room back at the hostel.

Her stop was approaching. She stood, straightened her

coat and skirt, and gathered her things about her. Her seatmate was departing at Clapham too, along with a dozen other occupants of the car, and the platform was crowded. Elaine shouldered her way through the mob, trying to cheer up. She wouldn't show a gloomy face to her mother-in-law. Griselda had enough to put up with already.

Elaine cheered herself resolutely all the way from the station to Griselda's dingy lodging house. She gave a penny to an organ-grinder's monkey, another coin to the ex-soldier who sat legless on a corner holding a pasteboard inscribed with, WHY DID I SERVE MY COUNTRY? and then, to much better effect on her mood, she caught the ball some urchins were tossing about in the street and threw it back to them, laughing.

"Dear Griselda, how are you?" The incident with the children's ball had helped her to arrive at Griselda's with her brightest face. Elaine kissed the cheek of the lady who reclined upon a shabby horsehair sofa.

Elaine could never get used to seeing her mother-in-law in this setting; to being let into a rundown rooming house by an overworked tweeny instead of into a gracious West End flat by the dignified butler who had regulated Mrs. Westwood's callers in bygone days. Oh, how Elaine hated wartime securities and stock markets and entails and everything that had led to the elder Mrs. Westwood's present distress—not to mention one's own.

"Darling, I'm ten times better for seeing you. Sit right down. I've asked Mrs. Gantle to bring up our revolting high tea as soon as you come in, and she ought to be here soon." Griselda laid aside a tattered volume of an old novel by Mrs. Braddon. She had a pure, aristocratic profile and a wealth of waving gray hair arranged in an old-fashioned way which was nevertheless most becoming to her. A limp and lacy wrapper that had first seen the light of day in Edwardian times still flattered her spare figure; and she smiled at Elaine from a pair of fine dark eyes, the eyes she had passed on to her son. His picture, in uniform, was one of those crowding the fringe-draped table beside the sofa.

Elaine glanced at Bingo's photograph with the usual stab of pain. Interesting to feel such a raw pain after three years. Though she didn't miss him as such—they had been together so little that she couldn't miss him in a daily life that had never really included him—she was angry still over the mere fact of his life having been cut so short. She felt a like anger whenever she saw one of those wounded ex-soldiers, amputees mostly, such as the one she had just given a sixpence to, who studded the streets of London asking for help or raving over the unfairness of it all.

Her musing was interrupted by a racking cough from Griselda.

"Better, indeed. You're worse, aren't you?" Elaine glared at her mother-in-law.

"It's only a little cold," Griselda said, suddenly furtive and guilty.

Elaine had opened her mouth to probe further when the inquisition was interrupted. Mrs. Gantle, the landlady, entered with a laden tray. Since it was laden only with tea things for two and two portions of beans and toast, her preparations and bustling didn't take long. Elaine could see the merest edge of a grimace on Griselda's face at this final indignity: The working-class high tea, rather than a proper afternoon tea followed hours later by a proper dinner. But even Griselda had to admit an early evening meal enabled an invalid such as herself to get to bed at a reasonable hour.

Mrs. Gantle was a friendly woman, tiny and sixtyish with a keen gaze. The three exchanged small talk while she set out the dishes, talk touching on weather, the coming peace celebrations, the king and queen. On her way out Mrs.

Gantle looked Elaine straight in the eye and said significantly, "Better hope it don't get into madam's lungs. I know them doctor bills is something awful, but the way she coughs of nights . . ." She and her voice trailed off together.

"At least someone in this house is honest," Elaine muttered, pouring tea.

There were two spots of color on Griselda's chiseled cheeks; whether from embarrassment or illness, Elaine didn't know. "She's a meddling soul, though I suppose she means well. But I've been resting until I can rest no more. What better way to get over this, whatever it is?"

Elaine was mortally afraid it was the influenza still. She had no idea how someone so frail as Griselda had survived the dreadful scourge that had been fatal to so many more robust people only last winter. The doctor had assured them that, Griselda's weakness notwithstanding, the disease hadn't gone into pneumonia, but Elaine didn't quite trust a doctor of the caliber Griselda was able to afford.

"You ought to go down to the country for fresh eggs and milk and that sort of thing, not to mention a few weeks out of the Smoke, as we Londoners say. Anyone would cough in this weather. Go down to Berryhill. Mother would love to see you, and your lungs would thank you."

Elaine then braced herself for the customary polite refusal. She never failed, on her visits, to offer the hospitality of her family's country home, and Griselda was always just as sure to refuse with thanks what she saw as well-meant charity. They had not been family long enough for her to accept such largesse, especially from in-laws who were nearly as hard up as she was herself. She had been Elaine's mother-in-law only for a few weeks when Bingo died.

"Visit Berryhill? I might do precisely that," Griselda said in a strange tone; the voice of someone barely holding back a secret.

War Widow 13

"You will?" Elaine was delighted but amazed. "Why will you?" she added, with a hard look.

Griselda rummaged among medicine bottles, Jeffrey Farnol novels, and other litter on a nearby hassock until she came up with a large, cream-colored envelope. "Because I've been invited. Your mother means to give a house party in the grand old manner, and she's been kind enough to include me. I've nothing to wear, of course, and precious little to tip the servants with, but I might simply forget my vanity and go for the fun of it."

"What is this all about?" Elaine held out her hand for the envelope and Griselda released it with a mischievous smile.

Elaine shivered as she scanned the letter. Reading this was like traveling back through time. Her mother wrote graciously, in the way she always used to when inviting society to one of her famous Saturday-to-Monday gatherings. Entertainment was to be lavish; people from the worlds of art, music, and literature were confidently expected to attend; this and that friend would be so delighted to meet Griselda at Berryhill. Every phrase was indistinguishable from pre-war years until the postscript. Then all came clear.

We can't hold it together anymore, Griselda dear, Elaine's mother scrawled, *but I'm determined to go out in grand style. We had hoped to let this place, save it for Louis and live on the rent, but we haven't had a nibble. The next step is trying to sell up. But I will not until I've entertained one last time. Don't tell Elaine.*

Griselda shook her head, still looking amused. "As for not telling you, your mother ought to know I'm not to be trusted. Daphne always was too naive." She began to scoop up beans on toast in an animated way that would have delighted Elaine had she not been so suddenly upset.

"Naive isn't the half of it," Elaine said with a shake of her own head. " 'Don't tell Elaine' indeed. I was going down to the country that weekend. Did she think I wouldn't notice a houseful of guests?"

"I believe she's thinking more along the lines of you not stopping her extravagance until it's too late," Griselda said between bites. "Do you suppose she's planning to do the whole thing on credit?"

"I can't imagine she has any left." Elaine took her own beans and toast and proceeded to make short work of the homely dish. The two women ate in silence until the plates were empty. Griselda poured more tea and passed the biscuits, also in silence.

Then, "Poor Louis," Elaine said, sighing as she gathered the dishes and put them on the tray. "He won't have anything left to call his own."

Griselda looked distressed at mention of Elaine's young brother. "Sometimes entails are a good thing," she mused. "In my own case, the system was unkind, but if only your Berryhill were entailed on the male heir he couldn't lose it."

"Things simply aren't done that way anymore," Elaine said. "Not in our family, I mean. You Westwoods are pretty old-fashioned." When Bingo died during the war, his closest male cousin had inherited his house and land in Derbyshire, and his mother Griselda had been displaced. Her private fortune was gone in unwise patriotic speculations made by her husband Colonel Westwood before his own death, only a month before Bingo's, also in the war.

Griselda Westwood had been holding it together in this furnished room on the tiniest of incomes for three years. Her daughter-in-law, who had worked for the Voluntary Aid Detachment through the war, had been living in a London dormitory with other volunteer hospital ward maids even before her marriage to Bingo and hadn't really had a home to be displaced from. After the war was over and the need for amateur nurses passed, Elaine had moved from the VAD quarters to the Businesswomen's Hostel without missing a beat; and she had been an awfully good sport about it. Yes, Elaine flattered herself that she had kept revoltingly cheerful in the midst of sorrow and worry and endless care.

"Well," she said briskly now, trying not to think of how mortally tired she was of being brisk all the time for the benefit of this or that person. "I don't suppose I could stop Mother's fun if I tried. So, since we're going—what shall we wear?"

Chapter Two

The next morning, when Elaine pushed past a limp aspidistra to enter the sordid little parlor where she and her fellow respectable women took their breakfast—toast and a boiled egg, with jam on a good day—the landlady surged across the worn-out carpet.

Mrs. Beasley was tightly corseted and large, with iron-grey hair and an old-fashioned shirtwaist from which dangled all sorts of chains, some supporting watches, some keys, some lockets, all of which gave her the look, from a distance, of a dignitary who had received many decorations.

"Mrs. Westwood," she said in her overly refined tones, "I trust your gentleman friend will be told, in future, that no callers are allowed after eight in the evening."

"Gentleman friend? I don't have one," Elaine answered at once, mystified.

Mrs. Beasley sniffed. "I doubt a stranger would have appeared clutching flowers and demanding to leave them for you. I do not hold with that sort of thing, as you are aware, and I did my best to convince the fellow you didn't live here. I did this for your own good, you understand, as well as for the reputation of my establishment. Such wild-eyed young men, no matter how respectable they look, are never welcome within my doors. I trust you will remember this." She gave Elaine a steely glance from behind the monocle she affected—perhaps because it, like her other ornaments, could be attached to the bosom of her shirtwaist by a chain.

Elaine shrugged and tried to smile. "I can't imagine who this person was. I don't know anybody 'wild-eyed,' or anybody who would bring me flowers except perhaps my brother, and I don't suppose this visitor was a lad of sixteen. He probably wanted another Mrs. Westwood or Mrs. West-something else."

"Such is my hope," Mrs. Beasley returned. "He mentioned he had been searching the lodging houses in this area. I sent him on to the Henderson woman's establishment in the next street. I suspect she allows lodgers of the sort who attract"—she let a shudder shake her impressive form—"male attention."

"I'm sorry you were worried, but I truly don't believe it was anything to do with me," Elaine said in her most conciliating tone. She and Mrs. Beasley parted with cold bows; but they always did, and this represented no lessening of their mutual cordiality. Mrs. Beasley cherished no warm feelings for any of the females who lodged with her. Since Elaine paid for her room on time, and her only sin had been to have a name similar to someone who had been sought out by a gentleman carrying flowers, she didn't believe the incident would jeopardize her standing over the long term.

Out in the cool spring breeze, as she hurried along the pavement, dodging traffic on her way to Borderfield's, she passed a florist whose lush wares exploded out onto the street from a dark and gloomy interior. She recalled her landlady's experience with the flower-bearing gentleman and chuckled; it was amusing to have caused the Beasley bosom to heave in disapproval, though she really did think the man with flowers had wanted someone else. Thanks to her mother's everlasting interference she had would-be admirers, but nobody in her home circle knew where she lived in London. She kept her address a well-guarded secret, partly out of embarrassment, partly out of a wish to avoid precisely such a situation as had so offended Mrs. Beasley. At least she knew her mother well enough to be sure that no promising suitors would be sent to Mrs. Beasley's undistinguished Businesswomen's Hostel. The family had pride left, if not funds.

Only when she entered her place of business did Elaine get her first inkling that the man who had invaded her hostel bearing flowers might indeed have had something to do with her. When she passed the switchboard the female operator, a cheerful cockney whose dream was to sing on the stage, gave her a conspiratorial wink. One of the mousier male clerks stared hard before he remembered to look away with the proper lack of knowledge at her existence the men usually displayed to the women in the office. Miss Rothwell, the personal secretary of Mr. Borderfield himself, a very grand female whose success in business Elaine much admired, gave Elaine a quizzical look from behind her pince-nez when she passed her in the corridor. One of the office boys snickered.

This was the last straw. Elaine grabbed the collar of the boy in question. "What in the world is going on here, Tim? One would think I had a live ferret protruding from my hat." She glanced down at herself in belated concern. If she did have something amiss with her personal appearance, she would have done much better to have asked a woman; but she could see nothing out of the ordinary about her neat and dull ensemble.

War Widow

The boy, one of those leggy adolescents all teeth and sticking-up hair, winked at her as the switchboard girl had done. "Surprised you had a gentleman, that's all," he said in an innocent tone. He fled with those cheeky words.

She approached the corner where her small desk stood, preparing herself for anything. A gentleman? Then these looks and disrespectful remarks must have to do with the mysterious visitor to Mrs. Beasley's. He had brought the flowers here, no doubt. She *didn't* know anybody who would give her flowers or who she would wish to give her flowers. But since most of the women employed by Borderfield's seemed to be gathered in front of her desk, clearly something unusual had occurred.

The chattering females parted for Elaine and fell silent in a way that made her feel she was taking part in something on the stage. The desk was buried in iris and hyacinth. She couldn't even see her typewriting machine.

"Isn't it exciting?" Katherine Marsh, the young woman who worked next to her and was her best friend in the office, gave Elaine a twinkling glance.

"My dear, it's too romantic for words," added Miss Plumb, a gray-haired, diminutive creature in a fussy, high-necked shirtwaist. She had been the first female employee of Borderfield's, long ago in the time of Victoria. "Do you know what it means? Youngsters often don't."

"Who delivered them?" Elaine asked, looking around the circle.

"There's the difficulty," Katherine said with a sigh. "It was only a florist's boy. But you have this note." She held out an envelope of heavy grey paper, and Elaine took it. *Mrs. Westwood, Borderfield's,* it said. The hand was one of those bold, manly strokes one read about in novels.

Elaine broke the wafer with her fingernail and unfolded the paper inside. A very short message was written in the masculine scrawl. She looked up. It seemed dozens of eager eyes were upon her, but there were really only half a dozen or so ladies. She saw no harm in reading the note aloud. It was mystifying enough.

" 'I beg you to take the message in these poor flowers to heart,' " she read, then passed the note to Katherine. There was no signature, no greeting, even. Soon the others were cooing over the strong, decided handwriting and the utter romance of an anonymous gift of flowers.

"But what is the message, exactly?" Elaine asked of no one in particular.

The elderly Miss Plumb gave a misty smile. "The language of flowers, don't you know, my dear."

Elaine didn't. She shrugged her confusion. The language of flowers sounded like a charming bit of Victoriana to her.

"An iris means a message. Hyacinth means sorrow. Apparently the young man is sorry for something he did," Miss Plumb said tremulously.

"Oh!" Instantly Elaine saw it all. She saw, in particular, that man who had caught her in the corridor the day before.

An editor came by just then, looked at the orgiastic floral display in disbelief, and managed to disperse all the office females without saying a word. Katherine slid into her chair at the desk next to Elaine's and whispered, "Well? Is he handsome?"

"Very." Elaine busily rearranged flowers to allow herself a workspace. "Tall. Dark hair and lovely gray eyes."

"And what did he do that he had to be sorry about?" Katherine's words were sly, and her eyes held a glint of curiosity in which blended more than a little respect. She was about Elaine's age but very aware that Elaine, as a widow, was vastly more experienced in the ways of the world, though Katherine too had nursed in the war and been through many losses. Elaine was vaguely amused by this attitude and tried to act as worldly wise as Katherine would like her to be.

"What did he do? Why, what you would suppose," she answered shortly, rolling a piece of paper into her typewriter.

"No!"

Elaine saw belatedly that her friend had taken her words the wrong way. "Oh, it's not so bad as that. He merely tried to maul me about; he didn't succeed. It happens often enough to both you and me simply because we have the brass to work for our livings and aren't fifty and dressed in sackcloth."

"Well, it doesn't happen that often," Katherine said in a considering, wistful tone.

"But I must say, I'd like it if every man who tried to insult me sent flowers. It's rather embarrassing, but it's fun." Playfully, Elaine threw a handful of blooms onto Katherine's desk.

Katherine laughed and gathered up the flowers. "I'm going to put these in a glass of water. What are you going to do with yours?"

"I don't suppose there are that many water glasses in the house. The poor things will have to die a quick death."

"Heartless creature! I suppose you're used to flowers. Deb balls and that sort of thing." Though Elaine offered up no confidences about her past, Katherine had more than once hinted that she suspected Mrs. Westwood of being one of *them*—the upper crust. Katherine, though she pinched her accent and put on what airs she could, came from a working-class family.

Elaine, for her part, wished her friend wouldn't care about her supposed background. As always, she pretended not to notice Katherine's curiosity. She wasn't going to give a detailed description of her social position—surely the war had seen to it that such empty things as titles and position didn't matter. Elaine thought of socialism and spring flowers throughout the long morning, with a worried feeling on both subjects.

It had belatedly occurred to her that this floral onslaught, rather than simply embarrassing her for the day, might have a bad effect on her job. Her status as a widow made her respectability automatically in question, no matter how standoffish she acted toward the men she encountered. Now someone might get the idea that she was being sent flowers in thanks for some decidedly unrespectable favor.

Or perhaps receiving flowers was against some Borderfield's rule she had not known existed. Elaine knew herself to be a natural worrier, and she gave in more and more to this weakness as the day went on, but nobody came to tell her she was being sacked. Nobody came near her at all, for she was working on a lengthy typing project she had been handed the day before by one of the junior editors. At noon she had one of the office boys buy her a bun from a teashop and continued working, having a vague idea that extra efficiency might counteract the spectacle she had inadvertently made of herself.

At the end of the day she jammed her hat upon her head and left as quickly as she could, abandoning the wonderland of blue, white, and purple blossoms to their fate.

Katherine walked out with Elaine, the former clutching the flowers Elaine had given her earlier. The two made their way in the general direction of the bus which would carry Katherine to Putney, where she lived with her parents. Katherine wondered aloud whether she ought to let her mother believe she had a beau. Elaine wished that she could have had just a fistful of blooms to decorate her dismal chamber, but there would be no sneaking them into the hostel. She silently cursed Mrs. Beasley's infernal refinement.

"I say!"

Elaine stopped in alarm at the voice, a familiar voice she would never in her life have associated with the streets around her office, though with its proximity to Covent Garden and the theaters she shouldn't have been surprised.

In resignation she turned to face her distant cousin and sometime suitor, Rollo Saxonbury, whom she hadn't seen in ages. "Rollo! How are you?"

Crowds swirled around them as Rollo began to chat. "I say, what are you doing in town? Thought you'd be grubbing away down at Berryhill with your mother. Haven't you ever heard of family feeling? Don't tell me you're still doing that job nonsense." He showed a lot of teeth and gum in a smile. Rollo had a pleasant horsey face and a shock of pale brown hair that resisted all efforts of brilliantine. He was dressed in impeccable taste, as always, though on him taste didn't always come off as such, and he carried a thick brown-paper-wrapped package. Books? Most unlike Rollo.

"We ought to get out of the line of traffic." Elaine led the way to the side of a building. Katherine as well as Rollo was following her. She would have to make an introduction and probably end up telling Rollo where she worked. She didn't think she could bear it if her cousin started to twirl his natty cane around the office at Borderfield's. He would chatter and tell her co-workers all about her. He would pester her to do what he saw as the right thing—quit her job, marry him, whatever struck him at the moment as most likely to get a reaction. Elaine didn't know if he loved her, as he sometimes claimed, but he adored annoying her.

"Katherine, this is my cousin Rollo," she said in what she hoped was a tone sufficiently cold to all parties. She always liked to emphasize her blood ties with Rollo in hopes of squelching his romantic forays. "Rollo, this is Katherine. We work together at one of those job things you respect so little."

"Smashing." Rollo grinned down at the two young women and tipped his soft hat. "Delighted to meet you, Miss . . ."

"Marsh," Katherine answered with a swift glance at Elaine.

"Rollo Saxonbury at your service, Miss Marsh."

Elaine had the feeling that had traffic permitted, he would have swept a theatrical bow. Rollo always did give one the feeling that he should be dressed in a manner Elizabethan or Cavalier and be traipsing about on some stage. She had the further feeling, from the look in Katherine's eyes, that the other girl thought Elaine had been reluctant to make this introduction because of some delicacy of class distinction that put Katherine on the other side of the dividing line. Elaine sighed.

"What in heaven's name are you doing in this part of town, Rollo?" she asked in an injured tone.

"Why, what should I be doing but looking to my own interests?" Rollo winked and tapped the brown paper package he held. "These are grandfather's racing memoirs, don't you know, and some publisher Johnny hereabouts gave Mum the idea he'd have a look-see and put 'em into print. Lots about the horses and whatnot, and while I don't suppose anybody cares to hear about a horse from fifty years ago, there's what you'd call gossip and scandal too, and that's what appeals. Mid-Victorians at play."

"Oh." Elaine did remember stories of her great-uncle as a racing man and *bon vivant* who had been in and out of every stable and bedroom in the country. Also current in the family lore was the rumor that the old gentleman had written everything down. Somehow word of this must have got out and elicited an inquiry. "I'm surprised Aunt Pen would agree to such an invasion of the family's privacy."

Rollo winked again. "She didn't. I was there when Mum was telling off the publisher chap, and I decided, well, one's daily bread is quite as important as the family dignity, don't you know, and how else are we to hold together? So I took the manuscript out of the library where it's been moldering, and here I am."

Elaine thought it unfair of Rollo to be taking such a poverty-stricken attitude when she knew very well he had a small private income adequate to a bachelor's needs. So did his mother, whom Elaine called "aunt" by courtesy, have enough to keep up her flat in Mount Street. All of that came from Aunt Pen's marriage settlements, luckily for that branch of the Saxonburys. Rollo needn't act as if he was as near disaster as Elaine's own family.

"You might hold together quite well if you got a job." Elaine noticed, as she snapped out this reply, that Katherine was standing by looking much too interested. "I'm sure we're boring Miss Marsh," she added, linking her arm through her friend's. "We must be off, Rollo. Interesting, as always, to see you."

"You're too late for the publishing offices, Mr. Saxonby," Katherine added helpfully, resisting Elaine's efforts to move her along. "It's closing time for most."

"There's always tomorrow," Rollo said with a shrug. "What say we—"

"No, Rollo." Elaine's hand was firm under Katherine's elbow. "Good-bye."

"Good-bye, Mr. Saxonby," Katherine called over her shoulder as she allowed herself, finally, to be maneuvered down the pavement. "What was all that about?" she then asked in a cranky way. "My arm isn't half bruised. I'm sure I didn't try to put myself forward to your grand cousin, if that's what's eating you."

"Oh, stop that. I would take you to meet the king if I knew him. But I might have guessed you'd think I didn't want you to meet Rollo for that reason, my dear. You're far too sensitive." Elaine was glad to note that Katherine hadn't heard Rollo's name correctly. She cast about in her mind for some way to avoid more disclosures and settled on the annihilation of the young man's character. "I don't want to be crude, Katherine, but I wouldn't introduce my cousin to any young woman I know. He has a terrible reputation as the worst sort of rotter, and women hate him."

"If they hate him, how did he get that reputation?"

"Oh, I didn't mean he's a lady killer, merely that he knows nothing of morals, and he's not above the occasional cheat." Which was perfectly true. How could he take his grandfather's manuscript from under his mother's nose? Elaine hoped that the publisher, whoever he might be, would decide against mid-Victorian scandal.

"Perhaps he wants reforming," Katherine was saying.

Elaine glanced at her friend in alarm, a glance which Katherine, looking back, swiftly misinterpreted as she continued, "But I'd understand if you want to keep him to yourself. Cousin, and all."

"Good heavens," Elaine muttered. "I know young men are scarce, but . . ."

"What did he do in the war?" Katherine asked abruptly.

Elaine wished she could say he had done nothing, a sure way to quash any woman's interest in a young man these days, but she couldn't be that mean to Rollo. "He was in the infantry, only he came out of the trenches fast because of being shell-shocked and spent most of the war in recovery."

"Oh! He shows no sign, does he?"

"No." Elaine realized that Rollo never did give anyone a reason to suppose that he had ever had an experience more upsetting than picking a loser in the Derby. She paused now to consider whether beneath Rollo's determinedly trivial personality there lurked some of what the war had done to every other man. He hid it away completely, if so. Perhaps too completely. "He probably has that faculty of putting unpleasant memories altogether out of his mind. Sometimes I wish I could do that."

"Lots of the old soldiers are forgetting the war right now and going in for good times," said Katherine with a wise look, "and I can tell you it ain't—it's not good for them. All they've been through will come popping out sometime, and they'll be in a fine fix."

Elaine had to agree. She wondered if her cousin could really have shelved the entire war in some far-off corner of his brain. Should she begin to worry now about Rollo's feelings and mental state, not merely about his devious schemes? This latest one would no doubt infuriate his mother and shock the rest of the family. She sighed. She had enough family members to fuss over without adding Rollo to her list.

"Perhaps we'll see him again," Katherine said. "Here's the bus stop. Cheer-o!" She waved her wilting handful of hyacinths and was gone.

Noticing the blossoms reminded Elaine of what had happened to herself earlier in the day. A message of sorrow, indeed! Was her encounter with that man entirely over? Now that he had apologized in such a public way, he had no reason to contact her again. She supposed she might see him in the offices of Borderfield's; if so, she would give him a cold nod. She would never speak to him again.

She wondered why this resolution didn't cheer her.

Chapter Three

Elaine made a few minimal purchases of the feminine and frivolous type, absolutely necessary if she was to participate in her mother's country house weekend party, and then went over the contents of the stocking she kept hidden among her underpinnings. She wasn't too surprised that her remaining funds wouldn't stretch as far as train fare and still allow her to pay for her lodging that month.

In order to go home to Sussex for the house party she so dreaded yet had been carefully preparing for, she would be forced to beg a ride with some likely guest. And who more likely than Rollo and his mother? They had a large and comfortable Rolls Royce which would easily hold a third.

But a telephone call to their flat in Mount Street revealed that Aunt Pen had given up the car and was going down by train, which led Elaine to wonder if that branch of the Saxonbury family could indeed be suffering the sorts of financial reverses that would lead Rollo to hawk his grandfather's racy memoirs to the highest bidder. Elaine had been so sure the memoir sale was merely some selfish start of Rollo's, perhaps provoked by gambling losses or other debts of the sort young careless men were bound to run up. But giving up one's car was a serious thing in Aunt Pen's circles.

"Then I'll see you on the three-forty-five?" the older lady said brightly.

Elaine reflected that she couldn't expect Pen to stand her young relative to a ticket as a matter of course. And even if Elaine could afford to take the train, she would have to go by a later one than three forty-five, after her job got out; she couldn't share what would doubtless be a first-class compartment with Pen but would be traveling third class; and lastly, however it might feed the family hopes of a match, she had no choice but to say what she next did.

"How is Rollo going down?"

As she had feared, Aunt Pen's voice developed that matchmaking lilt so obnoxious and so familiar to Elaine, and she soon heard the whole story of Rollo's newly acquired second-hand two-seater—a poor substitute for the departed Rolls—a young man's sporting vehicle which scared Pen so badly that she wouldn't think of rattling her old bones in it all the way to Sussex, but which Elaine, being a brave young thing, would find a charming experience. Rollo would be round at whatever time she said to get her at—but where exactly was "round?" Here the speculative tone grew until it seemed to fill the speaker of the telephone.

"I'll be staying the night before the party with Griselda Westwood in Clapham," Elaine said quickly, then gave the number of her mother-in-law's lodging. Best, as ever, not to let the extended family, especially Rollo, know one's London whereabouts. He wouldn't be a favorite with Mrs. Beasley, and Elaine would hate for Rollo's mother to sympathize with her too much over the sordid qualities of the Businesswomen's Hostel. Aunt Pen had the vague impression that Elaine stayed with friends when puttering about at her little job, and Elaine's pride made her fail to confess that it was otherwise, troublesome though it would be to carry her things to Griselda's on the tube. She had better start tonight and do it in two trips.

Pen was chatting on about Elaine's kindness in giving Griselda her company so often. "You're such a lovely girl. So charitable to keep in touch as you do, even though Bingo—oh, I'm sorry, my dear. Tell me, how is that dear Griselda Westwood? Do you think she would be insulted if I offered to pick her up in a cab and take her down to Berryhill with me? I know the poor thing can't afford train fare, and I could put it to her that I need the company. Which I do."

"You're an angel, Aunt Pen!" Elaine cried. A worry she hadn't even considered had been unexpectedly taken off her chest.

The next day but one found Elaine and Rollo tearing down country lanes in a small Swift two-seater that buzzed along like an angry bee. The business of driving in such a breakneck manner left Rollo with no leisure for any attempt at romance aside from the perky suggestion that they might surprise all the assembled company by coming down to dinner the first night and announcing their engagement.

"I don't think cousins should marry," Elaine shouted in answer, over the roar of the machine, one hand on her small hat. "You know that, Rollo."

"Lot of rot," Rollo shouted back. "I'd hardly even call us cousins. You only harp on that to put me off."

He was right, of course. Elaine only called his mother "aunt" because she was of an age with Elaine's own mother and it had seemed proper when she was a little child. Actually she and Pen were second cousins, which would make Rollo second once removed, or something. Her eugenics argument wouldn't hold up to scrutiny, but she was surprised

Rollo was astute enough to have thought of that. Elaine glanced at his profile, nearly visible though much encumbered by driving goggles and a large cap. He ought to meet some nice girl. She truly believed his affection for her didn't extend beyond the comradely, but still, she would hate to hurt him if it did. Marriage to him, after all, wouldn't be that horrible. They annoyed one another in a manner that boded well for future companionship, in that neither one of them would expect too much; they both liked a joke; but surely there ought to be something more for a young man on his first matrimonial foray.

Elaine didn't think the world of romance owed her anything. She and Bingo had lived their wartime idyll, and some women—many of the women in Britain, come to that—would ask for no more. She would not be selfish and take someone she really didn't want out of the small pool of English manhood, even if it would please the family.

She turned her gaze from the unpromising sight of Rollo out onto the Sussex downs. The day was one of those that make English people react with such a combination of reverence and smugness: A perfect example of the spring weather that got right into one's bones and made one scorn the thought of life in any other place in the world. A light wind to move the fluffy clouds about, a rocky field with cattle grazing, a glimpse of thatched cottages as Rollo roared his auto down a village street, and hedgerows thick with varicolored blooms—surely no one could ask more of weather, or landscape, or anything!

A noisy and smoky rattle down the drive and through the overgrown park and the house appeared, that curiously pleasing mélange of every style from that of Elizabeth's reign on into the early part of Victoria's, when the Saxonburys had mercifully stopped building on before the worst of the Gothic revival took hold. The mellow brick and stone of the house, a castle really in all but name, ivy-coated, ruffled all round by the shrubbery where the moat of the earlier fortress had once been: All this was so beautiful in itself, and so dear to Elaine, that she couldn't conceive of its passing out of the family. As the little car slowed at last and puttered to a stop at the front sweep she was dashing tears out of her eyes. If only there was something she could do!

"Jolly," said Rollo, referring to heaven knew what—the journey, the arrival, the fact that Elaine's mother and a clutch of other people were surging forth from the old front doorway to meet them—and Elaine brushed sentiment aside. She couldn't afford that. She was at home now.

Settled into her old room and clad in the one good dinner gown she possessed—a recent gift from her godmother in Paris and a treasured acquisition—Elaine took a last peek at the wavy image looking back at her from the Regency-era cheval glass and prepared to descend. Her mother had rather hustled her up the stairs when she arrived, obviously trying to hide the fact that something unusual was going on, and Elaine didn't know exactly what would await her in the drawing room. Mother did know that, thanks to Griselda, news of the house party had been "spilled" to her daughter, and she had chosen to react by never meeting Elaine's eye.

Elaine made sure her hair was tidy. She liked the dress, though she wished she wasn't obliged to wear it so soon in the weekend. A floating dull-blue silk, picked out with silver, it did surprisingly nice things to her eyes and light hair. She was pleased with the unstructured style that skimmed the body so gracefully, though her mother was always mourning that the new fashions didn't show off either Elaine's tiny waist or her bosom. Elaine would retort that the era of women's prospective fertility being exaggerated by dress was mercifully over—gone out with corsets. She only

War Widow

hoped now that nobody would notice the shabbiness of her good evening pumps.

She would never admit it to Mother, but she was looking forward to this gathering in a way. She liked parties as well as anyone and wished she wasn't cast as the evil fairy at this one. But she was so used to curtailing her family's good times that she knew everyone, at least her immediate circle, would expect her to be disapproving and surly. She would surprise them by saying nothing. Mother could hardly be in worse trouble, and if she wanted to go out with a flourish, one might as well not cavil. Elaine had done that for years already, advancing one scheme of economy after another, to more or less effect. Time to call a halt.

Putting her things away, looking out for any item of clothing that might be useful for the next few days from the back of her girlhood wardrobe, and mourning the fate of Berryhill had taken some time, and Elaine was late for the pre-dinner gathering. As she puttered about in her bedroom, which looked out on the walled garden in back of the house, she had noticed the faint sound of many doors opening and closing, of motors halting off in the distance, of strange voices coming from every direction.

Still, when she walked into the drawing room she wasn't prepared to find it, what her young brother might have called, "packed to the gills" with a crush of humanity. Everyone was in evening dress and most held glasses of sherry. The effect was festive and cheerful but astonishing. Elaine wandered about in a daze. Yes, they had bedrooms enough for most of these people, and some of them were neighbors who wouldn't be staying the night. But the sheer manpower required to care for so many guests was staggering. Mother must have hired the whole village. And paid them in what? Empty promises, or illegal proceeds from some entailed jewelry?

Her brother Louis was suddenly at her side, appearing as if by magic out of a throng of strangers.

"Shouldn't you be at school?" she asked sharply before she could stop herself. She instantly regretted the remark; she wouldn't be the stern older sister quite yet. "Lucky you could get down for the weekend," she added in a lighter tone. She knew Louis was not an enthusiastic scholar and that Eton bored him profoundly—or so he said.

"Yes, lucky," Louis said, not meeting his sister's eyes. That was getting to be a family failing. "How about a better greeting? You'd think having to attend this brawl would get me some points with you."

Elaine stood on her toes and kissed her brother's cheek. "Who are all these people?" she then whispered, biting back complaints about how much it would cost to feed them all on champagne and lobster. "They don't look too Bohemian, so perhaps Mother has passed through her artistic period."

"They're literary, some of them," Louis said, rolling his eyes. He and Elaine were evidently brother and sister. His hair was as light as hers, his eyes as blue, and there was a strong facial resemblance allowing for her femininity and, on his side, a masculinity still budding but likely to make him a golden deity among the ladies someday. The expression on his face was still that of a young person to whom disillusion has not come; Elaine recognized it from some of her own early photographs. She noticed how sweet he looked in his evening clothes and wondered if Mother had gone further into debt to buy him such a well-fitting ensemble. And was he even old enough to be here? She looked askance at a woman passing by in a particularly low-necked gown that was also backless.

"Literary would seem to be a bit cleaner than the painting and sculpting crowd," she said. "They look just like the county, except that I don't recognize them." She raised her hand to wave and gave a bright smile to a dowager across the room whom she did recognize and who was very "county." "But isn't this all rather boring for you, Louis?"

A footman in the Saxonbury livery, one of the villagers hired for the occasion, approached and offered Elaine sherry, whisking the tray away from Louis' outstretched hand with the same motion. "Thank you, Thomas," she said with a little smile as the man retreated.

"If I'm to be treated like a child, I should say it's a bore." Louis turned on his heel and stalked away in an evident mood of adolescent pique. Elaine wished the footman hadn't been someone who'd known Louis from the cradle. A tiny glass of sherry wasn't too much to ask if Louis was to be made to truss himself up in his best clothes and attend an adult gathering that could have no charms for him. Elaine watched her brother disappear into the Victorian-built conservatory, which seemed to be as full of people as the drawing room. Was the dining table really big enough for this lot?

"Mrs. Westwood. This is the surprise of my life, and a most pleasant one."

She turned at the sound of a male voice and found herself looking into the face of the man she had last seen accosting her in the corridor at Borderfield's.

"Thank you for the flowers." She felt her color rise at memory of that encounter. He had actually held her. He was as good-looking as she remembered, his dark hair and chiseled features set off remarkably by the black and white of evening clothes.

He looked eager and admiring and very glad to see her. Those eyes of his were as compelling as she remembered.

"Will you come away somewhere with me?" he asked. "Do you know this house at all? I have something I must get off my chest, and I can't say it in public."

Of all the things she might have expected him to say, that

wasn't it. She hesitated, trying to think of the proper reply. "Mr. . . ."

"Marchmont. Allan Marchmont, at your service."

"Mr. Marchmont. I have to say that our last private interview doesn't lead me to risk another with you. I do like flowers, but I'd as soon you didn't have to send them more than once."

"How charmingly old-fashioned of you. But I deserve every prim word."

She laughed. "I have to say you do."

"Won't you come anyway? I swear you'll be safe from my fiendish ways. I knew Bingo, you see. In the war."

Such a serious look came into his eyes that Elaine, without further thought of banter or even of doing the proper thing, led the way at once to the study her father used to inhabit, and which Louis wouldn't ever use since they would have to sell up. She passed familiar people along the way, people who said, "Elaine, darling!" and started towards her, but she waved them away with smiles and kept going until she had closed the door behind herself and Marchmont.

"Elaine is a beautiful name," he said when they were alone. No fire had been lit in the grate of the book-lined room, and the air was chilly and slightly musty. Elaine felt the gooseflesh rising on her arms; or could that be nervousness rather than cold?

She shrugged. "My mother had a Victorian schoolgirl's weakness for Tennyson. I've always thought it was a pretty soppy name. One doesn't want to go through life linked to such a weak character as the Lily Maid of Astolat." She paused and gave an apologetic smile. "What a thing to go off on. I think my name's pretty enough, and my mother couldn't help what she read."

He shook his head, smiling at her. "You're an interesting character, Mrs. Westwood."

War Widow

Again she felt a sort of chill; this time she was nearly certain it had to do with this man. How could she react like a ninny simply because she was alone with him? Resolutely, she told herself to stop it. "Interesting? Me? I'm afraid not. I haven't anything to be interesting about, no talents or great skills or anything of that sort. I'm merely a war widow trying to make the best of it."

He moved closer; a subtle movement and very slight, but suddenly it seemed to Elaine that he was looming over her. She stepped back. "Which brings us to Bingo," Marchmont said. "I knew his fiancée was named Elaine, of course, but I had no other information. I saw your picture, thought what an appropriate name it was for such a beauty—forgive me, you do look like a sort of Lily Maid—and I worried for both you and him when you were married after he was wounded. I'd seen so many of my friends do the like thing. War leads to those sorts of quick ties. Deathbed marriages and rash promises; regrets, perhaps, on the part of the one left behind who hasn't even begun married life."

"Hardly quick in our case," Elaine said in a repressive tone. She knew what he meant when he said "married life," and such a subject was much too intimate to comment upon even to tell him off for mentioning it, but she wished she could ask him how he dared make assumptions and generalizations. "Bingo and I had been engaged since I was eighteen. The only reason we didn't marry then is that I was in mourning for my father. So we did it at last rather than at first." She looked at the floor, her mind going back to that ceremony in hospital when she was twenty-two: She in her VAD uniform, between working shifts, clutching a bouquet of violets some fellow nurse had got her, and Bingo just able to sit up, joking and smiling at her.

He had insisted on the marriage, and so had she, thinking it might bring him comfort. At least he had never known that his wish to give her extra security by the legal tie had been useless. Word hadn't come of the loss of his family fortunes when they were married that bleak day, and Bingo died believing he had taken care of Elaine's future to the best of his ability.

"I didn't know it was an attachment of longstanding," Mr. Marchmont was saying. His sympathetic tones had mutated into something that sounded rather like annoyance. Elaine wondered why the length of her engagement should rile him.

"Did you have something to say to me in private?" she asked.

"Yes." He put his hand into his pocket. "After the crash, when both he and I thought he'd die on the field, Bingo gave me his pocket watch for you. I'm ashamed to say I've kept it until now. There's no excuse for my not seeking you out. None but—"

"Lady Elaine."

Elaine started. She hadn't noticed the door open; but of course her mother's faithful but underpaid butler had passed thirty or more years in service in which he had learned how to open doors silently.

"Yes, Norton?"

"The countess requested me to seek you out, you and the gentleman, and inform you dinner is served." The butler's eyes made a slight movement which didn't quite qualify as rolling them.

"Who is to take me in, Norton?"

"The bishop of Leeminster, my lady, or the head of the Panic Press. There was some doubt in her ladyship's mind as to which must take precedence. One hears they are both single gentlemen."

Elaine gave her old friend a conspiratorial smile and turned slightly to include Mr. Marchmont in the joke. To her surprise, Marchmont's eyes had suddenly grown cold, and

War Widow 39

he was giving her a look she didn't hesitate to interpret as contempt.

He extended his arm as the butler retreated. "Will you allow me, *Lady* Elaine?"

Oh! So that was it. He hadn't known who she was, and now he thought she was a fraud, a silly aristocrat playing in the working world out of boredom. She had seen this attitude before. Elaine lifted her chin and took the offered arm.

As she and her now icy escort moved through the halls of her ancestral home, she experienced a twinge. Typewriter girls didn't have titles, for heaven's sake, so she didn't use hers at Borderfield's. That was the beginning and end of the matter.

She resolved to be as coldly dignified as Allan Marchmont. She wouldn't ask about the pocket watch. Let him keep it another three years, or forever. Relics couldn't bring comfort. She knew that well enough.

Chapter Four

Allan relinquished his lovely companion to a dignified and middle-aged gentleman as soon as they reached the drawing room. He couldn't tell if the man was the bishop or the publisher, so haughty was his bearing and so respectful Lady Elaine's manners.

He wished above anything that he hadn't let Michael Parkington talk him into accepting this invitation. Country house parties were never Allan's delight, but when Michael assured him that the head of the publishing firm would blame Michael if he couldn't deliver the latest lion to the Countess of Berry's doorstep, Allan had given in easily enough. He had no weekend plans. He was a bit flattered to think of himself as the latest lion.

People were forming up for the march to the dining room, and his hostess, Lady Berry, approached him with a youngish woman in tow. "Ah, Mr. Marchmont. I'm so delighted to present you to your dinner partner, Miss Ann Averil. Miss Averil is one of the major poets of the new school, you know. She has been compared to the Brontës and all that sort of person. I must speak to both of you later, I'm so fascinated

War Widow

by your work, but for now duty calls. If you young things will excuse me?"

Left alone with her, Allan bowed to Miss Averil, a lank female of about thirty whose steely glance and long banged bob of light-brown hair made her look like an ill-tempered male child of the last generation. "Have you known our hostess long?"

Miss Averil shrugged. "I've only met her once before today. One of the gushing sort, but I believe she has a reverence for anything literary that's rather touching. It's in the family, I expect. She told me that in her father's house in Cornwall there's the portrait of an ancestress of hers who starved herself to death on account of Lord Byron." She paused, looking at him hard as they joined the procession to the dining room. "Aren't you that war photographer? The book that just came out?"

"Yes."

"How could you think that anyone wants to remember the war when the country wants nothing more than to forget?" He thought she was beginning a rant until she looked at him with respect. "But we mustn't let ourselves forget. How could you *know?*"

He bowed his head, surprised at her attitude: Was this the secret of his little book's success, that people really did want to keep the recent horrors in their memories? "I was urged to publish by a friend of mine. Also, as you must know if you're familiar with the work, I concentrated on what I call genre subjects, peasantry and soldiers at leisure and the like, rather than the battle scenes I don't care to remember myself. You can't be more surprised than I that the thing is developing a sort of vogue."

His companion's fingers clamped down on his arm. Her next words betrayed that this was her way of showing a sort of affection or comradeship. "And to think we are together tonight, and I was one of the first in my group of friends to discover you. It isn't so much the photographs for me; it's the text. You're a poet, sir, though I know you didn't mean to be. You must try, with your next work, simply to write without using the crutch of pictures."

Crutch of pictures! Allan bit back the urge to deliver a lecture. "I'm flattered, ma'am. But I assure you the captions are straight from the shoulder, as it were, as plain as I could make them, with no thought of the poetical. I haven't read a poem since I was at school."

"I mean to get you reviewed in the *Poet's Times*."

"Thanks, but I'm sure such a respected literary journal would give my scratches short shrift. Some of my photographs, though, are in a gallery in Shepherd's Market. My editor thought it would be a good idea to show them while the book is new."

Miss Averil looked interested. "I'll have to see them. You've written captions for everything on display, of course?"

He had, but he somehow hated to admit it to this would-be colleague. The thought of himself as a poet was too ludicrous for words. He wondered if this woman, to whom etiquette would require him to devote himself for half the meal, was on some sort of mission to add to her number. One would think poets would want fewer rivals, not more. "Thanks for your interest. I'm ashamed to say the war hasn't left me much time to keep up on my reading. You can be sure I'll seek out your poems immediately when I get back to town."

"Oh, thank you! But that's not necessary. I always keep a copy of my latest volume in my bag." Miss Averil delved into the beaded pouch in question and emerged clutching a very small, blue-covered volume embossed on the cover with the words *The Wilted Soul.*

"I'm honored, ma'am." Allan put the mercifully light book into the pocket of his evening jacket, where it bumped against Bingo's watch and reminded him of Mrs. Westwood, the hard-pressed war widow.

"How well do you know Lady Elaine Westwood?" he asked casually.

"Her ladyship's daughter? Not well at all. A rich society madcap who is having a fling with the workaday world, or so the story goes. With unemployment as it is, one would think such young women would seek their thrills elsewhere as a matter of patriotism," Miss Averil said with a movement of her long nose that was perilously like a sniff.

"She's a widow. Perhaps she's working to forget her troubles," Allan suggested, wondering if that could be the case.

Again the nose of his companion made a slight upward journey. "There are charitable societies that could use her help if she merely needs to keep busy. Remind me to autograph that book for you after dinner, sir. It will be my pleasure."

He nodded, wondering only a little at the poetess' lack of charity towards one prettier and better-connected than herself, and murmured commonplaces as they were seated at an impossibly long table and the meal began. He could glimpse Lady Elaine and her bishop/publisher down the row, too far away for him to overhear what she might be saying. He kept the conversation with Miss Averil off his own future as a poet with difficulty, but finally struck conversational gold when he asked her what was the greatest influence on her own work. He was able to relax, nod as though he were listening and contribute the occasional key word while he puzzled about the Westwood woman.

He hadn't encountered up to now the society girl who plays at real life, but he had heard enough about the breed to scorn it—even if, as he hoped, she was not being frivolous but somehow acting out of bereavement. He felt, somehow, that she had played him a trick by masquerading as an office girl of the ordinary type, someone he might have taken out on the town and charmed into his bed.

The fact was, she had put him in a damnable position. Bingo hadn't helped. By referring to his fiancée only as "Elaine," the late Captain Westwood had misrepresented the entire situation. Had Bingo been more forthcoming about his betrothed, Allan wouldn't now be a guest in the house of the woman whose son-in-law had died through his own stupid error. He wouldn't be sitting at the table with the widow, whom he had idealized for years.

The point in the meal now arrived when people commonly turned to the person on their other side for a fresh go at conversation. Allan took a good look for the first time at the female on his left, a thin elderly lady dressed with an outdated elegance. "I'm sorry, young man," said this lady in a well-bred, rich voice of a slight hoarseness, "I didn't catch your name when we were introduced. You must forgive an old woman's carelessness. But I'm not too old to appreciate a good-looking male." She gave him a charming, dimpled smile.

Had he been a few decades older, he would have been enchanted. As it was, he was most favorably disposed towards this example of Edwardian or perhaps Victorian grace. "I'm Allan Marchmont. Here as one of the literary people, though I'm afraid my book is mostly photographs."

"How intriguing! I wish I could say my invitation was due to my accomplishments in the literary field. I'm a great reader, but I'm afraid it's never gone further than that. I'm Griselda Westwood, Elaine's mother-in-law. You know dear Elaine, of course?"

Allan said the proper thing, but his heart sank, and a crushing weight of guilt descended on his spirits. His dead comrade's mother, his mother-in-law, and his widow under

War Widow 45

the same roof; all in blissful ignorance that they were socializing with the man who had caused their loved one's death.

In the train the next morning, speeding back to London, Allan cursed his own cowardice. He had thought it little trouble to stand up to the Boche for years on end, but three English women had made him retreat within the space of twenty-four hours.

Closing his eyes in remembered pain, he tried not to relive that crash in enemy territory: He the pilot, Bingo along by special dispensation since he was going for his flying certification. When the plane went down they had by some miracle not been killed, crashing into a hay-filled barn. Bingo had been thrown clear. Allan tore himself out of what was left of his plane and hurried to his friend, crouching in what cover there was, and he and Bingo had time to exchange but a few words before—

The train's whistle as it approached a station brought him mercifully out of the dismal reverie. But it was only to relive last night's intimate conversation with his hostess after the interminable dinner. For some reason, Countess Berry had thought him an ideal listener, and when she happened to catch him brooding alone on the terrace, she poured forth all her hopes and fears for her children's futures into what she assumed was a sympathetic ear.

Young Lord Berry was only sixteen, but his mother feared more than anything another war, or even worse, a designing woman. Allan had been introduced to Lord Berry and agreed with the fond mother that the fledgling earl was certainly likely to be the prey of countless women in a few years' time.

He hadn't been able to take so lightly the countess' tender worries over her widowed daughter. Elaine and Bingo Westwood, it seemed, had been childhood sweethearts of the most devoted sort; and their deathbed marriage, tragic though it was, the only fitting end to a story which knocked Romeo and Juliet's tale into the realm of the commonplace. Even after three years, Elaine's heart was in the grave. Otherwise why would the girl be so reluctant to marry again, no matter how many suitable men her mother threw at her head? Lady Berry simply knew that her daughter, with her managing disposition, would find true happiness as a wife and mother. She confided frankly that Elaine couldn't marry anyone she hadn't yet met; and thus Lady Berry had to introduce as many possible husbands as she could find.

Allan thought he intercepted a significant glance from the lady when she made these remarks and didn't know whether or not he should be flattered that she might see him, along with the bishop and the publisher, in the light of a suitable match for her daughter.

He tossed on his comfortable if ancient bed that night in the bachelor's wing of Berryhill. He admitted he had harbored a platonic admiration for Elaine ever since Bingo had shown him her photograph years ago. Perhaps his feelings had not been so platonic. After Bingo's death, with the watch and photograph kept carefully for her, he had meant to seek out this Elaine Westwood and—what?

Make her fall in love with him, of course. He assumed her attachment and marriage to Bingo was one of those hasty wartime affairs. Knowing they had been married on Bingo's deathbed, it seemed unlikely they had consummated their union or that it had been motivated by more than pity on Elaine's part. He had expected, in short, without knowing anything definite about the young woman, that he might be in the running as the widow's first love.

Lady Berry's maternal agonies over her daughter's wartime tragedy had put the lie to these assumptions of his. That

War Widow

they had been unconscious up until the night before made them no less ridiculous, and himself no less a fool.

Impossible, under such circumstances, to remain at Berryhill. He rose early, made a trunk call, and invented a sudden family emergency. He was on his way to the station before the rest of the house party had groped its way down to breakfast.

He would miss a concert, a poetry reading, and a fancy dress ball which he hadn't brought clothes for. Since he had only come to Lady Berry's gathering on the instigation of his publisher, he would let the publisher handle any complaints from the countess.

Allan doubted whether Michael's "Old Beaky" knew that he harbored in his employ the daughter of the woman for whom, according to Michael, the old man would do anything. It seemed that "young" Mr. Borderfield—so called because, though his age was over eighty, his father had been the founder of the firm and had kept it in hand until the age of ninety-two—nurtured a violent admiration for Lady Berry that Michael thought rather funny. Beaky's reverence for nobility and mature female beauty could only be assuaged by laying at the Countess of Berry's dainty feet each and every literary lion she wanted to meet. And she had mentioned that new photograph book and the charming young war hero who had authored it. Hence Michael's orders to deliver Marchmont or else.

War hero! Allan shuddered and looked out of the window. They had arrived at Victoria, and all was a-bustle as passengers from the train hurried about their town business.

Allan sat up straight. A tall young man with golden hair, dressed in a lounge suit which fit as though he was about to grow out of it, was passing by the window. The fellow's expression was grim and determined.

But what was young Lord Berry doing in town when he

was supposed to be at his mother's house party down in Sussex? Allan had noted the young man's sullenness of the night before—especially during dinner time, when he had an elderly duchess at his right hand and the leading female novelist of the day at his left—and surmised that he was bored with the entertainment and had made the sensible, if adolescent, decision to clear out.

It was none of Allan's business what Elaine's young brother might be up to in town.

And there was definitely no reason for Allan to rise quickly from his seat, leave the compartment, and follow after the earl as though he were being paid to shadow him. That he did so gave him a twinge of guilt; he was invading the young man's privacy. However, this particular young man was Elaine's brother, and he had the look of someone who was up to no good. Allan had been an adolescent boy in his time, and he remembered how every adult around him seemed to assume he was plotting some mischief—which he often had been.

Lord Berry hastened away on foot, heading north towards the Park; and Allan followed, having quickly paid a porter to see to his luggage. He was glad the young earl had decided to walk. After the train ride, Allan was glad of the exercise. Keeping a good twenty yards between himself and the object of his attention, he let the breezy day cool his brain as he dodged autos, horse-drawn carriers of one sort and another, and the press of pedestrians. Everyone seemed to have taken the opportunity for a Saturday airing. The flower sellers were hawking daffodils; the cab drivers and others on the road seemed to curse each other with jovial voices. In the Park signs of spring were even more evident, and Allan strode after his quarry through fresh greenery, maneuvering around horses and prams in good humor.

The Park was already behind them. Lord Berry strode

purposefully up Piccadilly, Allan still at a discreet distance to the rear. The earl turned off into a minor side street and mounted the stairs of a narrow house. Here Allan halted. Feeling subtlety to be a waste of time, he addressed the porter.

"Bookmaker's establishment?" he queried with a nod of his head at the only nameplate on the door, that of a firm called Colliers, Bingley and Biddleton. Could be anything, he supposed, from a firm of solicitors—though far from the City if that were the case—to moneylenders. He rather supposed it was moneylenders or bookmakers.

"No, sir," the elderly porter returned, looking bored.

"What, then?"

"Domestic employment agency, sir."

"Oh." Allan was completely stumped. Perhaps Lord Berry was on no sinister errand at all, but had come up to town to fulfill some commission for his mother. His furtive air could be explained by embarrassment. But why couldn't such business have been conducted by telephone or letter?

Allan gave the porter a tip and then stood waiting not far from the doorway to the establishment. Might as well make an utter fool of himself now he'd come all this way. The porter gave him one or two suspicious glances from under beetling brows, but made no remark. Allan watched the passing parade of humanity, observed the change in the sky from light blue to an ominous grey, and kept waiting.

Finally his patience was rewarded. Lord Berry came down the stairs and out into the street at a fairly fast clip. There was a new set to his shoulders, Allan thought; as though he were saying "So there!" to the world.

"My lord!"

Berry spun around. Allan marveled that he should address a lad with such a term of servile respect, and that the lad should be so used to it. But that was England for you.

"Have we met, sir?" asked Lord Berry with the merest hint of disdain. It was clumsily done, and he topped off the effort at aristocratic severity by blushing.

"At your mother's party last night. I'm surprised to find you here instead of there."

"What about you?" shot back the earl after a moment of thoughtful silence. "You cut out as well. Or were you only invited for the evening?"

"Come in here." Allan pointed to a confectioner's. "We'll have some tea and talk about it." Berry looked less than thrilled. Allan knew he would probably get a better reaction if he were to take his lordship into a club or somewhere else where manly drinks could be got; but there was nothing of the sort in the street, and he wouldn't give the boy manly drinks anyhow.

Willing or not, Lord Berry followed after Allan. There was evidently still enough of the schoolboy in him to make him obey his elders. When they were established at a table and Allan had ordered everything the shop offered, Lord Berry's eyes brightened considerably. Being a boy, he would have a boy's appetite—constant and undiscriminating.

Allan waited until the first scones and slabs of heavy cake had disappeared from the other's plate. Then, "Would you like to tell me about it?" he asked in a tone of voice which he hoped implied that he knew all about the ephemeral "it" already.

Young Berry shrugged. "I've left school. I've got to get a job like anyone else. You might not know it, sir, to look at the way my mother throws a party, but the Saxonburys are going the way of all the other pre-war luxuries. We're washed up."

Allan didn't bother to hide his shock. The family was poverty-stricken? "But why should you say you must get a job? You're too young for that. I'm sure you should be going up to Oxford or Cambridge soon."

War Widow 51

"On whose ticket?" the boy asked bitterly. "Would have had fun at Oxford, but I'm not the sort to buckle down to any course of study. No, I know what I've got, and it's not much. No skill, not old enough for any proper occupation. But I'm over six feet high and my calves are something to look at, so I've done the only thing I could do."

Allan felt, somehow, that he should be understanding everything by now, but couldn't imagine what the boy was driving at.

"Footmen," said Lord Berry with a look down his aristocratic nose, "don't make a large salary, but if my sister can grub away in an office, I can stand about in livery with a powdered wig on."

Allan nodded in his soberest manner, suppressing the desire to laugh and wondering just how horror-struck Lady Berry would be if her only son, with his muscular legs shown to advantage in silk stockings and knee breeches, appeared to take her cloak some evening at a great house. "But won't you meet your own acquaintance if you go into service in the kinds of houses that have footmen?"

"I've told the agency I'll only work for the new-rich," the young earl said. "They seemed to know who the new-rich are. I supposed there would be some about, even with most everyone so hard up in these days."

Allan knew he must handle this delicately. So many new thoughts about the Saxonburys were coursing through his brain. This changed everything about Lady Elaine's behavior. Apparently she was keeping a stiff upper lip and doing her best for her struggling family. A grand girl, that's what she was. He might have known nobody with eyes like that could be a social butterfly playing at being a working girl. How brave of her to let her highly born friends think that was what she was doing.

A hundred schemes to help her fought for position in his

mind. But Allan knew he would help her most at this moment by talking her young brother out of his mad start. He was willing to wager any amount that she was not struggling and stinting herself, living at a sordid Businesswomen's Hostel, in order to let her brother throw away his future.

Allan cleared his throat and looked shrewdly at the youth across from him. "Why domestic service? If a job is necessary, why not get one of the proper jobs that young gentlemen of your class do get? Even at your age, fellows of good birth go out to some of the colonies, to work at a tea plantation or farm in Africa or some such."

Young Berry smiled, a startling, attractive smile that put Allan in mind of his sister. "It takes years to make any money that way, and I'd never save my home. You see, I'm not a complete dolt. I can sell my story to the films after I've worked in service a bit."

"I see. The earl's adventures below stairs." Allan paused a moment to admire the lad's cleverness. Lord Berry was doubtless feeling rebellious, and in one stroke he might make his mother, sister, and other relations panic; achieve the sort of notoriety that young people often seemed to want; and have a lark. "I have to say I see hardly any objections to your plan, except that your scheme to expose yourself rather contradicts the notion of saving the family dignity. Yes, most of it is soundly thought out."

"Really, sir?" Evidently the young man had expected a lecture from any adult to whom he confided his ideas, for he stared at Allan in surprise. A frown appeared on his brow; perhaps he was thinking about the family dignity Allan had mentioned. Possibly he hadn't thought of it before.

"Yes. There's the little matter of your education, but you can let that go. Probably you'd prefer to pass over the university years and get right out into the world."

War Widow

"Exactly so, sir. And as I've said, there's no money to send me anyhow."

"Footmen in these days do hardly any heavy work. You might be bored without any real tasks to put your mind to, and only the society of other servants."

"The man at the agency said footmen often train for butlers."

"A noble profession, to be sure. But what would your mother say to all this?"

Lord Berry looked down. "She can't say much, not without money to back it up, and we haven't a groat."

"Have you only run up to town for the day, or is this plunge into domestic service somehow related to your mother's weekend party?" Allan spoke carefully, casually. He hadn't yet tried to be mentor to a young man. In the war it had sometimes happened by accident, but he had never sought to give advice.

"Were you in the war, sir?"

Clever of the youth to answer a question with a question. "Yes. Why?"

"I wasn't. I don't mean to imply I miss not having slogged around in a lot of trenches and been shot at and gassed, but . . . in a way I do. Those of us who were at school, we were too young even to lie about our ages and sign up. We missed the biggest thing in our lifetime. We have to do something now. Something out of the ordinary."

Allan was silent. He didn't exactly know how to respond, and he believed the flood of eloquence would continue if he but held his tongue.

He was right. The earl took a breath and continued. "Everybody at Mother's party has been in the war; or if they haven't, it's touched them somehow. The duchess I had to take in to dinner lost two sons. We fellows can't have the war back now we're old enough, worse luck. But we must have something. At least I can work for my family."

Allan wondered if he ought to remind this lad that, at sixteen, he wasn't old enough even now to take active part in a war. "Tell me a bit about this family you're so anxious to save," he said instead to catch the earl off balance.

"Most agree that the family name, Saxonbury, refers to a Saxon burial site. So does the name of the old place, Berryhill. I had an old uncle who could've told you the very year the spelling changed from the kind of bury you do with shovels and the kind you pick out of the hedges; but I can't. And the title was called after the place, you see." Lord Berry recited this as though he was taking visitors through his mansion's state rooms on a public day.

"I see." Allan hadn't wanted to hear the history of the family name, but rather of the family—especially Elaine—but he supposed he would have to lead up to this by degrees.

"You're trying to distract me, sir," Lord Berry said next, giving Allan what would have been a shrewd look coming from a face less open and guileless. "I suppose you're trying to make me see sense by dwelling on my family. Next you'll be telling me how upset my mother would be. But you couldn't possibly understand. I believe you're one of the lucky ones. Came up from money and not all this blasted old blood."

Allan's family had indeed come into its own by Victorian energy on the Stock Exchange and in factories. They had been farmers down in Hampshire not so many generations ago. "None of that matters nowadays; or it shouldn't," he said.

"Precisely my point, sir." The young earl grinned. "What's wrong with a titled footman?"

"Perhaps what's wrong is that you're too impetuous to know your own mind. Once your name is notorious, it will be too late to go back and change into someone who doesn't want his story on the films."

Lord Berry frowned at this.

"Besides, your idea isn't even all that original. There are a lot of down-on-their-luck Russian notables, for instance, who have become taxi drivers and the like. Footmen, too, I'm sure. Perhaps your story wouldn't be newsworthy enough to make any money from a film."

"Oh." Evidently his lordship hadn't thought of that. "But I say, I can't take advice from you."

"To be sure not. It would be presumptuous in me to give advice to a peer," Allan said in a soothing tone. "I have an idea, though. Would it be enough like service if you were to accept the position of my secretary?"

"Your secretary? But what do you do, sir?"

A good question. Allan thought quickly, knowing he must come up with some duties for this secretary he hadn't thought of engaging until now. "Write letters," he said on an inspiration. "I mean to say, my secretary could write my letters. And I'm busy now with the photography book you might have heard of—the reason your mother wanted to meet me. There's a gallery showing of some other photographs, and business to be done soon enough for the next book, and I have some investments. You might take care of things for me." He paused, remembering he was talking to a lad of sixteen. "Message carrying and that sort of thing," he amended, shuddering at the thought of letting the boy loose among his accounts.

A large hand shot across the table, and Allan found himself shaking it. "When do I start?" asked Lord Berry.

"Well. Let us say, after your mother's party."

"You don't mean I should go back to it? Deadly dull stuff, sir, with all respect. There's to be a fancy dress ball. Torture." The earl shuddered eloquently.

"All the same, it's both of our duties to go back. It would be the act of cowards to stay away." Allan was wondering already how he could undo the invented message that had taken him back to London. "We'll make our first stop a fancy dress emporium."

"But I don't need a fancy dress. My mother insists I always go as my second name, and she has the rig down there ready to go. Does me no good to grow out of it, she simply has the thing redone."

"What is your second name?"

Lord Berry shuddered again. "Bedivere. From *Idylls of the King*, you know."

"Well, come along, then, my lord. Your first duty as my secretary can be to choose something for me." Allan grinned. "Something striking."

Chapter Five

Elaine had worn the gown spread out upon her bed at every fancy dress ball she had attended since she came out at the age of seventeen.

Designed after the pre-Raphaelite style of some of the Arthurian paintings of Lady Berry's youth, the Lily Maid rig was medieval in cut, fashioned of shimmering green silk. Elaine was always instructed to wear her hair down, in loose braids, which had become a bit difficult since she had bobbed her head a couple of years ago. Her mother came up with a wig in precisely Elaine's shade of blond which did more in the way of fairy-story hair than her own had ever managed. The false golden braids reached to her knees, quite as one read of medieval ladies' hairdressing. With the wig was worn a chaplet of silk lilies. Other lilies were poked about the garment at interesting places.

Since Allan Marchmont had been called away, Elaine saw no reason to take much interest in the evening's festivities. Not that she liked Allan, but he was undeniably good-looking and male, a friend of Bingo's with whom she might have shared memories of her late husband. And that stupid class prejudice of his would have been something to argue him out of. It would have been amusing, at least, to try.

A knock sounded at the door, and Lady Berry swept in. Elaine's mother was an older and stouter version of Elaine, as though her daughter's face were seen through a mist and her body in one of those trick mirrors. The countess' golden hair had that indefinite quality given by a brightening hair preparation that wasn't to be called dye but was not quite anything else. She gave a complacent look into the Regency cheval glass as she passed it. Though she demanded her children array themselves in the same outfits at fancy dress parties, Lady Berry indulged her own creativity and vanity in new ways for each such occasion. This evening she had selected an eighteenth-century gown that Elaine hoped came from the attics and not some expensive London shop.

"Beautiful as always, Mother," Elaine said, giving her a kiss. "Come to help me?"

"I can, dear, if you don't want Cooper. She did deliver the dress? Good. Better have Cooper, though; enjoy the services of a maid while you can. She'll be up in a few minutes after she runs a quick errand for me. I wanted to talk to you before the ball starts. You'll be opening the dancing, of course, but with whom? Do you have any preference?"

"Mother, I'm a widow, not a debutante. Isn't one of the cousins here? Or are you just trying to get out of having Goggle Winchapel open the ball, as she properly should?"

Lady Berry grimaced. "At least don't call her by that awful schoolgirl name. Miranda Winchapel will never open a ball at Berryhill while I'm mistress here. I can't even tell you what a reputation she's got since the war."

"I've heard it all. But you know the Duke of Wincastle's youngest daughter has to open the ball unless you want to throw the whole notion of etiquette out the window—in which case why would you be giving a ball?"

"But why does that slinking little *thing* have to be the ranking unmarried female? If you did it, everyone would understand a mother's fondness. You'd be opening my ball if you weren't married; and you're not married anymore; and I detest that girl."

"Then why did you invite her?"

"The odd thing is, I really didn't. She simply showed up with her mother. I didn't think the duchess would bring Miranda, and I didn't think Miranda would stand for anything so slow and sedate as one of my house parties. She's made fun of them enough times, as my friends have kindly informed me."

There was the real rub, Elaine knew, rather than any reputed fastness of the young woman she couldn't think of but as Goggle, this name having been fastened on Lady Miranda Winchapel when she was at school and used to go all goggle-eyed over the men in uniform stationed near her sedate female academy.

"I'm afraid there's no way out, Mother. I can't make a spectacle of myself. You really don't want me to. You want Goggle to sprain an ankle or worse."

"Too true." Lady Berry sat down on one of the tapestry-covered armchairs near the fireplace—gingerly, though she displaced a pannier even so. "Are you sure you can't help me out? It's my *last* party, you know, dear."

Elaine knelt down beside her mother, the thin silk of her kimono dressing gown spreading around her. "Isn't there really a way out, Mother? You were very wrong to give this party, you know, but I promised myself I wouldn't scold, and so I won't. But isn't there any resource we've forgotten? Any bit of property that would be worth something and might preserve this place until we can hit upon a permanent solution?"

"Such as Louis becoming old enough to marry an heiress?" Lady Berry shook her head. "Do you know he's left school?"

Elaine stared. "What? He gave me the impression he had come over for the weekend."

"He simply absconded. His housemaster telephoned me before Louis even arrived here. It seems the boy left a note requesting this term's fees be refunded."

"Oh, dear." Elaine sat back on her heels. "I knew our difficulties bothered him, but I had no idea . . ."

"Poor Louis must be distraught. I can hardly suggest he go back."

"Why not? He's still under age, and he must do what you say."

"But he's bound to fling our financial state in my face. And really, how can I insist when Louis is officially the head of the family?"

"And there is nothing to be done but to give it all up," Elaine said more to herself than to her mother.

"We're at the end of our rope, dear. You know how long we've looked for someone to take a lease on this house. I imagine all the prospective renters are as hard up after the war as we are. I thought my discreet words to our solicitor would instantly bring us a fairy-tale tenant right out of a novel, but it somehow didn't happen."

Elaine shook her head. She had really thought the same when they formed the plan to let the estate. In books, that all happened so easily.

"The house and furnishings will bring something. We've sold all the art that doesn't absolutely belong here to get us through the last couple of years," Lady Berry was going on.

"I couldn't bring myself to sell the Gainsborough or the Reynolds, you know, because they're of *family,* and I think they must go with the house."

Elaine was shocked at the mere idea of selling the Gainsborough or the Reynolds. She was quite as shocked with the notion of leaving them behind. "Give them to the nation when you sell up, Mother. Don't let some vulgar millionaire have them as part of the furnishings. That's really disgusting."

"The whole thing is disgusting," Lady Berry said with a sigh. "Augusta Damien, that old buzzard, has already had the face to ask me if the Ming vase from the entry has gone out to be cleaned. I didn't tell her the sum I got for it represented Louis' school fees and the servants' wages for the past year. But it was the last piece of that kind, unless, indeed, I start disposing of the chairs and tables to those small village antique shops one passes when out in the car; and that wouldn't amount to much, considering what it takes to run this place."

Elaine felt a now-familiar pang. The grandeur of Berryhill to be sold off piece by piece? No! Surely it was better to dispose of the estate, historic appurtenances as intact as possible, to someone wealthy who would care for it. An American, perhaps, would have the proper reverence for an old English artifact of this sort. She wondered uneasily if prospective buyers would be any thicker on the ground than prospective tenants.

"We should get rid of the car," she faltered.

"Let it all go together," her mother said with a wave of her hand. "Tonight I shall be happy surrounded by my literary lions. Have you met that devastating Allan Marchmont, Elaine? I had quite a talk with him last night. A man who understands what one is trying to say. I was disappointed to find he'd been called away this morning, but now—"

"Never mind Allan Marchmont, Mother. He's one of those people you'll never hear of again when once his one little book goes out of vogue."

"But, dear, he strikes me as someone who doesn't even want to be heard of now. A very private man, and one hears wealthy enough not to make money at all, though he has his interests in the city." Lady Berry sighed. "It would help if we had some of those."

But the earls of Berry had been more interested in farming, and gaming, and such investments as were likely to be wiped out by war. With a final regretful sigh that her daughter would not help her out by opening the ball, Lady Berry trailed away, leaving an expensive Parisian scent in her wake.

Elaine pushed herself up into the chair vacated by her mother and eyed the rig spread out on the bed. She should struggle into the tight back-laced dress by herself, but the temptation to wait for her mother's efficient maid was irresistible.

Elaine's descent into the Great Hall wasn't dramatic. How could it be when the hall was populated by every kind of historical and literary figure? She felt as inconspicuous as she ever had, though the Lily Maid costume was as striking as ever. More so, in fact. Elaine had noted that the bosom seemed to be cut lower than formerly, and Cooper had admitted to taking the neckline down a bit on Lady Berry's instructions.

The countess couldn't very well make her daughter wear a sign on her back that said, AVAILABLE FOR MATRIMONY, and Elaine supposed this was the next best thing, though according to Paris, bosoms were *passé*. She began to move through the crowd, saying a polite word to a Napoleon here, exchanging a compliment with a Cleopatra or Sophia Western there. A small orchestra, hired from Rye, was playing from the gallery, and the many guests looked interested, eager, and willing to be pleased. Elaine noted with amusement that some of the literary company, whom she would have thought above all this fancy dress foolishness, were wearing the most elaborate costumes. That female poet was got up in armor as Joan of Arc—the outfit did go with her hair—and the premier novelist of the day, a lady built on an operatic scale, had actually chosen to carry out the theme suggested by her physique and was wearing the horned helmet of a Valkyrie.

And there, surrounded as usual by men, was Lady Miranda Winchapel, a duke's daughter, in what looked like sackcloth and no shoes. Elaine approached the girl with the familiarity of one who had been in a higher form at the same school. "What are you got up as, Goggle?" she asked.

"Saint Clare," the young woman replied, striking a most unsaintly pose. Elaine noticed, as she was perhaps meant to, that the sackcloth was being worn over nothing at all; doubtless authentic to the character, but scandalous for opening a ball at Berryhill. Mother would simply have a fit. Lady Miranda's sleekly bobbed dark hair was unadorned, and she wasn't wearing lip rouge, though she hadn't been able to resist adding a touch of kohl around her eyes. Her lashes appeared to be naturally dark and unfairly thick.

"Is there a young man here who is being Saint Francis?" Elaine asked. "You might want him to dance with you first. You'd match so well."

"No; I don't choose my dress to match anyone. *Au contraire*. I'm the only woman here without something fussy on." Her long dark eyes traveled over Elaine, who refused to rise to the bait.

"You'll cause the usual sensation," she said with a patronizing touch on the other girl's shoulder. "Some of us don't care to stand out." Imagine bragging about being unsensational while bristling with lilies, wearing knee-length golden braids, and dressed in a tight silk gown with floor-length sleeves. Yet compared to Miranda, Elaine was invisible. "Don't you ever get tired of causing talk, Goggle?" she asked out of idle curiosity.

Lady Miranda's eyebrows lifted. "What an odd thing to say. How could one possibly get tired of being the rage?"

What else is there? were the words left unspoken. Poor Goggle. Elaine nodded as though she understood just what the girl was talking about and moved along, weaving her way through the guests and trying to act as the hostess' daughter should. She wondered where Louis could be. Perhaps Mother had told him he couldn't attend the party. If Louis did appear, he would have to open the dancing with Goggle Winchapel; he was the young man of the house. Mother might have sent him to bed for that very reason, especially if she had seen the Saint Clare get-up.

Elaine heard the orchestral fanfare which meant the dancing was about to begin. Lady Berry always opened with a waltz; it was one of her old-fashioned charms that she wouldn't yield the commencement of her balls to the two-steps and tangos of modern times. Elaine chose a vantage point on the second of the ballroom stairs to watch what would happen next. She could see Goggle's shining cap of dark hair across the room. The dance floor was clearing as all the guests instinctively moved to the sidelines to pair up.

"May I have this dance?" said a voice in Elaine's ear. She looked around to see a knight, dressed not in shining armor, but in the tunic and tights of a courtier. She looked down at pointed velvet shoes, then into the face of Allan Marchmont, surmounted by a jeweled cap. She was looking a bit down into his eyes thanks to being on the second step while he was standing on the ballroom floor.

"Who are you supposed to be?" she asked with a smile. He had come back! And he seemed friendly again. She wouldn't allude to the way he had become cold to her in the study, nor to the fact that he hadn't spoken another word to her all last evening.

"A knight," he shrugged.

Elaine's eyes fastened on the ornate "L" embroidered on his chest, and she blushed. Lancelot. Elaine in the legend had pined for him, but he had loved Queen Guinevere. He couldn't have chosen the costume to embarrass her, she assured herself. He had no way of knowing how she would be dressed.

"I want to talk to you about your brother. About Lord Berry," said Allan. "Can we dance and talk at the same time?"

"I've heard it's possible," Elaine replied. At the same moment that she adjusted her hand on his shoulder she caught a glimpse of Louis as Bedivere—like Allan, in knightly but unarmored costume, since Mother had always maintained that one couldn't dance in armor—setting off across the floor in the clutches of Lady Miranda Winchapel. "There's Louis."

"I brought him back. He'd gone to London."

Elaine shook her head as they began to move in time to the lush waltz tune, so outmoded and yet so much more graceful than any of the newer dances. "He probably went up like a sensible boy to avoid the ball, and here he's dancing with the most scandalous girl in London." She took a closer look at Miranda and Louis as they floated close to her and Allan. Drat, Goggle looked to be enjoying herself, even though Louis' lack of practical experience in the waltz was glaringly obvious. Louis was years too young for Goggle, who must be all of twenty-two, but perhaps robbing the cradle was a thrill she hadn't yet tried.

Allan stiffened. "I thought you'd prefer him here under your eye. His plan was to apply for a position as a footman."

"What!" Elaine lurched out of step, then felt Allan urge her back into the rhythm of the dance.

Allan said casually, "The young man seems to think he can save the family home by becoming a domestic—a footman—then selling his story to the pictures and collecting a tidy sum from the resulting scandal. 'Young earl belowstairs,' that sort of thing."

"What!" said Elaine again, but this time she managed to keep dancing.

"I'm sorry to hear your family is in such straits, Mrs. Westwood—Lady Elaine," Allan continued, seeming to Elaine to turn stiffer when he called her by her title. "I'm afraid the story going around differs a bit from the reality. Everyone seems to think you work for a living as a sort of lark. I'm afraid that's what I assumed too."

"Would that be so contemptible?" Elaine gave him a searching look, leaning back in his arms. "I know that's what people think. That's what Mother wants them to think, and I don't mind. She keeps hoping the family fortunes will turn, poor dear, and then my work *would* count as a lark. Well, if I were really a rich girl, I'd like to think I'd do something more with my time than dance and drink too much and run up dressmakers' bills. The war made me think that people ought to be doing something useful. All the time, not just when there's a war on."

"Wise words." The arms tightened again, as though in friendly affection. Elaine struggled to keep her mind on the conversation. "Your brother is somewhat of the same mind, but being so young, I suppose he didn't stop to think that he might help his family more by completing his education and learning to be really useful, rather than causing a brief sensation as a nobleman in service, or whatever he plans to call the film memoirs."

Elaine laughed. "If Louis was set upon doing something, how did you ever change his mind? He can be stubborn. It's a family trait."

"Simple. I hired him and ordered him, as my employee, to come back."

For the third time Elaine widened her eyes and said, "What!"

"I hired him as my secretary. Not as menial a position as he wanted, and hardly something he can sell to the films later, but it served to quiet him down for now."

"But do you need a sixteen-year-old schoolboy for your secretary?"

"Why not? There are many things he can do for me."

Elaine's head was swimming, and it wasn't because she was being twirled round a ballroom in the arms of a handsome man. Well, not altogether. She gazed up at Marchmont; she felt her body soften and draw nearer to him, almost of its own accord. "You're being so kind. What in the world could make you be so good to us, when I know you disapprove of me?"

His expression looked extremely guilty to Elaine, and his eyes shifted away from hers. "Disapprove of you? How could you think that?"

"Well, you became so very cold on finding out I had a title."

"It was simply my surprise," he said quietly.

Elaine had the feeling something more than mere surprise was involved. She remembered the icy fury in his eyes and barely controlled voice when he had called her Lady Elaine for the first time. Then there was his odd, intermittent stiffness right now.

She didn't think Marchmont came from an old, aristocratic family himself. Perhaps it gave him some kind of satisfaction to employ an earl as his secretary. She couldn't imagine her athletic young brother in that role, though the idea of Louis' stalwart young form in footman's livery was just possible to envision. But didn't gentlemen's secretaries write letters and do office work? She would be more suited to the position herself.

"Your taking my brother on sounds like more of a job for you than for him," she said with a smile of gratitude. "I have a feeling you'll teach him a lot."

"I expect he'll give me a new interest. I need one."

"Perhaps he can help you overcome your class prejudice," Elaine went on in a purposely musing tone. "You'll find an earl of the realm is nothing more than the normal young blockhead."

"What gives you the idea I suffer from class prejudice?"

She raised her eyebrows. "Oh, come now. You haven't been quite the same since you found out I had a courtesy title—even though you must know titles mean nothing anymore. First you were angry, and now you're holding me as though I'm made of glass, which I assume wouldn't have been your plan if a certain little blond typewriter girl had gone dancing with you that evening."

For answer he clutched her tighter, only for a moment, and grinned down at her. "You're not kind to remind me of my disrespectful behavior. I ought to be horsewhipped."

"I have a feeling it wasn't the first time you've tried to make up to a young woman to whom you haven't been introduced."

"You're right. I must say I usually did it to better effect in my wild days of youth."

"Which are naturally long past." Elaine seemed to be hearing herself from a long distance away; to be looking down on the spectacle of a medieval lady dancing with her knight. So strange was it that she should be flirting, actually flirting after all these years. She really hadn't consciously played the game since she was eighteen, and she had to admit it was fun. Also that she was woefully out of practice.

"I'm certainly venerable compared to your brother," Marchmont said. "He makes one feel a hundred years old. Tell me, should he live with me in town? Is he usually down here in the country, or does he have London quarters?"

"We lost the townhouse ages ago, and he doesn't have rooms. I'm sure Louis would love to be in London, and I'm quite as sure my mother would be horrified to have her son anywhere near the fleshpots of town. She doesn't like it that I'm there."

"I see her point. But I can assure you and her that I'll take good care of the lad—of his lordship. He can hardly be my secretary if he's nowhere near me."

"It will be funny," Elaine said with a laugh. " 'This is my secretary, Lord Berry'—and as if that wasn't enough of a surprise for the unwary visitor, in walks Louis, looking as though he's on his way to the cricket field or perhaps the nursery, depending on whether or not he's having one of his sophisticated days."

"Oh, does he have sophisticated days?" Marchmont was smiling as he steered Elaine to the edge of the dance floor. She noticed that the music was winding down. Though the waltz had been long, the usual thing for an opening dance at Mother's parties, she had barely begun to enjoy the sensation of being in his arms. Well, it was too late now. His hand dropped from about her waist, and there was Rollo bearing down on her, his determined expression at odds with his eternal *commedia dell'arte* outfit. He had no more originality in fancy dress than Lady Berry's children, but in his case Elaine believed that he had found the exactly right costume and didn't need to change to another.

"Do I have to relinquish you to Pierrot there?" Marchmont whispered into her ear. Elaine noticed that although he had released her from the waltz position, he was still holding her by the hand.

"Yes," Elaine said in sudden decision; for she noticed that Mr. St. Marle of the Panic Press, the middle-aged masher she had been stuck with at dinner the night before, was also threading his way through the crowd. At least Rollo was harmless.

"Come on, Elaine, it's a two-step next," Rollo said, grabbing her hand right out of Allan's. "Don't believe we've met," he added with a pleasant nod to Elaine's late partner.

"Rollo Saxonbury," Allan said in evident awe.

"Marchmont! What do you know? We were at school," Rollo explained to an amazed Elaine, his pleasant, horsey face breaking into a grin. "He was a couple of years ahead, of course, but he once saved me from being thrashed by the Duke of Montresor—those were the days." He sighed in reminiscence.

"Why were you being thrashed?" Elaine asked idly. She was fighting back her own surprise that Allan Marchmont and her cousin knew each other. She was riddled with class prejudices herself! Of course Allan could have gone to Eton as well as Rollo.

"A little matter of a debt of honor, or so the fellow said. I didn't really owe the duke any money."

Elaine, who knew Rollo well, backed the unknown duke in that dispute. But it had been nice of Allan to save a younger lad from disaster.

"Well, after Elaine and I jog about the room a bit, what say you and I lift a glass to old times?" Rollo said to Allan.

"To be sure, old man."

Elaine, still looking dazed by these revelations, two-stepped off with her new partner. Allan, left by himself, thought over the fact that Rollo's name was the same as Elaine's maiden one and decided they must be relations. She must be related to half the people in this room. Beastly for her. Out of the corner of his eye he noticed Miss Averil sidling up, a-clank with armor. Avoiding her eye, he escaped to the balcony. This was not the same balcony where he had mooned away the evening before until caught by Lady Berry and subjected to the story of Elaine's love life; but it would do.

He had plenty to think about: He had a renegade schoolboy earl as an employee; he was much too attracted to the said earl's sister; and in his pocket he still cherished Bingo Westwood's watch, which he meant to give to Elaine as soon as he could get her into some sort of privacy.

He felt extremely lucky not to be a confused young man, raised to believe the world was his oyster, yet finding himself at sixteen looking about at the ruins of his family's dignity. Perhaps he could guide Louis into a proper way of life: Pay for his schooling and call it part of the salary, perhaps. The young fellow ought to have his world widened at Oxford as others of his class were able to do.

Allan put that problem aside. More important was the question of whether Elaine would be willing to get to know him better. He had been almost certain she had been trying to tell him so during their dance. He had been daft to speak of her brother's problems when he had the rare chance to hold her in his arms; he should have spoken only of moonlight, roses, and how beautiful she looked in her gown.

But even though their talk had been serious and unromantic, he believed she was attracted to him. Of course, when she found out the real story about Bingo's death, she wouldn't give Allan the time of day.

There was no reason she should ever find that out, except for the very simple fact that Allan would tell her.

Chapter Six

Elaine got up late on Sunday morning, feeling a slight frisson of guilt for having missed matins in the nearby square-towered Norman church to which her mother, showing a surprising serious side, always made a point of shepherding house party guests. Attending services in the village church always gave Elaine a pleasant feeling of the continuity of life. She felt, when surrounded by the Saxonbury family monuments and eyed with friendly though gossipy interest by the villagers who had known her since childhood, that the world would indeed survive any amount of war and upheaval.

But the ball had been exhausting, and she hadn't heard her little bedside clock's bell go off, so dead was she to the world. Though Elaine hadn't managed to dance with Allan Marchmont again, the rest of the evening had been a blur of tangos and two steps with the county and the literary lights as all the male guests who could stand up made a dash for the daughter of the house—whether out of etiquette or for more flattering reasons, Elaine couldn't tell. She had been nearly as popular as Miranda Winchapel, and she hadn't

War Widow 73

even seen Allan from a distance. It was much more tiring not to see a man to whom you were attracted than it was to be actually with him.

She descended to the breakfast parlor wearing comfortable old country tweeds and found her brother sitting alone, dressed in riding gear.

"Where on earth did you find a horse—and riding clothes?" Elaine asked, staring at the ill-fitting jodhpurs and hacking jacket, not to mention the top-boots, encasing the manly frame of young Lord Berry. The selling-off of the Berryhill horseflesh, which had happened before the war as one of the first signals of impending poverty, had been one of the traumas of Louis' childhood and her own younger days.

Louis gave her a blissful look. "Marchmont hired some old plugs from the inn, and we went on a tour of the estate when the sun was hardly up. This is Father's old gear. Glad Mother hadn't given it away."

"Or sold it, more like." Elaine raised her eyebrows. "Why did Allan Marchmont want to look at the estate?"

"No idea. He said it was for the exercise, but he asked too many questions for that." Louis looked wise. "I think he was trying to find out if I'm as thick as I look. Since I'm to be his secretary, he probably wanted to know if I've had brains enough to pay attention to my own family estate up to now." He sighed. "It wasn't the most pleasant part of the ride, thinking how soon the old pile will go to strangers. Worse than when the horses did."

That was an understatement. Elaine squirmed. "Don't dwell on it, dear. You don't think Mr. Marchmont is wishing to buy the place himself? I believe he has money, but he can't be that rich. At least, I hope Mother's solicitors would insist on a top price."

"I don't think Marchmont is the country house type,"

Louis said in the tone of one pronouncing a great though unflattering truth.

Somehow, Elaine didn't think he was, either. She could see him in London, or perhaps traveling about in obscure and primitive corners of the world, but she couldn't envision Marchmont taking a country estate in hand.

"And where is he now? Did you tire him out so much that he had to go back to bed?"

"No. He's somewhere about. Said something about taking the horses back and making a few trunk calls. I offered to help, but he said while I'm here my duties are to my mother, not to him. What do you think of that?"

"I think it was the truth, as well as a charming compliment to Mother. Was she standing by when Mr. Marchmont said it?"

"No. Why? Do you suspect this fellow of not being on the up and up?" Louis gave his sister a shrewd glance.

"No, not at all." Elaine wondered, even as she reassured her brother on this point, whether she did altogether trust Marchmont. Except for their initial meeting, everything he had done had been a kindness. The fact that he was somehow displeased with her for being an earl's daughter could be explained away and, she trusted, overcome. Most importantly, he had been Bingo's comrade at arms.

Sounds of female twittering were heard outside the door. The other late sleepers were arriving. Kit Mannering, an old schoolfellow of Elaine's, entered the room along with Goggle Winchapel, Goggle's mother the Duchess of Wincastle, and a couple of other dowagers. Louis slid out of the room with the practiced air worthy of a much older man, and Elaine didn't blame him for not wanting to be the only male in the room. She played the hostess as prettily as she knew how, pouring coffee and tea and inquiring how everyone had passed the night.

The subject was Louis as the old ladies who had just been treated to a sight of his fleeing back praised his height, his likeness to the more dashing family portraits in the gallery, and his charming, shy manners. "He'll be a heartbreaker," warned one dowager, wagging a finger at Elaine.

"Devastating," Goggle added, helping herself to tea. "I say, Elaine, do you suppose the butler or someone could bring me the stuff for a Hell's Angel?"

"I'll ring." Elaine made a face, thinking of the concoction of brandy, raw egg, and cream which she had heard of but never tasted. It was supposed to cure people of having drunk too much. She gave Goggle a sharp look.

"If only dear Louis weren't so young," said the Duchess of Wincastle with a glance at her daughter that managed to blend irritation and speculation. "And had a bit more to work with in the way of income. I suppose this place is secure at least, Elaine?"

Elaine's hand froze on the coffeepot, but she made a quick recovery. "The place is as secure as most things today," she answered lightly. "I'm in town so often, I don't keep up with the details of country life as I should." All true, as far as it went. Nothing and nobody was secure in these days, and no matter how she tried to keep a handle on things from London, she ended up neglecting Berryhill. She hadn't known about her mother's latest adventures in selling off the Ming vase, for instance.

"What interesting times we live in, to be sure," the duchess said, turning her full attention to Elaine. "You must find it difficult to support your mother properly from London. I wonder what your father would have said if he knew his daughter was actually working in a sort of office instead of living at home."

"He would have wanted me to keep busy," Elaine said. "After Bingo died, and the war work was over . . ." She let her voice trail away.

As she had hoped, the duchess didn't continue to probe for the details of a young widow's ways of keeping her mind off her loss. Looks of sympathy came Elaine's way.

"Come on, Mama," Goggle put in. "Every young woman ought to have a flat in London if she wishes."

Evidently this was an ongoing debate with the Winchapel women. The duchess plunged in at what Elaine recognized as the middle of an argument. "Really, Miranda, there is a limit. If you're tired of our house in town, you can stay at your club perfectly well."

The company braced itself for the mother-daughter quarrel by loudly beginning to discuss other subjects so that they wouldn't obviously be listening.

"What a nice coat and skirt you have on, Elaine, my dear," said one old lady, reminding Elaine that her tweeds had gone through the war. "I do like to see a young girl in something modest."

"Do you know I heard a flock of geese go by my window at dawn?" said someone else. "I love the country."

"Marmalade, anyone?"

"And if you think a daughter of mine is going to expose herself and her family by taking a flat in Chelsea, of all the sordid spots . . ."

Despite everyone's best efforts, the duchess' voice rose above the throng. People began to cough and excuse themselves. Goggle, with long eyes half-closed in contrast to her chipper appearance of a few minutes ago, appeared to be the only one not listening to her mother. A footman arrived with materials for the Hell's Angel. Lady Miranda preferred to mix it for herself, which she deftly proceeded to do, cracking the egg with one hand. Those who were still in the breakfast room watched in fascination as the duke's daughter downed the concoction.

"You're amazing, Goggle," Kit said as she shrugged into

War Widow

her white cardigan, making Elaine realize uneasily that the breakfast room was not as well heated as it should have been. "You look as though you've had ten hours of sleep. Don't tell me it's all due to that vile drink you swear by?"

"It's quite a good drink," Goggle said. "Perhaps I'll have another later. Well, that was breakfast, Mama. I'll see you on the tennis court, Kit." She drifted out of the room, using a sinuous walk that was wasted without a man in sight.

"And she doesn't eat enough," said the Duchess of Wincastle to the room in general, rolling her eyes. "But pray tell me. Who on earth are these girls supposed to marry?"

A strained silence followed these ominous words. Elaine poured out more tea for the duchess. The war had definitely played havoc with the eligibles of society, many of whom were lying somewhere in France.

A cloud of gloom descended on the breakfast room, making Elaine feel a complete failure as a hostess. She laughed. "We'll have to find some rich Americans, I suppose. They can't have lost as many as we did, having got into the war so late. Besides, aren't there more of them in the first place?"

This was a lucky conversational hit. The ladies began to discuss such topics as Americans they had known, world politics, and the novels of Henry James. Elaine felt her shoulders relax and continued to pour tea and coffee for what seemed to her to be hours until finally the last lady posted off to some mild Sunday activity. This happened to be Kit. "Don't forget the poetry reading this afternoon," she said with a private wink as she straightened her tennis dress.

Elaine shrugged and gave a little smile. Her mother's habit of making her noted guests sing for their supper was a society joke.

Elaine spent what was left of the forenoon visiting the bedroom of her mother-in-law. Griselda hadn't attended the ball the night before and needed to be told all about it. She had enjoyed a luxurious rest instead, followed by breakfast in bed with plenty of eggs and cream. Elaine could see that visiting Berryhill had indeed been the right thing for Bingo's mother.

"And you're going to stay longer, aren't you? You can't rush right back to town; you're family. Now come over here and continue your rest," she said, plumping the pillows on the window-side chaise longue invitingly.

Griselda took the hint and came away from the wardrobe, where she had been puzzling over various garments. "You're right. Putting on clothes and going about would be rather a bore." Still in her dressing gown, she settled herself in the long chair.

"This view of the terrace will come in handy later on," Elaine said with a grin. "You can hear the poetry reading without coming down."

"There are drawbacks to any visit. Now tell me what you've been doing. Your account of the ball left something to be desired. Everybody in the world seems to have been there except yourself."

Elaine felt the need to be furtive and offhand; why exactly, she didn't know. "Oh, I was there. I danced with everybody."

"Such enthusiasm from a young woman who needs a little fun in her life. What is wrong with dancing all night? It would have done for me at your age."

Elaine sat down on the edge of the chaise longue. "Why should I need fun, darling? Leave all that excitement about balls and so forth to this year's debs."

"By which one infers that the person who interests you, if there is such a person, wasn't there last night," Griselda said with a sharp look.

"It merely seemed he wasn't there," Elaine said thoughtfully. "After our first dance, I could have sworn the man was hiding from me."

War Widow 79

"Aha! So there is someone. I'm so glad, dear."

Elaine looked into the eyes so like her dead husband's and was suddenly near tears. Griselda was really glad for her. She somehow found that so touching she could hardly hold back the sobs; and Elaine wasn't the crying sort.

Griselda seemed to understand her feelings. The brown eyes grew even softer, bringing Elaine perilously close to the point of no return. "It's natural for you to live, dear. Bingo would have wanted you to. But I've often worried that you won't meet anyone suitable, working for a publishing house. Writers are so hard up, and the men who work in the place can't be, well . . ."

"Suitable?" Elaine suggested with a smile "Oh, they'd be fine if they weren't all ninety or married or uninteresting. But as it happens, I did meet this fellow at my job."

"Oh?"

"But I don't think he's going to turn out to be 'someone,' as you put it. He doesn't seem to like me very much when all is said and done. Perhaps I've forgotten how to flirt."

"A girl as pretty as you doesn't have to flirt," Griselda said with a shrewd look. "I imagine you're mistaken about his attraction. He's probably afraid to approach you."

"No doubt," Elaine said dryly. "I have the same problem with the Prince of Wales."

"Who is this man?"

"Allan Marchmont, who wrote that new war book. The one that's all photographs."

"Mr. Marchmont?" Griselda's eyes sparkled. "But he's charming. I sat with him at dinner on Friday, and he was most attentive. I always say that one can tell who the real gentlemen are by their behavior to ladies they wouldn't wish to seduce."

"Griselda! What a way to put it."

* * *

"It seems to be true, but I don't get about much these days." Griselda laughed. "Well, he's very handsome, and he must have done something in the war besides take pictures, or he wouldn't be bringing them out. Not in these days." Not when those Englishmen who hadn't served were still being harassed by an indignant public.

"He was a flyer. Like Bingo would have been. He even knew Bingo."

"Oh. Have the two of you talked much on the subject?"

Elaine shook her head. "That might be part of the problem. I don't know how I'll feel when I do talk to him about Bingo, but it can't be left undone if I'm to know Allan—Mr. Marchmont better. Perhaps he feels the subject is too painful to discuss."

"Undoubtedly it is. But as you say, it must be done. Every time I speak to a young man who served with my son, I feel ten times worse; but then, in the morning, I'm so glad to know a bit more about how it was for him. It brings Bingo—William—closer for a moment, and that's a blessing." Griselda paused. "In the case of my husband, it's a bit harder to hear the tales; I don't know why. But I still end up being grateful."

"Griselda, you're a wonder. I think I'd feel the same. Everyone is so sensitive to my feelings that the few men I've met who served with Bingo hem and haw and don't say anything at all."

"Funny. They are probably gentler with young widows than with old widows or mothers," said Griselda. "But if anything helps, recalling their memories does."

Elaine nodded resolutely. She would catch up with Marchmont if she had to use a man-trap. They were long overdue for this talk that would make everything better—or worse, for she didn't know if her reactions and Griselda's would be the same.

She was suddenly eager to experience her own reaction. Perhaps that was the trouble with her memories of Bingo. She hadn't reacted enough. She had been presenting a brave front to the world ever since her bereavement. In the face of the war's wholesale slaughter of nearly everyone else's loved ones, any indulgence of grief had seemed selfish.

"I'll do it today, no matter what," said Elaine, getting up. "Will I see you later downstairs, dear, or do you plan to spend the day in your room?"

"I'll try to get down for the poetry reading since, as you point out, I'd be hearing it anyhow from here. It's at teatime, and one of my least shabby ensembles is a tea gown."

"See you then." And Elaine marched out of the room, determined to corner Marchmont as soon as possible. Perhaps this wasn't only so that she could talk about her dead husband. She wasn't in the mood to examine her motives too closely.

Chapter Seven

Allan was determined to find Lady Elaine and immediately have it out with her about Bingo, the watch, and the whole blasted war. After his early morning ride with young Lord Berry he prowled about the house looking for Elaine, admiring the old place's antiquity and the graceful lines of some of the rooms, and shaking his head over the signs of genteel poverty which couldn't be hidden from someone in the secret: Worn carpet; minor pictures whose frames did not cover up the darker wallpaper behind; columns which might once have held classical busts and now carried brave vases of flowers.

Moreover, he couldn't manage to find Elaine, though he diligently asked everyone he met if they had seen her. Lady Berry was particularly informative; she had a gleam in her eye. But why should a countess approve of a commoner's interest in her daughter?

Well, the war had been a great leveler, Allan was thinking as he followed Lady Berry's suggestion and looked for Elaine on the croquet lawn. There he got stuck in a conversation with the elderly vicar of the parish and the publisher of the Panic Press, who seemed to go by the name of St. Marle. The men were sitting in wicker chairs at the edge of the field, watching some players go at it with mallets and balls in the soft spring sunlight, and looking as though they didn't quite know what to do with each other.

"Dear little Elaine," Dr. Barnstaple, the vicar, said with a shake of his head. "She hasn't shown up for croquet, and she used to like it so much as a little child when she played with me and my dear, departed wife. I hope the London life isn't going to her head. You gentlemen might not realize what a gentle, country-bred girl Lady Elaine is."

"Indeed we do, don't we, March, old man?" St. Marle said with a wink in Allan's direction. St. Marle was a large and distinguished-looking man of forty-odd who somehow acted more like a duke than the publisher of the most scandalous books in London. Allan could sense a ruthlessness which he didn't like in someone who was interested in Elaine.

"It's Marchmont. Yes, Lady Elaine is a young woman who seems to enjoy the country," Allan answered. Actually, he didn't know if she loved the country or hated it.

"She told me she's stifled in London," St. Marle added, making Allan feel a great irritation that Elaine had ever told that bounder anything. When one looked more closely at the man, his dignified air was a discernible mask. He was really more akin to the moustache-twirling villain of stage and screen than to the aristocracy he superficially resembled. He doubtless meant the worst in his pursuit of Elaine.

"The poor dear creature," Dr. Barnstaple said with a shake of his genuinely distinguished white head. "If only she would see the light and stay down here to support Lady Berry. The countess sometimes has need of a practical mind."

"But we'd miss Lady Elaine in London, hey, March— mont? She only needs a quick run over to Paris now and then to clear the cobwebs. And I could see to that."

"To be sure." Allan held back the urge to punch the other in the jaw for such insinuating remarks. "I trust I'll see you gentlemen later? I'd better be about my business."

"Yes, finding Elaine, wasn't it?" St. Marle gave another detestably hearty laugh and a second broad wink.

As Allan left the scene, shaking his head, he nodded to Rollo Saxonbury, who came hurrying past looking very sporting and fit in tennis whites. To his surprise, the younger man halted in his tracks and rebounded a few steps.

"I say."

Allan nodded in polite response to this greeting and waited. Saxonbury was rather a nervous type, given to twitching about the eyes. The war? Allan didn't seem to remember the twitching from schooldays, when such habits would have earned their owner a notorious nickname and a world of torment. Now the fellow looked as though he had something to say over and above the ordinary borrowing of cigarettes and money that Allan associated with this style of idle aristocrat.

Saxonbury leaned forward in a confidential manner. "Thought I'd let you in on the news. Though Elaine doesn't realize it yet, she's to marry me, you know."

"I see."

"As long as you've got that straight. Cheer-o." And Rollo loped off in the direction of the croquet lawn, leaving Allan to wend his way in the opposite direction. What would possess the fellow to collar an acquaintance and make such a statement? Even if Allan's attraction to Elaine was obvious to all the world—and he didn't believe it was—Rollo didn't seem the discerning type. He had probably heard some gossip or other.

Allan frowned at the thought that he and Elaine could be the subject of gossip when less than nothing had happened between them. Could their dance last night have done the damage? Until the very end, when he had found it so hard to let her go, he hadn't held her too tightly or flirted with her obviously, at least nothing others would notice.

Elaine was eventually run to ground in a summerhouse where she was chatting with three other young women. Their high-pitched laughter had led Allan to the spot. After having searched so long and grown more nervous by the minute, he decided subtlety was not in order and stood bravely in the doorway of the place. "Lady Elaine. A word?"

"Do excuse us, Elaine," one of the young women said, and the three left at once, their pale dresses floating out behind them as they cast mischievous backward glances at Allan.

He grinned sheepishly at Elaine, who was looking at him in astonishment. "I didn't mean to scare them off so abruptly."

"That's all right." She gestured to a seat opposite hers. The round room was lined with a cushioned wooden bench and had a small table in the center.

Rather than take the seat she had pointed to, he found himself sitting down right next to her. The desire to take her in his arms became almost overwhelming; but he could hardly change seats now. She was gazing at him in something like curiosity, and he supposed this meant he ought to get on with the object of the interview. Immediately his hand went to his pocket. He held out Bingo's watch.

Elaine took the watch. "Yes, it's Bingo's. I recognize the Westwood seal carved on the case. You were starting to tell me about it the other night before dinner."

"Well, there it is, after three years. Sorry it took so long."

She was turning the watch over and over in her hands.

"Open it," Allan said softly.

She did. Her eyes widened, presumably at the picture of herself pasted inside, and she smiled and shook her head. "Before I bobbed my hair."

"You were as lovely then as now," Allan said, taking her hand, beginning to stroke the palm. Then, amazed at his own behavior when he was in the middle of a serious discussion about a dead man, he let go of her hand and drew back a little distance, to where the soft fabric of her dress wouldn't touch his leg. Desperately, he continued.

"As you might imagine, I thought quite a lot of that picture. Especially after Bingo's death. For a long time I thought of you only as his fiancée. He had referred to you simply as Elaine, and I didn't ask your surname. Then I heard Bingo had been married on his—in the hospital, and that would have made my search easier." He paused. "If I'd searched."

"Why didn't you? You say you liked my picture. Didn't you have a curiosity to meet me?" Elaine asked. She leaned forward, not making it any easier for Allan to remain detached and unemotional.

"I wanted very much to meet you. I planned in detail how I would meet you, return the watch, tell you things . . . but one of the things I'd have to tell would be what happened the day he was wounded."

"You were wounded also that day," Elaine said, as though she were prompting him to go on. "I've heard that much. Bingo was in very bad shape, but he could talk."

"Did you also hear that if it hadn't been for me, your husband would likely be alive today?" Allan knew his voice was gruff. He suddenly found it more convenient to look at the tiled floor than into Elaine's eyes.

"So that's it," Elaine said.

"That's a pretty big *it*." Allan made himself look up at her and saw her face; it held only sympathy, no anger that he could see. "Don't you blame me?"

"I blame the war. What happened that day?"

Allan took a deep breath, trying not to see the picture in

his mind. Elaine's hand was in his own again, and he had no idea of whether he had grabbed it or she had offered it. "I—I miscalculated somehow. We were shot down. The Hun in the other plane got a good aim at my arm with his pistol and rather blasted it. Bingo's legs were broken in the drop. I managed to get to Bingo; managed to drag him away into a nearby abandoned shed of some sort; even got some rags around the worst leg, to hold the bones in place, or so I thought, though I was bleeding from the arm so badly by then. I left him for a moment to reconnoiter outside; to see if any of our chaps were around. Nobody. Then, when I returned, I found he'd been shot and left for dead. One of the Boche must have been watching the whole thing, and a funny sight it must have been to the enemy. I—Bingo wasn't dead."

"I know. You nursed him, then I nursed him." Elaine smiled her gentle smile, reminding Allan why he had fallen so hard for her picture. "You didn't do a half bad job on that leg. It was the other one they had to amputate." She sighed. "Not that it mattered in the end. The shot did kill him eventually."

He looked down again, suddenly finding great interest in the sight of his hands clasping hers. How had both their hands got together? "I managed to drag him back across the lines, but it took too long. Fever, gangrene, heaven knows what. I'm surprised they got him home; surprised he survived the crossing, let alone hung on long enough to marry you."

"He was lucky to be transported right away by an ambulance unit. It happened only by chance. But what makes you think I'd blame you for Bingo's death? It seems to me he would have died a lot faster had you not been there."

"If he'd been paired with a decent pilot, one who could resist a foolish chance—I was playing cat and mouse with that German plane, and I lost. I was responsible for another life besides my own; I was an idiot. Bingo was full of promise. He was about ready to fly on his own, and chances are he would have been a sight better at it than I. He had that aristocratic sense of it being a not too important sport. Such fliers were the best of us all."

"I've thought of all those things. When a person dies you do go over everything that happened or that you imagine might have happened. You do want someone to blame. But you weren't flying for your own pleasure, were you? You ended up in a field hospital, didn't you, and almost died of a fever yourself, but even if you hadn't it wouldn't have made a difference. I eventually decided the whole war was simply beyond my grasp as a woman. I don't seem to think it's logical to spend years killing everyone in sight." She paused. "Even if one is on the winning side at the end. Our people are as dead as theirs."

"You won't get an argument from me there. How did you hear about what happened to me?"

"Bingo knew. One of his higher-ups contacted him with the details. Bingo didn't remember much of that day behind the lines."

"I imagine he wouldn't. And so he came out of his illness enough for you to marry. I don't suppose they would have married you to a delirious man."

"He was in his right mind, yes. He seemed to be comforted by the thought that I'd be taken care of," Elaine said with a shrug. Allan dropped her hands, thinking it was somehow wrong to be holding onto a woman who was discussing her marriage. "There was a bit more security in his family at the time than there turned out to be in the end. My mother-in-law is awfully hard up. There was an entail, and her husband didn't plan adequately for being blown up by the German Army."

"Oh." Allan's heart lifted a little, and he cursed himself

for being such a rotter that he was glad her marriage hadn't been a romantic affair but a matter of economics. It must have been a simple farewell gift from Bingo to the girl he'd been engaged to forever—perhaps since before either of them knew their own minds. . . .

"Elaine," he said abruptly, "I've got to tell you now that I hope you loved Bingo very much and were very glad to marry him. I'm a fiend. The thoughts that are going through my head make me ashamed. I can't even tell you what they are."

She looked at him wide-eyed. "Suddenly we seem to be having a very disconnected conversation. What on earth are you talking about?"

Allan was desperate to get out everything he wanted to say, yet knew he was making a hash of the conversation. He found himself grasping her shoulders. "Did you love him? You'd been engaged since you were eighteen, I think you said."

"Yes, I loved him." She didn't say anything else; offered no long explanations of how their love had come about.

"But you were separated during the war. You hardly spent any time together."

Elaine said softly, "He was my husband. I won't make less of him."

"You were right about one thing you said earlier," Allan said, standing up, his brain a riot of competing thoughts. She didn't hate him. On the other hand, she had loved Bingo. She wouldn't find it so easy to give her heart to another, no matter what her body seemed to be telling him now. "This conversation is becoming much too disconnected. Well, you have the watch now; you know something of my romantic fool's desire to idealize that image of you; you've forgiven me for virtually killing your husband, for which I thank you. In case we don't happen upon each other later on, thank you for a delightful house party."

Elaine's gaze had not yet wavered. "The war has really played havoc with you ex-soldiers. I don't believe I've talked to a one of you who can make sense of those days. I can't, and I wasn't even a soldier."

Allan searched her face, finding nothing there but questioning and what seemed to be a great desire to care. He couldn't look into that face again. He turned on his heel and left the summerhouse.

At teatime Elaine wandered down to the terrace, wishing she could kill Griselda. She hadn't found the expected peace and sense of well-being from talking over her husband's last days with Allan Marchmont.

At least she had the watch back. For the rest of it, she felt she was wandering in a wood with no way out. Infuriating though it was, Marchmont seemed to have given up on her once his mission to tell her about Bingo was over. Was it his guilt over Bingo's death? Could he only flirt with her, be friends with her, up until she knew the true story?

About twenty people were on the terrace, seated at the tea tables or perched on the brick wall that edged the flagstones. Elaine didn't see Marchmont among them. A couple of village girls in prewar maids' uniforms circulated with trays of sherry; Lady Berry was ensconced behind the large silver teapot at the chief table. Griselda, in a wispy tea gown, sat beside her hostess dealing with the hot water.

Elaine approached these ladies. "Is the poetry reading about to begin, or have I missed it?"

"Don't worry, dear, you haven't missed a thing." Countess Berry handed her daughter a cup of tea with milk but no sugar.

Elaine piled some tidbits from a nearby cake stand onto the saucer. "This is quite a spread, Mother. We are certainly going out in a blaze of glory."

War Widow

"My guests must never have anything but the best. Do try that paté on toast points."

Elaine grabbed for the toast and downed a piece. She felt a void inside, and unfortunately food was the only available nourishment for what ailed her. She doubted whether she would be able to feed her soul on the poetry to come.

Several studious-looking people were milling about at the edge of the terrace and clutching books. "Don't you have to announce them, Mother?" she whispered.

"They said they'd take care of it for me. Miss Averil mentioned something about a surprise."

A young woman with a bob of shoulder-length brown hair—the Joan of Arc from the night before—cleared her throat and held up her hands for silence. "Ladies and gentlemen!" she called out in a voice much suited to public readings. "As you know, I and several of my friends will be reading to you today from our latest works. But first I would like to make you known to a poet who came among us quite unsung. Ladies and gentlemen, here to read Mr. Allan Marchmont's work for you is Lord Berry."

Elaine and her mother stared at each other in amazement. Louis was threading his way through a by now very interested crowd; he was neatly dressed in his only good lounge suit; under his arm he held a copy of Marchmont's book of war pictures. Elaine had glanced over her mother's copy the night before and recognized the jacket from a distance.

Louis placed spectacles upon his nose with a flourish.

"Is there something wrong with Louis' eyes?" Elaine murmured to her mother.

"Heavens, no, they're perfect. I suppose those are plain glass or he couldn't look through them. But what on earth is the boy doing?"

Louis now surveyed the crowd with a youthful confidence more often seen in the peerage than in the general population.

He cleared his throat and his voice, which had always been very fine, rang out clearly. "As Mr. Marchmont's secretary, I have been delegated the task of reading from his work. I shall now begin."

Elaine flashed a look at her mother. The "secretary" business was doubtless news to the countess. Countess Berry was visibly under pressure; surely all that was holding her back from some outburst was a couple of centuries' tradition of breeding. So must an ancestress, on being told Bonaparte's invasion was imminent, have gone on pouring tea.

" 'An early morning on the river Marne,' " Louis recited from the first page of the book, turned it and went on. Elaine realized Louis was reading the captions from the photographs in *Pictures of a Year.* She realized further that, taken one after another, the lines had a poetic feel. She looked with a new respect at Ann Averil who had discovered this amazing fact.

Louis kept reading, and the guests sat spellbound by the young earl's voice reading the stark lines. Elaine wondered if there wasn't an added poignancy in the fact that the text was being read by someone too young to have been in the war. The voice of innocence, reading the words of experience. Yes, Miss Averil had been doubly wise to engage Louis as the reader. Elaine wouldn't have believed her brother would do half so well.

"He must do rhetoric when he gets to Oxford," Griselda whispered. "How the boy has grown up."

Elaine nodded absently, for she was listening to Allan's words. Louis came to the last lines, about a mine-blasted December field, and then closed the book to thunderous applause from the listeners. Elaine joined in with a will.

Louis bowed and gave a boyish smile, then handed off the book to Miss Averil and left the terrace rather quickly. Perhaps a hint of shyness had caught up with him.

Ann Averil raised her hand for quiet again. "Don't you agree with me, ladies and gentlemen, that Allan Marchmont should be known as a poet and not a mere photographer? I know you'll all agree with my decision to urge his publishers to bring out this poem by itself, without the distracting illustrations, in a special edition."

More applause.

"I wonder what Mr. Marchmont will say when he learns Miss Averil has referred to his photographs as 'distracting illustrations,' " Elaine said.

"He seems to me to be a diplomatic young man," Griselda answered, while Countess Berry merely rolled her eyes and shrugged.

"But I think he loves his photographs as much as these poets love their words." Elaine knew in her heart she spoke the truth and wondered how she could be so certain.

She was certain of nothing else about Marchmont.

Chapter Eight

Elaine had no time to brood over Allan Marchmont as she attended evensong, ate yet another festive meal and then, in the dark, motored back to London with Rollo, who showed a depressing tendency to propose. She gathered that Rollo had picked up the idea that Marchmont admired her and thought he should secure her before she was swept off her feet. Those were his very words, in fact.

"Don't worry your head on that score," Elaine shouted over the loud noise of the motor in the two-seater. "Allan Marchmont and I don't get along."

"So you say," Rollo yelled back, "but women never care about that sort of thing. Give them a cave-man every time. I shouldn't have told you how he saved me from a thrashing that time at school."

Elaine didn't want to end the trip with a sore throat. She let the subject drop and concentrated on Rollo's driving.

By the time he dropped her at Griselda's place, to which she had the key—for Griselda was going to spend more time down in Sussex, and Elaine's task was to ask the landlady to water the plants and see that Griselda's favorite stray cat was fed—Elaine's jaws were tired from clenching her teeth. If there was anything more hair-raising than driving with Rollo, it was driving with Rollo at night.

Even if it hadn't been too late to get in at the door, she wouldn't have undertaken the trek to her Businesswomen's Hostel when Griselda's bed and roof were ready to her hand. Elaine had a comfortable chat with Mrs. Gantle, Griselda's landlady, ate some biscuits and drank some hot milk which that lady kindly provided in exchange for a little gossip, and fell into Griselda's narrow bed. She would take her luggage back to the hostel in the early morning and then continue to the office.

Next morning she accomplished the planned program even while wondering, as she lugged her baggage on and off the Underground in the early morning mist and deposited it in her room under Mrs. Beasley's suspicious eye, if such trouble was worthwhile merely to keep Rollo from finding out where she really lived.

What with all this activity, not to mention a nagging feeling that Marchmont and she should somehow become friends, she wasn't surprised to find herself drooping over her typewriting machine.

"Hard weekend?" Katherine Marsh asked, wiggling her eyebrows. "Too much night-life?"

"Too much family life," Elaine replied. She declined to say more, though a part of her was itching to pour all her troubles into a sympathetic ear. She supposed that Katherine would be agog to hear that Elaine's family castle was to be sold and that the romantic flower-sender had turned out to have a connection with Elaine's dead husband. But Elaine was in no mood to handle even mild interest in her own doings. "How was your own weekend?" she asked instead.

Katherine indicated by a sharp look that she knew Elaine was holding out on her, then talked about a dance she had gone to with cousins, a shopping trip, and a married brother's expected child, stories to which Elaine listened with much interest. Katherine's life sounded so pleasant, so simple. At least she didn't have to depend on Rollo Saxonbury for her transportation.

"And I have my mum right taken in with those flowers you let me bring home the other day," Katherine said with satisfaction, rolling another sheet of paper into her typewriter. "I described your friend Rollo when she asked me who'd given them to me. Said it was a chance encounter in the street. Well, so it was, though he didn't give me the flowers."

Elaine eventually got through her Monday and Tuesday with the minimum of incident. Her fatigue decreased, as did her strange, uncomfortable feelings about Marchmont. On Wednesday evening she was washing out some stockings in her room when a sharp knock came at her door.

Mrs. Beasley's chief flunky, her gangly sixteen-year-old daughter Albertina, poked her head round the door. "Telephone for you, miss."

Elaine rushed with wet hands downstairs to the front hall, brushing past the girl with only murmured thanks. So few people knew how to reach her at the hostel that she expected nothing but tragedy from a telephone call. She couldn't remember the last time one of her family had contacted her in this way.

But her mother's voice was blessedly cheerful. "Dear, I have a job for you. A man wants to look over Berryhill, a man with an obscene lot of money, and you must help me out. I've just spoken with him on the telephone. Bring him down to see the place and help me charm him. He seemed so awfully keen on meeting my daughter. I'm afraid he gave me the feeling he wouldn't consider the purchase if you didn't drive down with him from London."

"What?" Elaine was certain she hadn't heard right. "Slow

down, Mother, I don't quite follow you. What has a potential buyer got to do with me?"

"You're a ladyship, dear, and he thinks titles are too utterly glamorous."

"Oh. An American."

"How did you guess? You will do it, won't you? I suggested Friday, since you would have to give your office notice tomorrow."

"Mother, don't you realize that if I take off a day from my job, I could be sacked? People simply don't say they're going to motor down to Sussex instead of coming in."

"Oh, I'm sure you can think up a good story. Only don't say anything about a death in the family, if you please. I always think those sorts of lies are unlucky."

Elaine sighed and leaned against the wall. "How did this happen? Why should you have a buyer for the house? You haven't yet put it on the market, have you?" Or was this another detail Lady Berry simply hadn't mentioned?

"No, but you know how such things get about. Americans must have their ears to the ground."

"They are already lying on the ground, rolling in their money, as Louis would say, so I suppose it's natural they should hear things others don't," Elaine said dryly.

"What? Oh, you're so clever, dear, but don't insult the man to his face, please. Simply look pretty and smile a lot and tell him all about the history of the house. Americans love that sort of thing. They can't get it at home."

Lady Berry knew a lot of Americans, who peppered London society, and Elaine believed her mother knew what she was talking about. "Are you so eager, then, for Berryhill to be sold?" she asked, unable to keep the wistful note out of her voice.

Perhaps wistful notes didn't transmit easily over the telephone wires. Lady Berry seemed to sense nothing amiss as she answered, "I'm eager for us to send Louis to university and keep myself, not to mention you, in some modest sort of style."

"I'm happy as I am."

"Nonsense. You must get back into the swim of things and meet more men. If you won't pay attention to those at my parties, we must look elsewhere. Bingo wouldn't have wanted you to mourn him forever, dear."

"Perhaps it's too soon, though."

"Three years is much too long, on the contrary. Will you do this for me? I've given the American your address and told him to be there in his car at ten o'clock on Friday."

"Mother!"

"You see, I have every confidence you can explain things to those people at your job."

"Well—what's his name?"

When Elaine entered the office next day, she had no hope of really getting leave to flit off on her mother's projects the day after. Lady Berry simply didn't understand the working world. The typewriters were nominally under the charge of one of the senior female stenographers, and Elaine had never yet gone to the said Miss Tarrant with a request of any kind. She knew nobody who had. In general, it was believed at Borderfield's and throughout the wage-earning world that nothing was serious enough to warrant staying away from a job.

Elaine believed this herself, and she wasn't surprised when her request to take the day for a family errand was met with a startled negative. More lighthearted than not—she would tell Mother she had done her best, and she would be spared an auto trip with a stranger—she was strolling back down the corridor after her short session with Miss Tarrant when a male voice hailed her from behind.

"Mrs. Westwood! Anything one can do for you?"

Elaine gave a polite nod to Mr. Parkington as he limped up to her. Miss Tarrant was his secretary, and it was a joke throughout Borderfield's how much the spinster mothered the cheerful young man.

"Why, no, thank you, Mr. Parkington. I'm perfectly fine."

He shuffled his feet a bit. "I thought, er, that is, old Tarrant's a bit of a stickler, what? I've told her you should have that day off. Why not, in fact? Didn't I hear you offer to stay late without pay until you'd made up the time?"

"Mr. Parkington! Were you listening at the door just now?"

His eyes sparkled shyly behind his pince-nez. "You've caught me out. But what I say, Mrs. Westwood, is that a fine, hard-working young woman like yourself ought to be able to take the time for a family emergency."

"To tell you the truth, sir, it's not that much of an emergency, and I can perfectly well tell my mother I can't get leave." Elaine hesitated. "I'm not particularly inclined to do my mother this favor, if you want the truth."

"Rotten luck," Parkington said with a chuckle. "I've got the Tarrant to set you free, and that's that."

"But can't you simply tell her not to bother after all?"

"Couldn't possibly, ma'am. I never go back on my word." And Mr. Parkington went on his way down the hall in rather a hurry, Elaine thought. She wondered, exasperated, why he had taken it upon himself to rescue her.

On Friday Elaine slept through breakfast, dressed carefully in her best coat and skirt without being rushed for once, and emerged onto the dingy hostel steps at about five minutes to the hour of ten. The day was cloudy but predominantly blue: The best sort of day for motoring, and the American was sure to have an open car. She was looking into her bag to make certain she had a scarf to tie round her hat when a small, purring sound reached her ears. A gigantic Hispano-Suiza was rolling to a halt at the edge of the pavement. Not an open car at all, but an extremely luxurious one, with a uniformed chauffeur at the wheel. The back door was already open and someone emerging before the driver could even bring the car to a full stop.

Elaine hurried down the steps and put out her hand. A large man, perhaps in his mid-thirties, in a dark overcoat and a dark hat, shook it heartily.

"Oswald Van Vliet at your service, ma'am," he said with a smile. He had a pasty, rather beefy face and sharp dark eyes. His clothes were as expensive-looking as his car and fit his bulky figure extremely well. "You must be Lady Elaine. Your mother told me all about you."

"I hope Mother was discreet," Elaine said with a laugh.

"Not at all," her new acquaintance said, taking her elbow to escort her to the car. He and his chauffeur settled her in with rugs and pillows, and he took his seat beside her. "She told me everything. How you're the family eccentric, which is why you're living in that dump." He gestured back at the hostel, which was disappearing as the quiet car moved majestically forward. "And how pretty you are. Underestimated there, though." He shot Elaine a certain look.

Her heart sank, and she made sure her knees were as well out of grasping range as they could be in the close quarters of an automobile. "So! You're interested in Berryhill," she said brightly. "Have you decided to settle in England, then, Mr. Van Vliet?"

"I never say never, but I'm mainly looking for investments over here," he said. She thought he glanced at her knee. She also thought he spoke in a repressive tone. She edged the knee in question even more into the corner and wondered what they could possibly talk about for a two-hour drive if she wasn't to question him about his purposes. She need not have worried. It soon became obvious that he meant to spend the whole drive down into Sussex in questioning her.

"Well. Lady Elaine." He did seem to like a title. "Tell me about the way things are in England. If you married an ordinary Joe, would you be a lady anymore or just a missus?"

"As it happens, I did marry an ordinary Joe," Elaine said with a smile. "Perhaps my mother didn't mention that I'm a widow."

"She didn't. War?"

Elaine nodded. "Were you involved in the war, sir?"

"You bet. Munitions. Came back over as soon as I could."

He kept asking questions, and she found herself telling him about nursing during the war, and country life in Sussex, and her court presentation, and a dozen other things.

She laughed as he helped her out of the car two hours later. "Mr. Van Vliet, I never would have believed I could know so little about a man after spending so much time with him. Did you really have to keep the conversation on me the whole time?"

"Just trying to get to know you, your ladyship," he said with an odd half-bow. "I'm an ordinary mug."

"Somehow I doubt that. But that's neither here nor there. I should have talked about the history of the house to get you ready, but I'll do it now. There are some ruins on the property that might go back to the ninth century, and—"

"It's all swell," he interrupted with a grin. Putting a hand on the small of her back, he shepherded her up the front steps, where Norton was already opening the door. Elaine thought Van Vliet barely glanced at the house, but he scrutinized the solid English butler with evident appreciation.

Inside they found Countess Berry in the small salon, looking her countrified best in soft tweeds. Elaine was surprised not to see Griselda and hoped she was resting in her room. She would run up to see her mother-in-law before she left.

A couple of spaniels belonging to the gardener—Lady Berry detested house dogs—provided ornamentation and conversation for the few minutes of greeting. Elaine had to congratulate her mother on coming up with all the accouterments an American would find necessary to an English country experience. She busied herself in stroking the dogs' silky heads while Van Vliet gave her mother what she believed Americans called the "once over." He had doffed his dark overcoat, revealing an impeccable suit of clothes, blinding linen, and a diamond pin in his tie. "You've got quite a place here," he greeted the countess.

"We're glad you like it," Lady Berry returned, looking somewhat dazed.

Van Vliet leaned forward, hands on his knees, toward Lady Berry. "Well, countess, the place is pretty snazzy looking. Could use a little fixing up here and there, but it'll do me just fine. Now I've got to talk to my partner, but I'm telling you, it looks good."

Lady Berry and Elaine stared at him. "Do you mean to say you're nearly sure about Berryhill?" Countess Berry said in a careful voice, speaking slowly as though not to a native speaker. "Without even looking at it?"

He blinked. "Why not?"

"Because you might look about and not like it," Elaine said. "Maybe the estate is too big or too small. Maybe you'll find the house too shabby to be worth fixing up. Maybe you won't like the neighborhood." She tried to think of every drawback. This was happening much too fast. "We haven't even put it on the market," she finished with a little sigh.

"Oh, don't worry about the money side. You'll get top price," Van Vliet said.

"But you do have to talk to your business partner first," the countess said, speaking firmly, as she might to Louis.

"Yeah. We'll be in touch." Van Vliet's eyes lit up as a maid wheeled in a tea cart. "Say, this tea business is a kick."

Lady Berry began to pour and ask the proper questions about milk, sugar, and hot water, and Van Vliet suggested that she give him whatever was the usual thing. Elaine gauged his appetite by his substantial size and passed him a plate of cucumber sandwiches and walnut cake. He began to eat with relish.

"Mr. Van Vliet," Elaine said sternly, when she saw that he was between bites, "after driving all the way down here, I insist that you see over the house and walk the grounds. You simply can't take a house you haven't seen."

"I wanted to take it sight unseen. But my partner thought I should come down and take a look."

"Thank heaven your partner is looking out for your interests," Lady Berry said.

"Besides, it's not like I'm buying it."

Elaine stared. "Then what have we been talking about?"

"Didn't you know?" Now it was his turn to stare. "I'm after a lease, you see. Need a swell place to entertain while I'm over here. A big place not too far from London. Two hours is kind of far, but on the other hand, this is one whale of a place you've got here."

"More like an elephant than a whale," murmured Elaine. "A white one." She glanced at her mother. "You didn't know he was thinking of taking a lease, Mother?"

"No! Perhaps I didn't understand your phone call properly, Mr. Van Vliet. We never came close to finding a tenant, and my mind was all on our new plans to sell."

"You can still sell, though we won't want buyers coming through while I'm staying here," he suggested.

As if they would, if they could get an income out of the house! Elaine and her mother exchanged happy, hopeful looks. Elaine thought the very suddenness of this spendthrift millionaire's appearance on the scene was highly suspicious, yet she couldn't quite see why she should think so, or whom she should suspect of what. She supposed she shouldn't be surprised. Life was like that, with nothing happening on a project for a long, long time, then everything suddenly coming together.

"Come along, Mr. Van Vliet," Elaine said. "Even if you're not going to buy, we'd feel terribly remiss if you couldn't tell your business partner what Berryhill is like. The short tour, but you must have one. Don't you agree, Mother?"

"Yes, my dear, take him round the gardens first. It looks like rain. I'll see cook about the luncheon. You will stay, Mr. Van Vliet?" Her mother had the familiar matchmaking look in her eye, Elaine noticed cynically. An American millionaire would be quite a catch.

"Whatever you ladies say." Van Vliet got up from his chair, putting aside his empty plate and cup. He beamed at them, whether at the prospect of yet more food or in anticipation of seeing a cavernous house in the company of a young woman who was being pushed into his arms, Elaine couldn't tell. At the moment, she didn't really care.

Chapter Nine

"How *did* you hear about Berryhill, Mr. Van Vliet?" Elaine asked on the way back to London, when he had finished praising her mother's excellent luncheon and hinting that the cook might go with the house—which Elaine was sure the cook would be delighted to do.

"Around," was his answer, with a wink; and no matter how subtly Elaine tried to phrase further questions, she couldn't get a thing out of the American.

Finally, probably in order to put an end to her curiosity, Van Vliet fell into a post-lunch doze as the auto purred its way up to London, leaving Elaine to think over what seemed to be her family's marvelous luck. For unless Van Vliet disappeared like fairy gold at the stroke of midnight, their salvation seemed a settled thing.

Louis would be delighted that a tenant had appeared at last—or if not delighted, he would definitely recognize it as the lesser of two evils. The money from Van Vliet would pay Louis' school fees and Countess Berry's keep in some modest abode. Maybe they could even get a little bit ahead.

Glancing at her traveling companion, Elaine wondered

hard about this unexpected savior. She and her mother had tried to question him on many things as they enjoyed a rare, lavish lunch which Elaine suspected was the cook's way of auditioning for the coming tenant; but he was either an expert at evasion or truly didn't know what they were getting at. After spending nearly a day with Oswald Van Vliet, Elaine didn't know a thing about him save for the small tidbit, which he had let slip out, that he came from New York.

Well, the Saxonbury solicitors would surely look out for the family interests, and whatever quirks Van Vliet was determined to keep hidden, perhaps they were only small, personal ones . . . although it would be rather glamorous if his business dealt with the kinds of shady goings-on that made films so exciting. Elaine only hoped he didn't have friends who would be hard on the furniture.

Her companion came to consciousness with a snort, making Elaine realize he had truly been sleeping and not just shutting his eyes, as she had suspected. "Well," he said with a friendly look at her. "I have a favor to ask."

"I'll do my best."

"Great. Then the thing is, I want you to go out with me. Never been out on the town with an English lady. Get you a break from washing your stockings in that boardinghouse."

Elaine stared. How could he know with such accuracy how she passed her evenings?

"I know a lot of girls," he said with one of his winks, to explain his clairvoyance. "Well, what do you say?"

Somehow, despite the fact that he had given her several looks of masculine appreciation, she hadn't expected the offer of an evening. "Certainly I'll come out with you," she answered, wondering what possessed her. Perhaps she was only trying to be nice to the man who, if all went well, would be solving her immediate problems.

It occurred to her that her landlady Mrs. Beasley would

have a fit if she could know. Somehow this thought made Elaine more determined. "It would be fun," she echoed Mr. Van Vliet's words.

On Saturday night Elaine dressed herself in her best. She assumed she and her escort would have dinner and perhaps go dancing. He hadn't mentioned the theater. Her Paris dinner dress once again came in useful, as it had during the weekend at Berryhill.

She went down to wait in the cheerless lounge and saw Mrs. Beasley sailing by, her ornamented bosom making a sort of jingling noise.

"Going out, Mrs. Westwood?" she asked, nostrils flaring with evident disapproval. She looked Elaine's costume up and down. "With a man?"

"In a manner of speaking, ma'am," Elaine answered cheerfully, glad that her velvet evening coat was already put on against the chill in the lounge and her décolletage safe from the landlady's scrutiny. "A friend of my family's. If he doesn't bring me back before you close the doors, I plan to stay at my mother-in-law's in Clapham." She handed over a paper she had ready. "Here is the telephone number of her house and the name of the landlady. It's a most respectable place, and Mrs. Gantle can confirm that I have permission to stay there."

Mrs. Beasley took the slip of paper without a discouraging word; but Elaine knew that she did not believe a word of this and assumed Elaine would be staying out all night for wild doings of an unspeakable nature.

Casual as she tried to feel about her only night out in London with a man since Bingo's death, Elaine noticed a slight flutter in her mid-section as she waited for Oswald Van Vliet's car to appear. She wondered how much more fluttery she would be if he were a man she was attracted to—a man such as Allan Marchmont. Resolutely she put all thoughts of that confusing man aside; it would be unfair to Mr. Van Vliet if his companion spent the whole evening musing over someone else. Out on the front steps, she breathed deeply of the brisk yet smoky air in the drab street, enjoying as she hadn't in years the anticipatory sensation of being outside in evening clothes before night had fallen.

At seven o'clock the Hispano-Suiza rolled around the corner. Elaine's heart leaped, although she would much rather have had it leap for the man inside than for the car, or more exactly, for the very fact that a car was appearing to bear her away on an adventure.

But this was quite enough, and she was smiling happily as Mr. Van Vliet, his rather bulky shape contained smartly in evening clothes, shepherded her into the vehicle while his chauffeur held the door politely.

"Well, Lady Elaine," Van Vliet said as they rode along, "I thought we'd do dinner at the Savoy, but our reservation's not till eight, so how's about a drink at the Ritz bar first? A lot of my pals go there."

"Whatever you like," Elaine said, determined to be agreeable and glad she was a widow who might do more or less as she liked. Girls did go everywhere these days, and she knew they had always been a little freer in America, but she was vaguely shocked at the prospect of doing all this without so much as another couple, if not a stern chaperone such as would have been fastened to her in her debutante days. As if she could have gone for "a drink" at all in the old days!

She needn't have worried, as it turned out. Though Van Vliet had called it a place where his friends went, the Ritz bar was full of people *she* knew, and by the time she had greeted three women from her debutante season and their escorts, she was feeling very much at home and extremely well chaperoned. Mr. Van Vliet stood by with a glazed, impressed expression as Elaine introduced Major Hollander, Lord Inglethorpe, and Sir Ralph Edmonds. How lucky that Bab, Gwyneth, and Eliza all happened to be out with important-sounding men. Eliza was even married to her baronet, giving Van Vliet the thrill of meeting another "Lady." Gwyneth, like Elaine, was a war widow, and Major Hollander was her older brother. As for Bab Playfair and Lord Inglethorpe, Elaine suspected there were bets laid on at the clubs over how long their courtship would take to come to the point.

"Any of you people care to join us at the Savoy?" Van Vliet asked the table.

Elaine was rather sorry when no one could—they would have been chaperones!—but she had no time to ponder on whether or not she should take one of the girls aside and urge her to come with them. The others were already making cheerful plans to join up after their own theater party and go dancing with Van Vliet and Elaine when three men, dressed in rather flashy lounge suits, entered the bar and were instantly hailed by Elaine's escort.

"Fellas!" He called them over to the table. "Just get in? These are my English friends. Lords and ladies"—with a quick, all-encompassing smile around the table—"these gentlemen are some business associates of mine."

Elaine looked up with a social smile as Van Vliet began the introductions. The three "fellas" were rough-looking customers, she thought, despite what were obviously expensive clothes. Like Van Vliet, they all happened to be substantially built. One of them, named Sanguinetti, was darkly handsome, evidently of Italian extraction. The others, called Brown and Porter respectively, didn't seem as English in looks as their names might have indicated.

Everyone pressed them to sit down—Elaine thought her English friends must be as fascinated as she to talk to such dangerous-looking Americans—and they squeezed three more seats in around the overburdened table, Sanguinetti pressing his chair close to Elaine's. He leered at her, and she had to edge away from the touch of his striped-flannel thigh, which unfortunately brought her into closer contact than she liked with Van Vliet.

"Lords and ladies, eh?" Mr. Porter said with a glance around. He was a solidly built, light-haired man perhaps in his thirties, with a shrewd eye and a nose which had evidently been broken at least once. Elaine looked at the nose and suddenly knew what all these men were like: The popular image of prizefighters. Could they be?

"Yeah, great, ain't it?" Van Vliet answered. "Now take Lady Elaine here"—he indicated Elaine with a flourish of his hand, which sported several large gold rings—"her ma's a countess. Just like in the flickers."

The Americans looked at her in awe, and Elaine smiled modestly, hoping her English tablemates wouldn't say anything nasty or quelling. She found the American interest in social details rather endearing, though she supposed it would wear on one after a while.

"You gentlemen are the ones who intrigue us," Gwyneth Halperin said with a giggle. "What part of America are you from?"

"Chicago," said Brown, his only contribution to the conversation thus far.

"The West!" Gwyneth sighed. "How romantic. I've read your Mr. Whitman."

The Americans exchanged blank looks.

"She always was brainy," her brother, Major Hollander, apologized for her with a shrug. "I've always had a fancy to visit America. Should I do better to go all across the country in a train, as one of the fellows did on his world tour, or stick to the eastern coast?"

Elaine was concentrating on edging as far as she could from the males on each side of her. Her shifting away from Sanguinetti made Van Vliet give her a sidelong look of speculation; inching away from Van Vliet brought her perilously near to the hairy hand of Sanguinetti, which rested in a predatory yet casual manner on his own thigh but which she knew was waiting for the chance to grasp hers. She felt no wider than a pencil.

This thought amused her as she let her gaze wander around the room. The Ritz bar was a dark and smoky place, and Elaine often wondered at its popularity; but then, she reminded herself, people did like to sit in the dark and to smoke. She glanced at a couple at a corner table, then away, then quickly back again, the resemblance was so striking . . .

"Louis!" she said aloud, jumping up from her seat.

One of the Americans nodded and said something about a place called St. Louis, but Elaine's English friends seemed to understand the reference at once. All turned in the direction of Elaine's shocked stare. The young Earl of Berry was seated with Lady Miranda Winchapel, looking very cozy. A glass in front of Louis probably held something unsuitable for a growing boy. Goggle Winchapel was dressed in low-cut red.

"Pardon me," Elaine said to Van Vliet, and wiggled out from between the chairs. She marched over to the table in question, threading her way through the crowded place, rehearsing with every step the dressing-down she was about to give her brother. He couldn't have seen her yet; he didn't look either furtive or guilty. She didn't think Goggle had noticed her, either, but Goggle wasn't known for noticing other women even in the least crowded and sunniest of places, let alone the Ritz bar.

Elaine remembered Louis had been in town all week, supposedly under the care of his employer, Allan Marchmont.

Well! Was this the sort of guidance Marchmont provided to an under-aged lad? Elaine would give Allan a large piece of her mind when she got through with Louis.

Nobody was more surprised than Elaine when she arrived at the table, smiled sweetly at her brother and Goggle, and said, "Lady Miranda! And dear Louis! Won't you join my friends? We'd love to have you. And my escort and I are going on to the Savoy. Can't you come with us?"

Louis gaped at her as though she was the most hideous of monsters. Goggle gave a faint but superior smile with her carefully reddened lips, in a shade identical to her gown. As always, she let her eyes run up and down Elaine's costume. Elaine was pleased to sense that her Paris dress, at least, seemed to have the fashionable Lady Miranda's approval.

"No!" Louis answered her invitation in a horror-struck voice to match his expression.

"We'd be delighted," Goggle said at the same time, rising. "Is that your table? Oh, I see Bab and the others. How cozy. Come, Louis, it will be fun to squeeze two more chairs in there. And dinner at the Savoy sounds good to me."

Though very young, Louis was every inch the gentleman. There was no way he could contradict the woman he was escorting. Meekly he followed the ladies back to Van Vliet's table. A waiter was dispatched to fit in two more chairs, a gentleman rose to give Miranda his, and introductions began again as the newcomers were presented to the Americans.

"Goggle, you are the limit," Eliza said, with a significant glance at Louis. "Are you out on some sort of a dare?"

Elaine hoped Louis didn't hear this remark. Due to the scarcity of chairs, he hadn't yet been able to sit down and was hanging about the edges of the group with one of the men from Chicago. She could hear him asking a boyish question about buffalo on the Western plains.

Lady Miranda merely looked mysterious and turned her attention to charming the strange men at the table.

Soon Elaine's friends had to run off to *Chu Chin Chow*, the fashionable musical, the Chicago visitors had plans of some sort, and when everything had settled down and Van Vliet discovered he was really going to have dinner with an earl as well as two ladies with a capital L, his joy knew no bounds. Elaine wondered if he would have some sort of attack when he found out Goggle was a duke's daughter.

She resisted the urge to take her brother's arm as they left the bar; she couldn't ignore her own escort to that extent. Instead she saw to it that she and Van Vliet walked behind so she could observe how the other couple behaved. She thought Goggle was rather hanging on Louis, but she couldn't fault his behavior from the back. He was polite, helping Lady Miranda on with her fur, ushering the ladies through doorways and doing the proper things with hats and gloves.

The trip along Piccadilly and down to the Strand was more comfortable than Elaine would have thought it would be. She had planned to stare hard at her brother the whole time, but Louis, in a jump seat, peppered Mr. Van Vliet with questions about the vehicle. He avoided his sister's eye, but in a most natural manner; and Elaine was reduced to enduring Goggle's drawling gossip about the latest society pairings.

"It seems odd that there is anyone left to talk about, with so many young men gone," Goggle said with a sigh. Then her eyes widened. "Oh, I'm sorry, Elaine, I didn't mean to remind you of Bingo."

"That's all right. It's been three years. You're very kind to think of it." She hoped she didn't sound as amazed as she felt at the notion of Goggle being kind.

"Well, here we are, girls—ladies," Van Vliet's voice

interrupted them eventually, and Elaine looked up to see that the car was at the entrance of the Savoy Hotel. Louis was examining the Hispano-Suiza's bar fittings and had to be poked before he was fully conscious of where he was. Then he sprang out after Van Vliet and turned back into the perfect escort.

"So you're really a lord, kid?" Van Vliet was saying to Louis as they entered the establishment and headed for the dining room. Louis admitted that he was.

Elaine tried to look at her brother with a critical eye and decided that he could pass for twenty-one, especially in the dim light of evening. He was tall and filled out his evening clothes admirably, thanks to his athletic habits and a lucky choice of parents. His handsome face, which to Elaine would never be anything but her little brother's, was less rounded than it had been a year before. Of course, being an earl didn't hurt his air of maturity, since Van Vliet was quick to inform the headwaiter of this phenomenon as soon as they entered the dining room. Louis looked embarrassed but straightened perceptibly.

Elaine grabbed Goggle's arm before they were seated at the table. "Lady Miranda and I will be back shortly," she said with a sweet smile at her escort.

Van Vliet nodded politely, respectful of female mysteries, and Elaine nearly burst out laughing when, on turning to walk away, she heard him say to the waiter, or Louis, "While the girls are in the can . . ."

Elaine closed the door of the ladies' room with a snap and decided to keep things fairly good-natured. There was a maid sitting on a small gilt chair and women going in and out all the time. "Whatever are you doing with Louis?" she asked in a low voice, trying not to sound accusing or as shocked as she felt.

Goggle shrugged. She had taken the opportunity to redo

her lips at the mirror, and she was looking into her own eyes as she said, "He's a very sweet boy."

"Of sixteen," Elaine muttered, not wanting to shock the maid. "There must be laws against this sort of thing." Somehow her resolution to keep the conversation light and non-accusing was coming to naught.

"He's an earl." Goggle shrugged again. "He's very presentable. And as we were saying earlier, there are so few left."

"There are plenty of people your own age or older. Some of them are even men," Elaine said, fluffing her own hair in the mirror, since she was there.

"For heaven's sake, I'm not doing anything with him but spend the evening. He's very sweet, and it doesn't hurt a boy of that age to be in love with an older woman."

"So now he's in love with you." Elaine returned her comb to her handbag. "You know he hasn't any money."

"I have," Goggle said simply.

She did. The Wincastle estate was one that hadn't been on the short end of the fortunes of war. Elaine wondered in a panicky way if Goggle could be meaning to marry Louis out of hand—in Scotland or something—with the promise of saving his home.

"You must be six years older," Elaine said. "That means so much at his age."

"But it means less and less as time goes by," Goggle replied. Elaine finally looked at the girl's eyes in the mirror and saw the light of mischief in them.

"Oh! You're not serious." Elaine gave a relieved sigh.

"Of course not. I do like Louis, and if in six years I'm still on the loose, he'll be over twenty-one and I'll be first in the queue."

"But in the meantime you might break his heart. Is he really in love with you? He seemed more taken with the car on the drive over."

"Yes, he likes my little sports car too. He's just a normal male." She hesitated and gave that mischievous smile again. "In many ways."

"You're still teasing—aren't you?"

Goggle's paint-rimmed eyes turned serious. "Elaine, I'm not going to take advantage of your brother. Do we understand each other?"

"I suppose so. But how did this happen? How did you and he ever meet here in town?"

"That's very simple," Goggle said, taking out a vial of perfume. Her scent was an exotic, patchouli-based one, of course. "I took a fancy to look at Allan Marchmont's pictures in that gallery, whatever it's called, in Shepherd's Market, and there was Louis on some sort of commission. Surely you know your brother is working for Mr. Marchmont?"

"Yes, it's a new thing." Elaine narrowed her eyes. "And you're interested in Mr. Marchmont's photography, are you?"

"Heavens, no. He's a very attractive man, and I hoped he might be there sort of standing by the things. I gather, though, that artists generally don't do that unless there's a party."

"As you say, men are scarce," Elaine said in a dry tone.

"They don't have to be scarce for Allan Marchmont to be attractive." Goggle had put away the perfume, and she now took a small brush to her shining dark hair. "And he has piles of money in the family, all from some little Victorian venture like paper boxes, but that doesn't matter these days." She paused. "Except to my mother, of course. And do you know Cynthia Bimberton, who is positively desperate for a man, actually found out that if you go back far enough in the Marchmont family, there's baronet blood?"

"Not really?"

"Yes, some old Hampshire family. A detail like that might fob off Mama."

"You're very thorough. I must say I'd rather have you go after Allan Marchmont than Louis." She was uneasily aware that she was not quite telling the truth.

"Good," Goggle said with a sharp glance from her long dark eyes. "I did wonder. You and he seemed very cozy the other weekend down at Berryhill."

"Nothing," Elaine said, shrugging. "He knew Bingo in the war."

"Oh. That explains it."

"What do you think of Mr. Van Vliet?" Elaine asked casually.

Goggle gave a shrug that was almost French, at any rate more expressive than any gesture of Elaine's. "Americans are another kettle of fish," she said in a reflective tone, as though she had considered the problem. "They aren't quite the same species, are they?"

"That's rather a harsh assessment. He seems nice, and he's very rich."

"But I wouldn't dream of encroaching on your territory, Elaine dear."

"He's only a business acquaintance, really. Feel free."

Goggle made no comment to this and rummaged in her bag.

"We'd better get back to the, er, men," Elaine said, noticing that Goggle was about to launch forth with a project involving her eyebrows. She found it hard to say "men" when her little brother was one of them. "You look perfect," she added to stop the proceedings.

"Oh, yes, madam, you do," put in the maid, making Elaine jump. She had totally forgotten that anyone else was in the room.

For an instant Elaine looked at herself and Goggle with an appraising eye in the mirror. Had they been better friends they would have made an excellent team, one fair, the other dark. Elaine should have been wearing black for the best contrast to Goggle's red, but the blue silk was surprisingly good.

Goggle seemed to read Elaine's thoughts. "They are a couple of lucky . . . men," she said with that telling hesitation, and led the way back to the table.

Chapter Ten

Back at the table, Van Vliet sprang up to seat the ladies. "I've been ordering the meal. Lord Berry here told me what you gals would like. No objection to caviar? Nor to lobster? Then there's some French thing the waiter told us we couldn't go wrong with. All set? Here, Lady Elaine, have some of these appetizer things. Lady Miranda? Good. Eat up, ladies."

Dinner conversation focused on England, mostly, from Van Vliet's tourist point of view. Louis was given the news that his host was going to lease the ancestral home.

"You don't say! Capital," was his assessment, as he shoveled in his main course. Elaine was relieved at such a practical reaction, but she might have hoped for a bit more sensitivity in a landowner. Well, Louis wasn't a very experienced landowner, at that.

"It's like *Persuasion*," put in Goggle. "Remember how Sir Walter Elliot had to let Kellynch Hall?"

Elaine's gaze riveted to the other girl. She bit back just in time a remark about her astonishment that Goggle had ever read a Jane Austen novel, or any novel, let alone remembered details and proper names from it. The males, of course, looked mystified at Lady Miranda's remark.

"Who did he rent it to?" Van Vliet asked, turning his sharp eyes on Lady Miranda with every appearance of real interest.

"Admiral Croft," she answered at once, as though it was an examination at school.

Van Vliet looked impressed to be in the same category as an admiral.

"Jane Austen aside, it's providential that Mr. Van Vliet should be wanting a country house and think of Berryhill," Elaine said.

The males looked more surprised at another strange name being brought into the conversation than they had at the talk of books, but neither asked about the Austen female.

"Berryhill is perfect," Van Vliet said. "The real old English thing. Not a moat, but you can't have everything."

"Wincastle has a moat," said Goggle.

"Oh. Your old family place?"

"One of them," Goggle answered with a shrug.

"I've got a couple of places myself, over in the States, but they don't have moats."

"I think it's marvelous that you are so fond of English history, being an American," Elaine put in, smiling at her escort. It had struck her that if he mused too long on the subject of moats he might begin to want one so much that he would give up the idea of Berryhill. "One gets the impression from books that Americans are always making money and think of nothing else. Yet every American I've met—mostly in the war—they were all very well-rounded people with a variety of interests." She hesitated. "Uppermost, of course, being the wish to go back home."

"Without getting blown up or gassed first," Van Vliet

agreed with a nod. "That was the first object in life, to stay in it, no matter where a soldier came from."

"You were in the war, sir?" Louis asked, his eyes lighting up. "You came over here?"

"You bet. Here and France too."

Louis sighed deeply, then began to pepper his host with questions. "But you say you wanted to get back home. Wasn't it exciting, being in the thick of it?"

"Well, sure, any man likes being in on the action, but on the other hand . . ."

"Were you a flyer? My brother-in-law was a flyer."

Elaine exchanged glances with Goggle. Strange how she and the younger girl seemed to be turning into allies of a sort. "Louis, dear, maybe Mr. Van Vliet doesn't want to dwell on the horrors of war during his dinner," she said, keeping her tone of voice light. Searching her mind for a suitable substitute, she added, "Tell us about your new job instead. My brother is secretary to a literary man," she told Van Vliet.

"Earls gotta do that?" Van Vliet asked with a frown.

"Earls without money do," Louis muttered with downcast eyes, his face reddening. Elaine perceived a struggle going on. On the one hand, he was an ill-tempered schoolboy whose sister had just chastised him in public. On the other, he was a man of the world who was earning his own living. When he looked up, the man of the world had won and enthusiasm was clear in Louis' eyes. "But having a job's not so bad. Marchmont has had me taking messages and things back and forth to the picture gallery to save him the trouble; and I read over the things he has to sign for his cousin's paper mill down in Hampshire. He's a sort of partner, but silent, he tells me. And he's letting me help him on his new project, taking pictures of the veterans around the city. Even let me take a photograph or two on my own and says he'll credit me if they come out all right."

"Really?" Elaine was impressed by Marchmont's kindness. "And does he dictate his letters to you? With a family business to see to as well as books, there must be letters."

Louis flushed. "He tried that, but there's a stenographer person he uses, a female, and he told me he's decided not to hurt her feelings by taking the work away from her."

"That was good of him."

"Marchmont, you say? A picture gallery?" asked Van Vliet. "I'll have to go see that stuff, if it's popular."

"It's most educational," Goggle said. "But tell me something really important, sir. Where do you think we should go dancing after this?"

"Somewhere dark," Louis suggested.

Elaine hid a smile. Her brother was evidently wishing for his youth to be less than obvious. Or—uncomfortable thought!—he wanted it to be dark so he could more easily take liberties with Lady Miranda though under his sister's supervision.

"They're all dark," Goggle said with a wave of her hand. "There's a new place, very much the thing. The Purple Club."

"But Mr. Van Vliet and I have arranged to meet the others at Ciro's after their theater," Elaine said. "Do say you and Louis will come with us." She wasn't going to lose track of Louis for the rest of the evening if she could help it.

"You wouldn't miss it, would you, ladyship?" Van Vliet gave Goggle a good-humored leer. "Maybe the purple place afterwards. The night is young."

Goggle gave an expressive shrug that did distracting things to her gown. "Purple would clash with my dress," she said with a laugh. "Ciro's it is."

* * *

War Widow

When Van Vliet's little party arrived at the nightclub, Elaine realized just how long it had been since she had been out socially. She and Bingo had gone dancing in London, but all that might have taken place a hundred years ago. The dances had changed, and the people seemed younger than before the war or even during it. Maybe it was the new, less structured gowns of the women; or maybe the all-for-fun look in the eyes of so many of the men.

The foursome paused in the doorway of a huge, darkened space filled with chattering people and waiters dashing about with laden trays. Elaine glanced uneasily at Louis, then sidled up to him and said, "We are drinking lemon squash from here on out, my boy."

Louis gave her a murderous look. "You too?"

"Me too. I wouldn't make you do it alone. We'll call it a family quirk."

Her brother seemed slightly mollified by the idea that she as well as he would be abstaining. Even Van Vliet, when ordering drinks in his expansive manner, didn't protest too much when the earl and his sister chose to forego spirits. He gave Elaine a private look which she thought expressed understanding or perhaps even approval of her solution to the problem of being out with a young boy.

"Let's dance, Louis," Goggle suggested when the jazz band struck up a tango. "Show me what you can do."

Elaine was also extremely interested to see what Louis was capable of in the tango line. He had been so very bad when he and Goggle waltzed at Berryhill. When Van Vliet suggested the two of them dance as well, she led the way to a spot near Louis and Goggle and prepared to observe them.

She observed them so closely that she missed a step; then she righted herself with the assistance of Van Vliet, who tugged her against his chest in a way she thought she ought to protest. But she was too interested in what the other couple was doing. Louis was actually holding his own. Perhaps that waltz at the masquerade ball had simply been too old-fashioned for a boy his age.

"The kid's got rhythm," Van Vliet said with a wink. "Don't worry."

"Is it that obvious I'm checking up on him?" Elaine laughed. "I apologize for being less than attentive to you, Mr. Van Vliet. I had no idea we'd meet my little brother this evening, and you're an angel to treat him so kindly."

"Call me Oswald," he said into her ear, causing her a momentary panicky sensation. Then he spun her out, letting go of her hand, and she found herself looking into the quizzical gray eyes of Allan Marchmont.

"May I have this dance?" he asked with a crooked smile.

"Someone else is already having it," Elaine said.

"The next one, then. Lady Elaine, I find I have to apologize to you. You were so understanding about the war—about Bingo—I didn't know how to go on that last time I saw you. You seem to bring out the coward in me. But I want us to be friends—"

"But that's what I want!" she interrupted, smiling.

"Excuse me, bub, that's my lady you're bothering—oh, it's you, Marchmont." Van Vliet clasped Elaine in his arms and took off across the floor with her, calling over his shoulder, "Wait your turn. She's my girl tonight."

"You know Mr. Marchmont?" Elaine asked in surprise as they glided around. Her cheeks were hot. Forgetful of her dancing partner, she had been standing in the middle of the floor with Marchmont quite as if the two of them were alone.

Van Vliet grinned down at her. "I didn't like to admit it when you people were talking about him earlier, but, yeah, I know him."

"From the war, I suppose?"

"That's right, the war."

The music wound to an end, and they walked back to the table. Elaine glanced about for Louis and Goggle and saw that they were staying on the floor.

Allan Marchmont appeared out of the shadows and held out his hand. "May I? I apologize, Van Vliet, for usurping your lovely companion, but it's only one dance and I'm by myself tonight. I deserve a treat, wouldn't you say?"

Van Vliet looked him up and down and said, "Bring her back quick, sport."

Elaine put her hand in Marchmont's and let him take her out to the floor, a good distance both from Van Vliet's table and from Goggle and Louis. As she put her hand on his shoulder and felt his arm go round her waist, she said, "I'm surprised to see you tonight, Mr. Marchmont, but glad."

"Why should you be surprised to see me tonight?" He smiled down at her and tightened his arm in what she sensed was affection; she could feel a pleasant current running through her body. "Somebody had to keep an eye on the young earl."

Elaine stared. "Is that what you're doing? But how did you know he'd be here?"

"I knew he was going out on the town with Lady Miranda Winchapel, and she is notorious—"

"That's the problem."

"As I was saying, the young lady is notorious for haunting only the newest and most fashionable places. This is only my second try after the Purple Club."

"She wanted to go to the Purple Club," Elaine said with a smile. "So you read the society pages, do you? An unsuspected vice."

He shrugged. "A man must keep up with what's going on. Besides, your brother told me all about Lady Miranda, and it was after that I looked her up. He was extremely excited about this evening, you know. I hope you haven't put too much of a damper on things."

Elaine drew herself up, ready to deny any such thing, but honesty got the better of her and she laughed. "We met them by accident and I arranged a sort of mutual chaperonage for the evening."

"Mutual?"

"I felt rather shy about spending the evening with Mr. Van Vliet and no one else. Luckily, we ran into friends of mine; also Louis and Gog—and Lady Miranda, who dined with us. And we're set to meet a half-dozen or so people here after the theater lets out."

"If you call all that luck, apparently I'm not to congratulate you on your new romance?"

Did he really not sense that she was attracted to him, not Van Vliet? Or perhaps he merely thought she was attracted to everybody. "I don't ask you personal questions, do I?"

"No, not that I've noticed."

Elaine felt the conversation was heading in an unfortunate direction, as so many of their conversations seemed to, and chose the moment to change it. "I started the evening extremely irritated with you, if you must know. I thought that you hadn't taken the proper responsibility for Louis. But I'm ready to admit I was out of line. I can understand you're not obliged to play guardian to someone you've so kindly employed. There is a limit."

"No, you were right the first time. If I bring a boy up to London, a boy of that age, I have to keep an eye on him. I'm here because I was sixteen myself once."

"So was I. And that's why I attached myself to him like a burr."

"If you don't mind my asking, what has my friend Van Vliet got to do with you? I'm surprised you know him."

Elaine hesitated, debating whether or not to say anything.

She had a superstitious fear of somehow jinxing the wonderful news that Van Vliet was going to rent Berryhill, and it was the feeling that she should not give in to superstition that made her confess the whole. "He somehow heard Mother was thinking of selling our estate, and he offered to rent it instead. Isn't it marvelous?" She smiled. "In a way it seems we merely had to give up on finding a tenant for one to fall into our laps."

"It sounds like the solution you've been looking for. The estate might remain in the family if you're given a stopgap to get things into order. I suppose my new secretary will have the funds to get back to his studies now."

Elaine frowned. "We don't know how much money we'll have in hand. And I wonder if Louis will want to get back to his studies. The life of a man about town is much more appealing than being booted back into school."

"I'll talk to him if you like. Let him down gently. If I were your mother, I'd allow him to work for a while and get it out of his system."

"Excellent idea. I'll pass on your message." Elaine glanced across the floor at Louis, the happy cynosure of most eyes as the partner of Lady Miranda.

"And this plan of Van Vliet's will mean a lot to you, of course," Allan went on, smiling at Elaine as he turned her in time to the music. "You'll be able to quit your job and go back to the country."

"What?" Elaine laughed. "Oh, of course. That's the first thing I'd do."

He laughed with her, but his eyes were keen. "Don't tell me that if your family had the money, you'd work as you do and continue to live in a ladies' hostel."

"You know, I believe I would. Except for the ladies' hostel. I admit Mrs. Beasley is simply too grim. But I'd like a little flat of my own with a congenial flatmate or a large dog.

I got used to my independence in the war. I can't see giving it up."

"You can't?"

Elaine went on talking, enjoying the sensation of actually having someone listen to her plans; of having plans, for a change, rather than merely trying to keep body and soul together. "Perhaps I'd be constrained to live with Mother if she chose to settle down in London. I should seem so scaly and ungrateful if I didn't, and it would save expenses. I'll have to hope she prefers the country and gives me an excuse to stay put."

He laughed. "For a moment I believed you were serious."

Elaine stopped dancing. "But I am."

Allan gently got her moving again. "You promised me the whole dance, my lady."

They moved together for a while, keeping silent time to the music. Elaine began to relax, thinking he couldn't have meant to speak as he had. That languor he seemed to draw from her limbs made her relax against him.

He ruined the moment by asking, "You would suffer in a menial job if you had the wherewithal to go back to your real life? You really aren't joking?"

This time she kept dancing, but only with difficulty. "Mr. Marchmont—"

"Allan."

"Very well, Allan," she continued in a tight voice. "I don't believe you understand what you call my real life. Do you suppose I could suddenly revert to being an idle society girl? I'm afraid that's so long ago I can barely remember it. The war started when I was turning twenty, and since then my real life has been nursing and then typewriting. I never got the chance to set up house with Bingo, but I feel as though I had. If my mother needs me, naturally I'll go back to her if finances permit, but she is a perfectly capable person."

War Widow

"But can you like toiling all day for a pittance? I know what young women make in offices; it's a disgrace."

"Even more of a disgrace than what young men make, yes. What about you? Do you like toiling all day? You have wealth, I believe. Do you sit still every day and do nothing but think over your social life?"

"A man must be doing something, my dear Lady Elaine," he said, his arm stiffening under her hand.

"Oh, I see. And a woman must not?"

The music stopped, and Allan gave her a desperate look. "We aren't finished talking. Do you suppose we could dance again?"

"I hardly think so. I see no reason to prolong this." Elaine turned from him.

He grasped her arm. "Let me take you home. We could talk in the car."

"When I came out with Mr. Van Vliet? That would be the height of rudeness."

"I suppose it would." He sighed. "You must know in your heart I'm not such a clod that I would insult the whole of womanhood, but I'm afraid you think so."

She let a little smile appear. "I do."

"I merely meant to suggest that you ought to have a job more worthy of your talents. Such an ordinary thing as being a typewriter girl is surely beneath you."

"Oh. Perhaps if I were an artist or a literary person—a poet? A journalist?—I would be allowed my little quirk of wanting to have a job? I could have a studio and potter about and pretend to accomplish great things. Well, I haven't any of that sort of ambition, Mr. Marchmont. I simply enjoy earning my way with what skills I have."

He gave her a penetrating look. "And when you marry again? You surely won't hold to this plan?"

She shrugged. "Who knows? Perhaps if I marry, my

husband will be poor and need my help. Or perhaps he'll understand a woman's reasonable wish for independence. But remarriage is scarcely likely for most of us war widows. There are simply too many of us."

By this time the music had started up again. It was another tango, and Elaine wasn't about to perform such a dance in the arms of a man who was angering her more by the minute. She nodded in a mock-cordial manner for the benefit of any watchers and hurried back to the table.

As she approached, Van Vliet rose and pulled out her chair. "You and Marchmont were getting pretty close to a brawl out there, Lady Elaine. Want me to challenge him to a duel or something?" He grinned at her in a genial way that somehow touched her heart.

"No, thank you, Mr. Van Vliet—Oswald." She smiled back, wishing that people could choose to whom they were attracted. If she could only like Van Vliet in that man-woman way, she would show Allan Marchmont. But it was no use. She had a decidedly sisterly feeling for Van Vliet; there was a fascination with his American background, a curiosity having to do with his air of mystery, but he didn't appeal to her at all in a physical way. As for Allan, he seemed to call up every feeling of desire she had kept suppressed for years and many she had never known she possessed. She sighed.

"Don't feel bad," Van Vliet advised her. "He'll come around. Nobody could stay mad at you for long."

"What? I don't think you understand, sir—Oswald. Mr. Marchmont and I have nothing between us besides a bit of disagreement over the proper role of women."

"Uh oh. That sounds bad. Don't tell me he's not in favor of the modern woman."

"He seems to have become stuck somewhere in the

twelfth century, as a matter of fact," Elaine said with a shrug. "But it's nothing to me."

"Of course not." Van Vliet's sharp look caused Elaine to squirm. She somehow thought he might see much more than even she did. And that was definitely too much.

Chapter Eleven

Elaine's six friends of the Ritz bar showed up before the conversation between herself and Mr. Van Vliet could become more maudlin or reveal more of Elaine's confusion. She believed she had revealed quite enough as it was. Oswald Van Vliet was a strange man. He guessed her attraction to Allan, yet didn't seem to care.

Immediately after his argument with Elaine, Allan disappeared from the club. A bit resentful that he hadn't stayed to continue their battle, Elaine went back to her careful observation of Louis and Goggle. She couldn't quite tell if her brother was seriously infatuated with Lady Miranda or merely excited to be the escort of a fascinating older woman. As for Goggle, Elaine had to admit that the girl wasn't turning her full sensuous power on Louis; her manner was more mischievous than amorous.

More dancing and more drinks followed, with lemon squash for the Saxonburys. Elaine danced at least twice with all the men who ended up in their party and was happy to note that all the females were dancing with Van Vliet. She wanted him to have a good time on his night out with a 'lady.' Bab, Eliza, and Gwyneth were all nice enough to dance with Louis, too, though Elaine drew the line at taking the floor with her brother. He was already undergoing the humiliation of spending the evening in her company.

Eventually the others had to go look in on somebody's sister's debutante ball, and Van Vliet's party declined to join them, though they were urged very genuinely to come along.

"You must come with us if only for the tourist value, seeing the very young London set at play," Bab Playfair said, looking up at Van Vliet in a languishing way that earned the American a resentful glance from Lord Inglethorpe. "White gowns and predatory mothers. I hear our deb affairs are nothing like New York. And Lord Berry would enjoy it."

"Would not," grumbled Louis into his lemon squash, reddening at the ears at the idea that he might like such a childish event. In reality, he was too young ever to have been to a coming-out ball. Van Vliet genially said that he would join them another time, and that there were plenty of white gowns and phony mothers where he came from.

Elaine's friends exited the club in a noisy way that made Elaine worry over what exactly they planned to do when they got to the sister's debut.

They had hardly got out the door when the three men from Chicago, who had been at the Ritz bar earlier, entered and made for Van Vliet's table with happy cries. Elaine didn't think Van Vliet was as thrilled to see his friends as he had been earlier in the evening, but she didn't know whether or not to take that as a compliment to herself. If he would rather be alone with her, they were already stuck with Louis and Goggle, and three more wouldn't make much of a difference.

Lady Miranda and Elaine spent the next hour or so being whirled about in extremely muscular embraces, though the man named Sanguinetti was the only one who could dance worth anything. Elaine was proud of her own agility in having protected her dance slippers from both Porter and Brown, especially when she heard a squeal of pain coming from Goggle. Then, quite suddenly it seemed to Elaine, one of the Chicagoans looked at a pocket watch and the three had to leave—though what sort of appointment they could have so late at night, Elaine couldn't imagine.

Lady Miranda did insist on stopping by the Purple Club in Soho next, but the foursome's stay there was blessedly short. The hour was very late, and Elaine was having trouble focusing her eyes. She had really become a staid, boring sort of person, she thought regretfully, noting how Goggle, despite having drunk champagne, still appeared bright-eyed and as lively as her languid pose would allow. Perhaps it was only old age; Elaine was three years older than Goggle.

As Elaine sighed over the unfairness of it all, of youth gone by before she had even noticed it, something fell heavily against her shoulder. Louis' head.

"That's about enough for tonight, ladies," Van Vliet said with a laugh. "Lady Miranda, you don't mind cutting your evening short?"

Goggle laughed. Red-lacquered fingertips reached out to stroke Louis' golden head. "Poor boy. We've worn him out."

"He's still growing. Needs his twelve hours of sleep," Van Vliet said. "Not all of us can be like you, your ladyship." Elaine thought he looked keenly at Goggle as he spoke to her. Elaine was struggling through her own fog of sleepiness only slightly less intense than Louis', but she felt like kissing the large American for rescuing her and her brother from Miranda Winchapel's zeal to dance all night.

"Come on, lordship." Van Vliet hoisted Louis to his feet. "Party's over."

"Over," Louis said in a strange, echoing voice.

"What a shame. But we could drop him by the Albany and then keep going. I know of a delightful party in Chelsea that ought to be in full swing by now. What do you say, Elaine?" Goggle's eyes were bright and restless.

"I'm afraid I'm as dead on my feet as Louis, or nearly so. Besides, it's after two. How do you do it, Goggle? I mean, Miranda?"

"I have a strong constitution. And I'm used to these hours. I could steal your escort, I suppose." Goggle looked at Van Vliet. "After he takes you home, he's a free agent."

Van Vliet seemed to color slightly in the dim light of the table candles. "Well, that's very flattering, ma'am, but, er . . ."

Elaine thought that perhaps he would go with Goggle if it weren't for her. "Oh, go on. Don't mind me. We've had our evening, and this could be your chance to see London society at play. If you're still conscious, why let me spoil it all?" It might do Van Vliet good to go to some bohemian party out in Chelsea. If he had stars in his eyes about London socialites, he'd see they could be as obnoxious as anyone else when they played too hard. "I'm sorry I tire so easily," she added with a smile.

Van Vliet looked hard at Elaine, then subjected Lady Miranda to an even more searching stare. "I believe what I'll do is take all of you home."

"Could you at least drop me in Chelsea?" Goggle put on a wheedling tone. Then, looking more closely at the man's implacable expression, she shrugged. "Oh, never mind. I can always take out the car when I get home."

At this Van Vliet looked truly alarmed. He exchanged a quick glance with Elaine which she couldn't quite interpret, then shepherded everyone out onto the pavement where his Hispano-Suiza was waiting.

Louis managed to hold his head up and walk under his own power, but his eyes were tiny slits, and Elaine couldn't help feeling sorry that her young brother's big evening on the town was ending in such an unprepossessing way. Not that Louis seemed to mind. He curled up into a corner of the back seat and unabashedly began to snore. Miranda shook her head ruefully and continued to give Louis the occasional friendly pat while Elaine tried to look on severely but only succeeded in yawning.

Van Vliet handed Louis over to Allan Marchmont's valet at the Albany, then returned to the car where Elaine was settled down in the corner so recently occupied by her brother, under a lap robe, and Goggle was busying herself with a powder puff and compact in another. Elaine managed to be polite and sincerely grateful for the lovely evening she had been treated to. "I don't know how to thank you," she said sleepily to Van Vliet. "I haven't been out since Bingo—I mean, I don't get out at all anymore, and that's no doubt why I'm such a sleepyhead. No stamina."

"It's probably just your personality," Goggle suggested, smiling sweetly. "Some people do better at firesides."

"Lady Elaine, you've got plenty of stamina for two or three in the morning," Van Vliet said with a frown at Lady Miranda.

"Thank you—Oswald." Elaine smiled at him dreamily. The car eased to a stop. She looked out the window and noticed, in some alarm, that they were in front of her Euston hostel. She had assumed Van Vliet would be taking her home last of all. Now Goggle Winchapel would know where she lived; and would Elaine ever survive the ensuing gossip among the fast set?

A very faint sound, something like a purr, caught Elaine's attention. Goggle, for all her vivacity of a few minutes before, had fallen fast asleep in her corner of the car.

Van Vliet leaned over to whisper, "Thought I'd take her home last to make sure she gets in. I'll hang around her house if I have to, see that she doesn't go out driving in her condition. She might get a second wind. They often do."

Elaine reached for his hand to clasp it. "You're a wonderful man. Thank you so much again for the evening; for entertaining Lady Miranda and my brother too; for everything." After a moment of hesitation, she brushed a kiss against his cheek. Then she hopped out of the car before he could get out to assist her and waved at it as it pulled away.

She had been standing alone on the pavement for a couple of minutes in a sleepy haze before it occurred to her that she was in the wrong place. She had forgotten to tell Van Vliet she would have to be driven to Griselda's room in Clapham at this time of night. She looked up at Mrs. Beasley's fortress. Her bed was in there, but she was as cut off from it as though it were a thousand miles away. If she knocked on the door, she would be ejected from the place come morning—or possibly even before. Elaine had observed Mrs. Beasley's methods with young women who tried to bend the rules of her establishment.

"May I be of some help?"

The sound of a voice quite near her almost made Elaine scream, but luckily for the tranquility of the neighborhood she merely jumped. "Mr. Marchmont. Is that you?"

He was definitely beside her, taking her arm, a comforting, dark, solid presence in the forbidding chill of early morning. "I waited here for you to come back. I don't believe I convinced you to accept my apology for the things I said earlier in the evening."

She was fully awake now, thanks to the way he'd startled her, but still not thinking at full tilt. She had to ponder for a moment to remember what he was talking about. "Oh, that's right. Your notion that I shouldn't have an ordinary job; your lack of respect for females who earn money in unglamorous occupations. All of that." She sighed. "I was rather angry with you, wasn't I? But it doesn't seem important at the moment. Do you have a car?"

She could see in the faint light cast by the street lamp that he was amazed by her non sequitur. "I do. But why . . ."

She hated to ask him for a favor, but it was that or try to walk on her own to Clapham—or at least until she found a cab. The Underground had closed long ago, and she had on thin slippers. "I was so tired in the car that I forgot to have my escort take me to the place I'm staying tonight. I can't get in here, you see." She indicated the house that was so much less than home to her. "There are rules about coming in late, and this is later than anyone has ever tried. But I already told my landlady that I plan to stay at my mother-in-law's out in Clapham. If you could possibly give me a lift—"

"Of course. You don't even need to ask. I'll take you there at once. But how could Van Vliet leave you without making sure you got into the house?"

"If he had, you couldn't have accosted me on the pavement. I jumped quickly out of his car, if you must know, and sent him on his way. He still had to take Lady Miranda home."

"I see." But it was apparent from the look on his shadowed face that he didn't really.

The story of her evening was too complicated to explain, but she had to give her escort the proper credit for his true gentlemanly behavior. "He was so kind to take care of my brother, Lady Miranda, and me all evening. And he seemed so genuinely worried about Lady Miranda that I was touched."

"Worried about Lady Miranda?"

Elaine was afraid she shouldn't say anymore; she tried to be as vague as possible. "She was still feeling quite awake and wanted to go to a party in Chelsea. She said she'd go by herself, in her car, and Mr. Van Vliet wanted to make sure she didn't. He didn't think she was in any condition to drive."

"He was always a good fellow. Chivalrous." Allan nodded sagely and began to steer Elaine down the pavement to a Daimler that glowed silver in the street light. Matter-of-factly he tucked her up inside under a fur lap rug, and Elaine let herself be taken care of. First Van Vliet, and now Allan treating her like a piece of china. She could get used to this despite any feelings she might have about the rights of women to take care of themselves. One could earn one's living and be cosseted occasionally, couldn't one?

Weariness was trying to invade her bones again, but set against this was the excitement of being with Allan. Oh, but she was angry with him. She mustn't forget that. Her eyelids began to descend.

"How do you know Mr. Van Vliet?" she asked sleepily.

"The war."

"Oh, of course. I forgot. But what does he do these days? How did he make his money? I couldn't get a word out of him."

"Americans are often men of few words." The light was dim, but Elaine could see that he was smiling.

"You do know something. Is he a gangster?" Elaine demanded, wondering where such an idea had come from. Of course, she was thinking of those friends of Van Vliet's, the prizefighter-looking men from Chicago who had danced her and Goggle up and down Ciro's with such determination, if not skill. She felt a pleasurable little thrill to think she might have been spending the evening with dangerous people.

"Rather a harsh word, Lady Elaine. I thought you liked him."

"I do." She also noticed, through a deepening fog, that

Allan hadn't really answered her question. "Very well, keep your mystery. Or his mystery."

"A wise decision, my lady. Now, where to?" He started up the motor, which was low and well-bred in the style of the Hispano-Suiza, nothing at all like cousin Rollo's engine.

She gave him Griselda's address and leaned her head back against the seat.

Next she felt a gentle touch on her cheek. "Lady Elaine. Elaine. We're here."

She had fallen asleep. Elaine woke up in a mixture of embarrassment and surprise to find Allan's face mere inches from her own.

He leaned forward and kissed her gently. Then he closed his arms around her and kept kissing her, not that gently anymore.

She was still in a half-conscious state as she wound her fingers into his hair and pulled his head closer, kissing him as deeply as he was kissing her. Had she been dreaming about doing this very thing?

He drew back, taking her face between his hands. "Are you awake?"

She was now. "Why do you ask?" she said with a smile.

"I'd like to think you'd remember this." He bent forward and kissed her again. "Much more pleasant than scrapping, don't you think?"

"Yes, I do." Elaine sighed and curled up even closer to him. "It's been so long since I—I'm very glad."

She felt him retreat a bit and respected him for respecting her. But when he said, "I'll see you to the door," in a stiff voice, she knew something was wrong.

"Not right now." She leaned forward to kiss him again; surely the mood of a moment before could be recaptured.

"I'm afraid I must." Allan retreated behind the wheel. Suddenly, the atmosphere between them was that of people who had never touched. "I shouldn't have taken advantage of you in this way. You're tired; you're not thinking clearly. I should have remembered that Bingo—that you—I'm sorry."

"What?" She was silent for a moment, then said quietly, "Bingo is gone, Allan."

"No one knows better than I." His hands were trembling on the steering wheel.

"Do you think it's so wrong of me to want to be close to someone again? Is that it?"

"Not wrong of you. Wrong of me. I can't explain myself, Elaine. But I beg your forgiveness."

What a time for the war to intrude. Elaine glanced at Allan, at his frozen face, his whole stricken aspect. What had made him draw back, when he and she were both alive and so terribly attracted to each other? Why did it make such a difference that she had been married to his dead comrade?

She suspected this was no time to try and talk him out of it. Giving his cold hand on the wheel a short pat, she let herself out of the auto.

Chapter Twelve

"So. What do you think?" asked Rollo.

Elaine dragged her mind with difficulty from its constant preoccupation with Allan Marchmont and frowned. "I think you're mad, Rollo." She took a piece of batter-dipped fish from the newspaper-wrapped bundle by her side and bit into it hungrily.

When Rollo showed up at the door of Borderfield's at lunch hour she had every intention of snubbing him and sending him about his business until she spied the fish and chips in his hand. There was nothing Elaine liked better, and perhaps Rollo knew this.

A sudden change of heart ensued, and she agreed to accompany him to a little square where they sat on a bit of wall cheek by jowl with other lunch-goers and made short work of their treat.

Then, as soon as Elaine's guard was down, Rollo proceeded to tell her the piece of news that had brought him into her part of town in the first place: That none other than Borderfield's was to publish his grandfather's racing memoirs.

War Widow

"We'll have to keep it from the mater," he said conscientiously in reply to Elaine's major concern, wiping his fingers on his handkerchief.

Elaine seized the fine white linen square without ceremony and wiped her own hands, all the while glaring at Rollo. "It can't be kept from her. She's bound to notice a book all over the shops with her own father's name on it."

"Father-in-law's," Rollo corrected her. "Mum's father died a respectable death by pitching over into a stream. Heart attack while fishing. Never went near a racetrack."

"She'll still be humiliated," Elaine muttered. "What are they going to call the thing?"

"*The Racing Saxonbury*. Has a ring to it, doesn't it? Implies there are all sorts of Saxonburys who do many things, when, as far as I can tell, none of us have done anything much."

He was forgetting the war, in which he had played a brave if brief part. But Elaine wasn't going to remind him of that. She was noticing more and more that men these days were trying to forget the war altogether rather than dwell on it. She had to respect their wishes, Rollo's wishes, in this particular. "At least Borderfield's is a respectable house, and there will be a dignified cover," she said. "But, Rollo, how could you?"

"It was easy, once I got that little friend of yours, that Katherine, to put in a good word for me with her boss. She says it was the least she could do for a cousin of yours, so I suppose it's really your fault, when it comes right down to it."

"No, we are not shifting the blame for this one on to my shoulders." Elaine spoke harshly, and her sigh was deep and depressed. "Though Aunt Pen will blame me very much, at that. Katherine helped you, you say? Katherine Marsh?"

"She's a nice little thing. Not only helpful but interesting.

She likes the pictures, too; the same ones I do. We've both seen *Intolerance* five times."

"You've been taking her to the pictures? Pretending to like her, I suppose. Working your masculine wiles on her." And there had been no sign from Katherine that she had any intrigue going on with Rollo—or with anyone. The whole world was devious, sly, and unworthy of trust. Elaine groped for another chipped potato, though she had considered herself finished with lunch a moment ago.

"I don't have to pretend. She's a likeable little thing. And most helpful, as I've said."

"I didn't know Katherine had any influence at work. Who was her 'boss,' as you put it? The one who helped you?"

"Some old fellow, nearly had to prop him up. Now what was the name?"

Rollo's description could fit several of the superannuated editors whose names were on their respective doors mostly out of deference to their past accomplishments. They didn't do much in the office nowadays, though they each had their days to come in and totter about, mostly out to lunch at a club and in to a meeting. Elaine named them, one by one.

"No," Rollo said cheerfully to each suggestion. "That's not it."

There was only one name left. Hesitantly, Elaine pronounced it. "Not . . . not Mr. Borderfield?"

"Yes, that's the name. Knew it was familiar. It's up on the door of the building too."

"Rollo, you are the limit. You mean to tell me you walked into my office and made an arrangement with the head of the firm?" Elaine's head swam. "Besides which, I didn't know Katherine had ever said two words to young Mr. Borderfield."

"That's what she called him too," Rollo said with a

snicker. " 'I'd hate to see Old Mr. Borderfield,' I told her. Clever, what?"

"It probably was clever the first several hundred times someone said it." Elaine was in no mood to be kind. However it had happened, Rollo had laid another family problem in her lap. Aunt Pen would have an apoplexy, Mother would do worse if half the things they said Great-uncle Montague had done—and written down—turned out to be true. The family's dignity would be in shreds. If Montague Saxonbury had been indiscreet, and if such stories made it into print, nobody whose relations had been named would speak to his descendants anytime in the near future. And if one quarter of the stories were true, this would mean ostracism from all of society.

"I must see the manuscript. I need to know how bad it is," Elaine said. "I don't suppose you've kept a copy, have you?"

Rollo shook his head. "Where would I get a copy? All I had was the original thing, heavy as lead it was, all written up in Grandfather's hand. I had to leave it with the old fellow, what did you say his name was? Oh, that's right, Borderfield. Same as the firm."

"At least you deal with the top brass when you do act."

Rollo smiled as if she had paid him a great compliment. "The thing is, Elaine, now that I'll have some money coming in, we can marry. We were only waiting for something to live on, you know. Something besides the mater, I mean." He chuckled.

"I wasn't aware I'd agreed to marry you in any circumstances." Elaine wished she hadn't eaten his fish and chips. She hated to owe him any favors.

As usual when the subject was their marriage, Rollo was matter-of-fact, imperturbable, and not about to be put off by Elaine's lack of enthusiasm. "No, you haven't agreed, that's the point. But now you can. What with all those fellows who buzz around you at your mother's parties, I'd better secure you at once. That's what Mum says."

"You don't do everything your mother tells you, obviously," Elaine said, thinking of the memoirs. "Why marry me?"

"Why, Elaine." Rollo looked hurt. "I thought you knew. I'm fond of you."

Elaine dropped her face into her hands. Just when she needed most to be cold and off-putting, he decided to disarm her. No, she simply couldn't understand Rollo.

"I'm sorry, dear boy," she said in a gentle tone, raising her head. "I probably won't remarry, and I can't marry you. You've never been married. You need someone who can give you her whole heart."

Rollo looked as sad as any puppy dog. "Oh. It's still Bingo. I should have known it wasn't long enough yet. But you'll come round, won't you? If I keep asking?"

What was this? Could he actually be in love with her? She didn't really think so. She was glad he thought she was still mourning Bingo; it would help. "I want you to meet another girl, Rollo," she said in a commanding tone. If he was really "fond" of her, perhaps he would obey her. "I want you to do it now. You're quite a catch, you know. You deserve better than a tired-out widow."

"But we understand each other. We're family; and you understand about the war. I want to marry a widow. I have to marry a widow."

Elaine was surprised at the intensity of his words, but it didn't stop her for more than a moment. "Oh, if that's all, my dear, you can walk down any street in town and come up with a dozen women who've lost someone in the war. Now I insist you do that. As soon as possible. You need to get married. If you need to talk about the war, a wife could help."

"Not I." Rollo was Rollo again, his vulnerability well hidden. "I'm comfortable as a bachelor, come to that. But you have to marry. Our mums are always harping on it. And I think they're right. You need to settle down. You're keeping late nights with foreigners—don't think I don't have my spies."

He had to be referring to Saturday night. Any number of their friends could have told Rollo Elaine had been seen out and about with Oswald Van Vliet. Elaine laughed. "If my one night out—with my brother in tow, at that—adds up to a life of dissipation, standards have really gone down since the war. Can we change the subject?"

"If you wish." Rollo took the last piece of fish and put the whole thing into his mouth.

Thoughts of what had happened after her evening with Van Vliet washed over Elaine. She couldn't keep her mind off that subject no matter how she tried. In fact, Rollo's news about the family memoirs had given her the most relief she had felt in days from her constant mental visits to the dark interior of that Daimler parked on a night-shrouded Clapham street.

How could she have done it? Not the kissing; she was extremely understanding with herself about that. Passion and attraction and physical proximity had all worked together, and she wasn't sorry. But how could she have given Allan the idea that she was still mourning Bingo? It simply must have been her fault, but she couldn't think how.

After nearly a week she hadn't seen or heard from Allan. She had expected . . . what? Another load of flowers; a note; a visit. Every time she had left the hostel or the office she had halfway thought he would be waiting for her.

Her fantasies always broke down when the time came for Allan to speak. He was the one who couldn't forget Bingo, not she. Was there any way out of it, a way that would lead to their understanding each other? Her mind had been working away at this problem, going round and round, not getting anywhere for days now, and she was getting fairly sick of it.

"It's time for you to go back. Katherine would have to, so I suppose you do too." Rollo broke into her thoughts with a look at his pocket watch. Elaine remembered Allan's wristwatch, a newer fashion Rollo probably didn't have the extra cash to buy.

"Thanks, Rollo. I'm afraid my mind was wandering."

"I should say so! I've told you half a dozen things, and you haven't said a word."

"Sorry. But to return to what we were talking about earlier, do you think I could get a look at the manuscript? Won't they be making a copy in the office?"

"You'd know best about that," Rollo said with a shrug. They rose and found a basket in which to put the crumpled, oily newspaper from the fish. With her hand tucked into his arm, Rollo guided Elaine through the midday crowds back to Borderfield's, where he left her at the door. She stood for a moment watching him disappear and wishing that there could be more satisfaction in an encounter with Rollo.

His confession about needing a widow to marry, someone who understood about the war! For Rollo, that had been a cry for help. Now what was she to do to rescue him? So many young men were having breakdowns these days; he mustn't join them.

Katherine was there at the next desk, just taking off her smart little hat. She smiled brightly at Elaine.

"So." Elaine folded her arms and tapped her foot. "Deep waters, Miss Marsh. You've been carrying on an intrigue with my cousin."

"You said you didn't want him," Katherine said in a sort of squeak, sitting down hard in her typing chair.

"Of course I don't want him. You mean you do?"

Katherine shrugged.

Elaine, suddenly weak-kneed, sat down at her own desk and looked at her friend with widening eyes. "You do like him. I was afraid of that, though I told myself that perhaps you were merely being nice to him. And you thought the way to his heart would be to get his manuscript published. But how on earth did you manage to interest young Mr. Borderfield in the project? Rollo says you actually put in a word with the old—with Mr. Borderfield."

"Easy." Again Katherine shrugged. "There weren't exactly words involved, you know. Your cousin was just using that as an expression. What happened was, I waited till Miss Rothwell had gone to the ladies' room, and then I sent in Rollo—Mr. Saxonbury—quick as anything. I knew he could do his own talking, and it happens Mr. Borderfield would like those memoirs. Or so I thought, him being about the same age as your cousin's grandfather."

"And you didn't realize that Rollo's family was completely against the project? It's a tell-all book, Katherine. Unless Great-uncle Montague has changed a lot of names and left a lot of others out, the family name will be dragged through the mud with that of every other family in high society."

"Doesn't that sort of thing sell very well?"

"That's the point. If nobody was likely to read it, why would the family care whether it was published or not?"

"I don't quite understand. Mr. Saxonbury told me he inherited all his father's things, and the memoir was part of the estate. So what would the problem be?"

"It's not a matter of legality; it's one of delicacy. Everyone will think Rollo's mother, who is known to influence his every move, gave her blessing on the project. They'll blame her for raking up a hundred old scandals." Elaine sighed. "Or they will if there are any good scandals to be found in the book. Oh, if only I could get a look at it and see how bad the damage might be."

"I'm sorry if your family won't like it, I'm sure," Katherine said stiffly, rolling paper into her machine. "But I don't see that it's anyone's business except Mr. Saxonbury's."

Elaine rolled her eyes. Infatuation had blinded the girl to every finer feeling, or possibly she didn't understand the magnitude of a society brouhaha: The gossip; the way all talk stopped when a person came into a room; the polite and not so polite ostracism of the persons who had displeased; the absolute despair caused to someone who thought society's approval was important. Someone such as Aunt Pen.

Not only that, Rollo had evidently trifled with Katherine's feelings to a shocking degree. The question was whether Rollo had done this deliberately.

Having put away her hat and purse in a drawer and folded her jacket over the back of her chair, Elaine finally reached into the wooden box on her desk for her afternoon's work.

Her hand trembled. She had picked up the first of a stack of yellowed notebooks, some in leather covers. There was a note clipped to the top. "Call this *The Racing Saxonbury*," was scrawled in a spidery handwriting. "Leave nothing out."

She tore the first book open and began to read, avidly. The handwriting was terrible, the ink badly faded. Apparently the diary started in Uncle Montague's schooldays. She deciphered the first page without finding anything of an obscene or racy nature; but then, according to the entry, he was only twelve. The story involved the housemaster, a maid, and several schoolboys with dreadful nicknames such as Squirrel and Widge—who, if the family luck held, would probably end up being future prime ministers.

Elaine was aware of a slight, female figure pausing beside

her desk. "Oh, how do you do, Lady Elaine," said the female. "So this is where you 'work.'"

Never had Elaine heard more clearly the quotation marks around a word. She looked up into the bespectacled eyes of the poet Ann Averil, one of those who thought Lady Elaine Westwood's little job was a society girl's lark.

"How do you do, Miss Averil?" she responded pleasantly. "I didn't know you published with Borderfield's."

"I don't. But Mr. Marchmont does, and I mean to see that my great mission is set in motion."

"What mission is that?"

"Don't you remember? To get his poems published in a true literary form without those distracting pictures," Miss Averil said with a dismissive wave of her hand, presumably at the "distracting pictures."

"But I understand that the work is to be taken together, all of a piece," Elaine said, just to be contrary. She had no idea of Allan thoughts on the matter; perhaps he was thrilled to be suddenly lauded as a poet as well as a photographer. She wished she did know what he thought about his work. She had read her mother's copy and looked at the sensitive photographs many times by now. Usually doing so made her cry over Bingo and the war, which she assumed was a good sign as to the book's value as a war document, if not as art for its own sake. If she were to get to know Allan better, they could discuss his work. All she could tell Miss Averil now, with any authority, was how he kissed.

She grew slightly pink at the thought.

"Be that as it may, Lady Elaine, my duty is clear. I'm going to see your Mr. Borderfield and demand he do as I ask. Not only is it for art, but the company stands to make a lot of money. With my literary introduction and some of my colleagues', this will be a work to be reckoned with. Do you know if there is a good portrait of Mr. Marchmont? For the frontispiece? There wasn't one in the photograph book."

"I've no idea, but he will photograph well, I'm sure of that."

"Yes." Miss Averil sighed.

Elaine looked at her sharply. She too? Was nobody motivated by art, or helpfulness, or anything else but a wish to be noticed by the opposite sex? Katherine and Rollo; Ann Averil and Allan Marchmont: Where would it end?

"Perhaps my young brother could help you," Elaine suggested. "Louis has become Mr. Marchmont's secretary, as you may remember. He might know of a photograph; or he could take one. Mr. Marchmont is teaching him about photography."

"Thank you. I'll keep that in mind," Miss Averil said crisply.

Then she marched in a determined way in the direction of the private offices. Elaine hoped young Mr. Borderfield would throw the woman out on her ear.

"Did that woman call you Lady Elaine?" asked Katherine in a small voice, from across the way.

Elaine sank back in her chair, wishing she could be transported, instantly, to a place where none of this would matter.

Chapter Thirteen

Allan tried his best to get Elaine off his mind. This wasn't easy with her brother under his eye. Not only did the two look alike, but Lord Berry constantly talked about his sister, usually in reference to some scheme of his she had managed to spoil, but oftentimes in a grudgingly fond way which indicated he knew she had his best interests at heart.

"It's not her fault she's had to become the family spoilsport," Louis mused one day, apropos of nothing, or so it seemed to his irritated employer. Had they even been discussing Elaine? No, the topic was a foray of Allan's into the dangerous territory of whether the young earl would soon be going back to school. This had reminded Louis of Elaine, who was always suggesting things that were no fun at all. "Somebody had to be sensible in the family," Louis went on. "It's sure not Mother, and I'm afraid I'm not it either."

"Well, never mind that," Allan said, fishing a paper off his desk. "Take this round to the gallery for me—oh, on second thought I'll go myself."

"Are you sure?" Louis looked longingly out the window into the grey day. The freedom of the boulevards was evidently irresistible to the young, even when the weather did look like rain.

"Very sure. Catalogue those new books while I'm gone, would you, milord? And make sure you order a good tea. I expect I'll be back by then." Allan jammed a hat onto his head. Soon he was pounding down the steps of his flat and out of the Albany.

In Piccadilly the wind was blowing, which helped to clear the head, and one would be safe from seeing Elaine. Since she spent all her time near Covent Garden in one of those jobs that didn't allow for free movement, she wouldn't be anywhere near Piccadilly on a working day.

The fact that he could scan the passing crowds in perfect safety meant less to Allan than he would have thought. He walked quickly up Piccadilly, looking neither to left nor right, then wound down a side street until he came to the narrow way—a passage, really—where the gallery was located in the heart of Shepherd's Market.

The Victoire Gallery was new, owned by a cousin of Michael Parkington's, a spinster deprived of useful occupation after the war who now spent her time discovering new talent instead of dispensing medication at one of the hospitals.

"She's a queer duck," Michael had apologized in advance. "Fancied herself a painter in her youth, but never got very far. Cousin Lucy's got a good heart, though. Any profits she makes, she means to use for the benefit of orphaned French children. A pity these gallery ventures never do make profits."

Profits or not, the Victoire Gallery generated a lot of paperwork, or so it seemed to Allan. He was forever fielding urgent messages from Miss Lucy Gabell, none of which turned out to have much urgency about them. The one he had stuffed into his pocket on leaving the flat was only the latest in a series of similar appeals. He had actually been finding the constant flow from Miss Gabell's pen helpful in his employment of young Lord Berry. One had to send the lad to do something, and trotting back and forth to the gallery, which boasted no telephone, made the young man think he was earning his salary.

Allan entered the modest door of a small shopfront where one of his large photographs of a ruined French wall complete with creeper and a perching cat was displayed on an easel. A spinster lady would pick that one, he thought with a chuckle every time he passed it. Propped in front of the easel was a copy of his book, open to the page with the same photograph. Inside, the gallery consisted of a couple of white-walled rooms, both of which were hung with Allan's pictures. Not the ones from the book, but others which he and Parkington had destined for the sequel. Besides the photographs, Miss Gabell was showing some tortured-looking busts by a new Belgian sculptor who was becoming the rage.

A gratifying number of people stood about in groups in front of the photographs, Allan noted as he stood waiting for Miss Gabell to find him. Her assistant, a ferrety young man, had raised a pair of sharp eyebrows at sight of Allan and headed for the back, so Allan was quite sure that he need only wait.

"Mr. Marchmont!"

Allan turned and found Miss . . . something, a young literary woman he had met out at Berryhill, bearing down on him from around a corner. He had a vague memory of a book passing from her hands to his; he hoped she wouldn't ask him how he had liked it. He wondered if he was supposed to remember her name.

Today Miss Whatever was fashionably clad in a chic coat and skirt, light spring furs, and a Paris-looking hat. Allan had the distinct feeling that such clothing wasn't usual to the young woman, who would doubtless be more comfortable in tweeds or the armor she had worn to the fancy dress ball.

He smiled in recognition and touched his hat, hoping luck would save him from having to reveal that he had forgotten what she was called.

"Mr. Marchmont! Oh, you've found Miss Averil all by yourself. I was about to send you a message telling you she was here and most anxious to speak to you." His luck was in. Miss Gabell bustled up, a gallant small figure in the batiky clothes of a patron of the arts, her curly gray head surmounted by an intricately tied scarf.

"Miss Averil," Allan murmured with a slight bow, then turned to the elder lady. "I came in response to another message, ma'am. When are you going to get on the telephone?"

"I don't need it when I can see your dashing young nobleman of a secretary—or you—if I write you an urgent message." Miss Gabell was the sort of woman who, in bygone years, would have accompanied most of her remarks with a swat of her fan. "Never mind the other thing. Here is Miss Averil, and here are you. Deal with each other now, if you please." She stood back, evidently waiting to see them do so.

"Mr. Marchmont, I've been here to the gallery many times, and I've transcribed the captions on all these photographs," Miss Averil said in an eager tone, taking his arm. "But that's not why I'm here."

"It's not?" Allan, still hazy on any details of his past acquaintance with this woman, wondered why the devil anyone would write down the captions of his photographs, then remembered some uncomfortable moments from that weekend party. This must be the woman who had tried to flatter him into thinking himself a poet. He hoped he wouldn't soon have to call her a nincompoop to her face.

"Miss Averil has been most faithful," Miss Gabell put in.

"She's been here at least five times in the last couple of weeks."

The younger woman's long face colored slightly; a becoming change, as she had before been quite pale. "I didn't know how to get in touch with you except through this gallery or your publisher," she said with an annoyed look. Allan couldn't tell if the annoyance was with Miss Gabell, for taking part in their conversation; with the publisher, for some unknown reason; or with Allan himself, presumably for not making it easier for her to contact him. Yet he could hardly have given her his card out of the blue on first acquaintance. He didn't think he remembered her asking for it.

"I've just come from Borderfield's," she continued with an unmistakable look of disgust. Miss Averil happened to have a longish nose most useful for looks of disgust. "That philistine of a publisher, who must be in his dotage from the look of him, has refused to bring out your poems without the photographs. Have you ever heard of anything so shortsighted! So foolish!"

"I'm afraid I don't understand," Allan said, keeping his voice pleasant and mildly interested. He exchanged a look with Miss Gabell, who shrugged.

Miss Averil sighed. He realized her fingers were still around his arm when she squeezed it, hard. "That stupid old man kept talking on about things that make absolutely no sense; about how putting out books has to do with making money. He was raving about some racy memoir he had just picked up. Can you imagine! When he has the opportunity to assist at the altar of poetry!" She paused. "Besides which, I assured the ridiculous man that he would make plenty of money on a text-only edition of your work."

Allan had to laugh. "I'm afraid I can't fault Mr.

Borderfield's skepticism. Such a book would be no more than a pamphlet. I remember now that you were kind enough to find some value in my photograph captions. But have you thought about how very brief they are?"

"Yes, I've thought of that, and that's why these new poems must be included, too, in the same volume." She gestured around at the walls, where his newer photographs hung, all with hand-lettered captions. Brief captions.

"But I'm afraid I don't remember authorizing anyone to bring my captions out in such a form."

"You can hardly refuse and go against the great goal of bringing art to the people," Miss Averil replied. Rather than let go his arm, she grasped him by the other as well, looked up into his eyes, and added, "You owe it to the world."

Allan wondered if there was any way out of this encounter without hurting Miss Averil's feelings. Had she any sense of humor?

Miss Gabell meanwhile had cleared her throat in a meaningful way and was sidling off. Allan couldn't stand for the older woman to think that he and Miss Averil had personal reasons for wishing to be left alone. He gently removed himself from the poet's grasp and said, "I thank you for your good opinion, ma'am. Am I to take it that you bearded that hundred-year-old throwback, 'young' Mr. Borderfield, in his very den and lived to tell the tale? You're truly a heroine of the first order. Isn't she, Miss Gabell?" he added to make sure he wasn't left alone with the young woman.

Miss Gabell looked back and twittered something, and Miss Averil looked pleased. "I tried to do my best for you even in the face of universal contempt. Lady Elaine Westwood, whom I saw at her little typing desk in the offices, didn't seem to think much of my chances." She frowned. "I don't suppose that woman would have done

War Widow 159

anything to turn Mr. Borderfield against us? For nefarious reasons of her own?"

"I don't think so. Isn't she merely a typewriter there?"

"Yes, maybe so, but they probably give her every consideration due to her rank. And I've heard that Mr. Borderfield is in love with her mother, Lady Berry," Miss Averil said, her voice dripping with suspicion.

"Oh, yes, he's positively enamored," Miss Gabell put in, jangling her bracelets. "It's been all over town for decades. Too bad about the age difference. And of course, the discrepancy in rank. Imagine going from being a countess to being the wife of a publisher."

"I'm prepared to acquit Lady Elaine of all nefarious plotting against me," Allan said, rather dazed at these confidences. "What reason could she have? And while I'm sorry Mr. Borderfield didn't go along with your ideas, Miss Averil, I have to say—"

"You have to say that you'll change to my publisher." Miss Averil interrupted him with an eager look; he could sense that she had almost reached out for his upper arms again, but restrained herself at the last minute. "Hammly House is sensitive to the poetic soul, and since I'm one of their authors, and I've written an introduction of your work for the first edition, there should be no problem."

"Except that I decline to leave my present publisher. I only brought out my book in the first place as a sort of favor—or perhaps it was more like a dare—well, it's all due to my friend Michael Parkington, whose connections to Borderfield's are numerous. Not only does he work there, his mother's maiden name is Borderfield. So you can see the difficulty."

"Mr. Parkington wouldn't want to stifle your poet's soul," Miss Averil said thoughtfully, making Allan fear for

Michael's tranquility. He would ring him up later on and warn him against this determined female.

"Why are you so set against Lady Elaine Westwood?" he asked.

Miss Averil stared and Miss Gabell, who had been about to wander off again, perked up with interest. Allan realized belatedly that the question was somewhat of a non sequitur.

Miss Averil tossed her head and fiddled with her fur. "I don't think anyone with a fine mind could be 'set against' the lady, as you put it. There is so little to her. She may be working for a lark, but that only shows she hasn't any feeling for the higher things in life. Why couldn't she take on some sort of charity or literary patronage if she wants to keep busy? It's practically un-British for her to take a job from a working-class young person simply because she finds herself bored."

"Has it never occurred to you that she might need the money?" Allan asked.

Again Miss Averil stared. This time it was she who exchanged a glance with Miss Gabell, one of amused indulgence. "You were down at Berryhill when I was," she said. "Do you think she needs the money?"

"And even if she didn't, she scarcely qualifies as immoral in taking off the market one ill-paying, menial job." Allan warmed to his subject. "Is it your premise, Miss Averil, that young women who happen to belong to a certain class in society should sit on their hands until they catch a man?"

"The business about taking a job is an eccentricity in the family, dear," Miss Gabell said to Miss Averil. "Why, young Lord Berry is working as Mr. Marchmont's secretary. It's the most cunning thing. I'm in love with the boy, looking so serious about his business as he does when he comes in here. And I'm sure neither you nor I, my dear, would cavil at the thought of a fellow woman taking work. Why, now that the dreadful war is over, what have we got but work to fill our days, our minds, our hearts?"

Miss Averil glanced at the gallery owner, then at Allan. With no further ado she burst into tears and ran from the gallery.

"Oh, dear," Miss Gabell murmured as the front door slammed, startling the other patrons. "I should have known by the clothes. Not to mention her antagonism toward Lady Elaine Westwood, who I understand is a very attractive young woman whose name has been linked with yours."

"What should you have known?" Allan asked, completely mystified.

The lady explained. "That young thing's fixation on your work is not only due to an interest in poetry. It's you she's thinking of."

"Surely not."

Miss Gabell was wearing the sage expression of one about to impart a great truth. "She's in love with you. Nothing could be clearer. She has always looked tweedy and unkempt until today, when she had the possibility of meeting you. She came in here insisting that I should find a way to bring you out to see her on a matter of life and death. Or if she didn't say life and death, she said it was important enough to warrant fetching you at once."

Allan shook his head. "Then we may take it that I'm not the latest thing since Byron? She simply likes me?"

"Something like that, Mr. Marchmont. Though I must say that I think she has a charming idea about the poetry—I mean, the captions. They are really very good."

Allan thanked her, took care of the other matter which had brought him to the galley—one involving his signature on the back of a photograph which had been sold—and wandered out into the streets. A blighted romance he hadn't even known about! Life was sometimes too complex for an ordinary man.

Was it possible that Ann Averil's evident dislike for Elaine was a sort of female jealousy? No, that couldn't be right. Miss Gabell was too romantic to know what was what.

He stalked about aimlessly, watching others duck into tea shops—for it was that hour—and wondering why he hadn't done it.

Not duck into a tea shop. There had been only one "it" on his mind for days now.

He had been kissing Elaine, as he had wanted to ever since meeting her, and he hadn't taken the opportunity to keep on kissing her, to tell her he loved her. He had rejected her because she had been married to his friend.

He crossed over into the Green Park and sat on a penny chair.

Elaine had really loved Bingo. She might excuse Allan for Bingo's death, might blame it all on a nebulous "war," but he knew in his heart that Bingo would have survived longer were it not for his own mistakes. It was almost as though he had got rid of Bingo to rob him of his wife. That wasn't the truth, of course, but . . . his guilt had overwhelmed him there in the car with Elaine; and now he sat in the park alone.

He sat up straighter as the rain began to beat down on him through the lime trees. His name had been linked with Elaine's, Miss Gabell had said. He could overcome these guilty qualms. He wouldn't let the war blight his whole future life.

He had every reason to hope for a better future. If there was anything to be said for his record with Elaine, it was that it could hardly get worse.

Chapter Fourteen

Elaine ended up sneaking a volume of her great-uncle's diary out of the office. Not the earliest one, for schoolboy doings failed to interest her, but one in the middle. She spent the evening reading it and marveling. The style left a lot to be desired—but the content!

Perhaps, Elaine thought, her uncle had been too busy naming names to consider his syntax. The journal volume she had selected dated from the 1870s and went into amazing paragraphs of detail about the circle of the then Prince of Wales, most of whom were ancestors of her mother's friends and Aunt Pen's. This was aside from the racing stories, most of which bored Elaine but contained frank accounts of which outwardly virtuous member of society had caused this or that race to be rigged.

This one slim volume was enough to cause twenty scandals and another score of lawsuits. And on her desk at the office were many more slim volumes that were possibly worse. Mr. Borderfield had made a lucky catch, if sensation was his aim.

Borderfield's had always been a respectable, even a staid

house, notably lacking in the luridly colored paper-covered novels and thinly disguised society tales brought out by other firms such as the Panic Press. Perhaps young Mr. Borderfield was truly in his dotage.

Elaine lay back on her narrow bed, turning over carefully the yellowed pages covered with flourishing, faded handwriting, and wondered what to do. By the merest chance she, not Katherine next to her or Olive down along the corridor, had been chosen to type up this manuscript. If Mr. Borderfield had any idea she was related to Montague Saxonbury, surely she would never have been selected. She did have the reputation at work for being able to decipher difficult handwriting; there was probably no more to her "luck" than that.

However, the chance to do so had come to her, surely it was fated that she try to save her family's dignity. Her mind flitted from one possibility to another. She could simply put initials where Uncle Montague had put names. She could substitute euphemisms such as "a well-known peer" or "a lady in society," as the newspapers did.

Or she could burn the diary and say it had been stolen off her desk.

Her stockinged feet fidgeted, turning circles in the air, as she pretended to mull over these possibilities. She couldn't do anything, and she knew it very well.

Mr. Borderfield had ordered her, his employee, to type the manuscript and to leave nothing out. She had to follow instructions or leave her position. If she satisfied her own sense of propriety and substituted initials for names, she would have to write up another list as a key for the inevitable time when she was directed to put back the names.

As for destroying the memoirs, she couldn't do that. Not only was the diary Rollo's property, despite its lack of literary skill there was something appealing, something lively and jaunty about these tales of long-ago society. Great-uncle Montague did, in his way, make the past come alive. The memoir had a primitive sort of art. And it was beyond Elaine's poor powers to destroy a work of art.

She closed her eyes, wishing she could ask the advice of Allan Marchmont. Would she never stop thinking about that man? She was obviously never going to see him again unless she went to him; and her pride wouldn't allow such a thing.

A knock at the door made her start. Nobody could be visiting from outside at this hour, and even visits between the various rooms were discouraged, though of course this rule wasn't adhered to.

With the thought in mind that whoever was there would need her help and probably her discretion, Elaine went close to the door and murmured "Yes?" in an undertone.

"Mrs. Westwood! Open up at once!" came trumpet-like tones, and Elaine, amazed into obedience, turned the key and opened the door to Mrs. Beasley.

It being after ten at night, the landlady had doffed her usual formal attire of shirtwaist and unfashionable skirt and was clad in a fuzzy dressing gown of Scottish plaid, her hair in greyed braids. Elaine stood aside for her to pass into the room, noting as she did so that a frightened-looking rabbit of a girl, hair done up in rags, scurried off down the dark hall: Mrs. Beasley's daughter and chief slavey, Albertina.

"Alone, are we?" Mrs. Beasley snapped shut the door, looked around the plain chamber with an air of suspicion, and glared at Elaine.

Elaine wondered for one panicky moment if Mrs. Beasley had discovered the spirit lamp hidden under the bed; but then she realized the landlady was accusing her of much darker doings.

"Of course I'm alone," she said with dignity.

"I don't suppose even one with your wiles could get anyone in past my defenses," Mrs. Beasley remarked, crossing the room to twitch open the window curtain.

Elaine shook her head in exasperation. The window opened onto a blank brick wall. Perhaps the girls with rooms at the back of the house, where the chimneypots were, had a chance of sneaking a man in somehow, but she would need a rope ladder. "What exactly are you accusing me of?" she asked in a meek tone which she judged would be most likely to pass as respectable with the landlady.

"Sheets can be tied together, that sort of thing," Mrs. Beasley was muttering, half to herself. Then she turned to face Elaine. "I see you don't have anyone in here with you now, but I have no reason to suppose you haven't violated my establishment with male visitors at other times."

"What in the world would make you think so?" Elaine asked, more curious than angry. Of course Mrs. Beasley was unreasonable. She had started out that way when Elaine first met her, and she would end that way; whatever wild accusations she might make revealed more about her character than that of the accused. Still, she had to have had something to set her off on her flight of fancy.

"My own daughter is my witness," Mrs. Beasley said with an eloquent sniff. "She tried to keep your sordid secret for days, but I finally wormed it out of her."

"Oh?"

"Oh, yes. Albertina has some misguided sense of loyalty to you which I cannot understand. It took me almost a week to get out of her that you had been seen conferring with a man outside this establishment in the dead of night last Saturday." There was an ominous pause. "Long after my curfew."

Elaine opened her mouth to ask why, or how, Albertina could have been in a position to observe another's movements so late at night, but didn't say anything after all. The girl was well-punished by having to live with such a mother as this.

"Why should it matter what I was doing outside your establishment, as you call it?" Elaine asked with her haughtiest look. "You know that I stayed at my mother-in-law's that night, because I did get back from my engagement after you'd locked your doors. I was talking to the friend who ended up driving me to Clapham."

"A likely story! I've had enough of your shabby-genteel sort, you thinking you're too good for the place, you with your lying ways and your mincing good manners. You'll leave at once, do you hear?"

"I should hardly wish to stay after that outburst," Elaine said calmly, wishing she wasn't so tired. So class prejudice was at the root of this. Mrs. Beasley realized that Elaine's cultivated accent wasn't put on, but natural to her; or perhaps Elaine's having been picked up by that large, rich car of Mr. Van Vliet's had put her beyond the pale in this house. Whatever the exact cause, she was powerless to do anything about it. Powerless and much too weary.

"I'm not aware of what I'm supposed to have done, but I presume that, since you aren't either, no explanation will be forthcoming. If you'll excuse me, ma'am? I must pack."

"See that you do," Mrs. Beasley said with an awful frown. She swept from the room and shut the door with a resounding bang.

Elaine opened it and shouted down the hall, "You can return the rest of the month's rent, since you're chucking me out. Or shall my solicitor call on you?" As she closed the door again, more gently than the landlady but vigorously, she could hear the satisfying sound of other doors opening up and down the corridor and the excited twittering of female voices.

Most of the other women in the hostel were congenial sorts, and some of them came in to commiserate with Elaine, telling stories of their own about Mrs. Beasley and other tenants she had ejected from her house on the flimsiest of pretexts. She was agreed by all to be a woman of little stability, no matter how solid and matter-of-fact she appeared. Every once in a while she would hit upon some random lodger as the target of her wrath, and this time her eye had fallen on Elaine. There was nothing to be done about it except for Elaine to get her money back, if she could; and the women hoped wistfully that she would really try this through a solicitor. Mrs. Beasley deserved trouble.

One of the lodgers helped Elaine by sitting down on a suitcase. Another folded all her blouses for her. One cynical young woman made the laughing observation that Mrs. Beasley hadn't stayed to make sure nothing of hers was stolen: She furnished the rooms so sparsely that there was nothing worth taking.

Elaine bequeathed her spirit lamp to the last visitor and sat down on the bed, clad in her outdoor things. It was really very late. A cab would have to take her to Clapham, and she would have to trust to Mrs. Gantle's understanding when she got there. It was one thing to stay over in Griselda's room for the occasional night by special invitation, quite another to show up unannounced with bag and baggage. And Elaine didn't want to live in Clapham even if there should be room in Mrs. Gantle's house. It was much too far from Borderfield's.

She toyed next with the thought of telephoning Rollo and having him take her to his mother's. There would be no harm in his knowing where the hostel was now that she was moving out of it, and Aunt Pen would love to have her. She would think an engagement between Rollo and Elaine was imminent, but Elaine could nip that in the bud, and she would have a place to stay and a real breakfast. In the morning she could make other plans. Yes, that was much the better idea.

In the back of her mind was the traitorous thought that she could call on Allan Marchmont; that he would somehow make everything right. She resolved not to think of it. She would get out of this fix by herself, without help from any man—except Rollo, who was family and didn't count.

Down in the front hall, which Mrs. Beasley dignified by the name of lobby, the landlady stood guard over the telephone by the stairs. "No, you don't." She stepped forward as Elaine started towards the instrument. "You'll go out in the street without one of your men friends to help you, and no two ways about it."

"Reflect a little," Elaine said with a weary sigh. "If you don't let me make arrangements to get away, morning will find me huddled on your steps, either that or a passing constable will have asked me what I was doing out so late, and I will have told him. And may I trouble you for that money you owe me?"

"Think you're above us all, don't you? I know for a fact you're no better than you should be."

"How could you possibly know something I don't know myself?" Elaine asked with a hysterical giggle, thinking of Allan. She wished, yes, she did wish devoutly in this moment that she was really "no better than she should be" and could nip off to her lover's flat.

"Very well, make your call to your seducer," Mrs. Beasley said, moving away from the telephone. "To think my establishment should see this day."

"The money?" Elaine called as Mrs. Beasley disappeared through a doorway leading to the basement.

Though Elaine felt years had passed in the last hour, it was still not yet midnight, and to her relief, Aunt Pen answered the telephone in the voice of someone who had not yet gone to bed, though she did sound wary to receive a call so late at night. When she recognized Elaine's voice, her own fairly bubbled over the wires in her happiness to be of service. "Rollo will be right over. Where did you say you were?"

Elaine gave the address, endured Aunt Pen's shocked gasp when she heard it, then rang off. It took her only two trips to drag her bags to the front steps. Several of her former fellow tenants came creeping down the stairs to say a final farewell or to promise to meet her for tea in an ABC near Covent Garden the next week. Of Mrs. Beasley and Albertina there was no sign. Elaine supposed she could storm back to their private quarters and demand the money owed to her, but she felt it would be much more useful to get her mother's solicitor to send a threatening letter. She would love to scare the Beasley woman badly, if she could.

"I say, this is rather a rum go," commented Rollo fifteen minutes later, as he helped her to load her things into his little auto. "Don't tell me you actually lived around here?"

"Not around here. Here." Elaine indicated the Businesswomen's Hostel with a flourish. "Not only that, I'll be finding another similar place as soon as I can."

"No! Too dismal, old thing." Rollo assisted Elaine into the passenger seat and hopped behind the wheel. "Mum will insist on keeping you, and it's just as well. I'm promised to a fellow down in Kent for the next couple of weeks, and she'll need the company. Maybe she can talk you into marrying me. I'm not having much luck."

Elaine decided to ignore the comment about marriage; but it was just as well that he wasn't going to be at home for the next little while. They roared away south to Mount Street and his mother's flat.

War Widow

Mother and son lived in a block of flats converted from several Georgian houses. Elaine had always admired the charm of the narrow rooms and high ceilings, imagining life in the gracious days when the original houses had been built. The flat was spacious; Elaine knew there was an untenanted bedroom. Pen Saxonbury kept only one servant in the house, Rollo's old batman, who did double duty as butler and Rollo's valet and had quarters off the kitchen. Female help came in by the day when help could be got. Aunt Pen's favorite topic of conversation, aside from the hoped-for marriage between her son and Elaine, was the servant problem.

"There isn't a properly trained girl left in the whole of London," she chatted to Elaine, by way of explaining why the sheets in the chintz-trimmed bedroom to which she led her young relation hadn't been aired in the half-hour between Elaine's call and her arrival. "Nobody wants to live in, and precious few want to be domestics. All of those jobs in factories and buses during the war simply spoiled the girls."

"You should bring someone up from the country," Elaine said absently, eyeing the bed with satisfaction. She could see nothing to apologize for in the crisp white sheets and puffy satin quilt. "I do appreciate your taking me in like this."

"Dear Elaine! Could I do any less? I know your mother would gladly shelter Rollo from the storm."

As though on cue, a brisk spring rain began to beat against the narrow windows of the room, making it seem even cozier to Elaine's tired senses. She swayed a little.

"Why, my dear, you're all in. I'll send Mills to you with hot milk," Aunt Pen said in understanding, leading Elaine to a chair near a cheerful fire of gas logs. "He can leave it outside the door if you want to undress right now."

"Perhaps I'd better," Elaine replied, leaning back. "I'm

very tired. But I'm so grateful. I'll explain everything in the morning."

Aunt Pen tiptoed out.

A suspiciously bright shaft of sun struck Elaine's face. Her eyes flew open, and a panicked glance at the clock on the tiny mantelpiece told her it was already an hour past the time she was supposed to be at the office. Though she washed and dressed quicker than she ever had in her life, fifteen more minutes went by before she skidded into the breakfast room, only to find that Pen had only just sat down and Rollo wasn't even out of bed yet.

"Your office?" Aunt Pen said with a blank look. "Oh, my dear, I hadn't any idea that you'd want to go in when you were in such a state last night. It can't be good for you. Shall I have Mills ring up the people at your job and tell them you'll be resting today?"

"No, thank you, but I'd better use your telephone myself and get a message in that I'll be there as fast as possible." Elaine was already calculating the distance from Mount Street to Covent Garden. A bus, if she knew which bus to take; or she might simply run for it. There was no use in her giving a lecture to her hostess about the importance of going to one's job every day. Despite a fair amount of war work, Aunt Pen had reverted to a lilies-of-the-field philosophy as soon as the armistice was signed.

Elaine dashed to the telephone and did a good deal of fast talking to the switchboard girl at Borderfield's. Perhaps the fact she had never been late before would excuse her this time. Then she hurried into her outdoor things and prepared to plummet down the stairs.

"My dear girl, what are you doing? What about your breakfast?" Aunt Pen, followed by Mills, the manservant, emerged into the hall just in time to see Elaine. "You simply can't rush off without something in your tummy."

"No time for that. I must get to the office." Elaine held clutched to her side the volume of Great Uncle Montague's diary that she had been reading the night before, and she proceeded to move it unobtrusively under her coat.

"At least wait for Louis. He can take you there."

"Louis?"

"I sent for him because I thought you'd like the support of your whole family around you at a time like this," Aunt Pen said. "I still haven't got it quite clear what happened to you last night. Remember that you did promise to tell me in the morning."

"But I didn't know I wasn't going to wake up in time," Elaine said unhappily.

"See? You did need the sleep."

Elaine found nothing more difficult to deal with than the logic of someone who was advocating what she herself most wanted. She would love to be able to sit and have breakfast and explain every detail of last night's contretemps; she would like, in fact, to be as detached from the practical side of life as Aunt Pen appeared to be.

"Louis is on his way here, and you must wait for the boy," Aunt Pen said as though there was no question about the matter.

Elaine sat down on the stairs in defeat.

"I had in mind your sitting at the table and eating a muffin. Mills?" Pen motioned forward the manservant, a middle-aged individual tending to stoutness, and indicated he should help Elaine to her feet.

"Thank you, Mills, but I'll get up by myself in a moment," Elaine said with a little smile. The former batman retreated to a distance.

"I don't know what to do with you modern girls. You'll have your own way in everything. Though I've had my suffragist moments, I wonder if giving the vote to giddy young girls can be at all the thing. Perhaps only women of forty and over should vote."

"Then the men would have it their way. Who would vote if they had to admit to being over forty?" Elaine said with a laugh. "You forget, Auntie, we have to be over thirty now. The newest cause is getting the age reduced."

"It still gives girls the wrong idea," Aunt Pen said in a voice laden with doom. She was probably thinking of the servant problem again.

Elaine put her elbows on her knees, her chin in her hands, and simply sat on the stairs. There was a knock on the door somewhere below, and Mills disappeared. He would be letting Louis in, and Elaine knew she could make her brother go with her to Borderfield's without delay. Aunt Pen's explanation would have to wait until the evening. Elaine couldn't face losing her job on top of everything else. She prayed she hadn't lost it already.

A door opened, and Allan Marchmont appeared at the bottom of the flight of stairs.

"Well," he said, eyeing her. "So it's true. I didn't really believe you'd move in with Rollo Saxonbury."

Chapter Fifteen

Elaine looked down at Allan in confusion. How on earth had he come here? She remembered how only last night she had felt the urge to call upon this man for help; and now here he was—accusing her of reprehensible behavior. "Why should you think I moved in with Rollo?"

"Because this is his house, and here you are."

"I also moved in with his mother," Elaine said with a superior smile. "And they are my relations. Why is this any of your affair?"

To her surprise, Allant's expression changed from accusing to dismayed. He sank to one of the steps at the bottom of the flight of stairs. "I've done it, haven't I?" His voice was muffled because he was turned away from her, but she heard it all the same. "When your brother told me you'd moved in with my old schoolfellow Rollo, I naturally thought—I know you're related, but I also know Rollo wants to marry you."

"How do you know that?"

Allan turned around on the step to give her a rueful smile. "He told me when he warned me off."

Elaine rolled her eyes. "I'm not going to marry him."

"Now, dear, let's not be too hasty. You know you haven't quite made up your mind."

Aunt Pen's voice came as a complete shock to Elaine. She had somehow assumed that she and Allan were alone in the world. Now she realized that not only Aunt Pen but Mills stood on the landing just above the step where she perched. Both looked much too interested in what was going on.

Elaine looked down at Allan. "Did you come in your car? I must get to Borderfield's as fast as possible. I'm very late."

"No, but I can easily get you a cab." He rose from the stairs and held out a hand to her. She stood and gathered her things, not forgetting the book jabbed under her elbow, and rushed down to meet him.

"Thank you for everything, Aunt Pen," Elaine said over her shoulder. "I'll explain it all this evening after work. I promise."

"But what about Louis?"

"Give him breakfast," Elaine said, darting out the door.

Out in the cool air of Mount Street, Allan smiled at her and said, "Louis isn't coming. I hope Mrs. Saxonbury won't be disappointed. I convinced him to let me take his place."

"I don't really know why Aunt Pen summoned him. Some muddled idea of family solidarity in my time of trouble. But I was going to make him take me to work at once, and she wouldn't have had a chance to entertain him. Do you realize I'm over an hour late? They probably won't stand for this at Borderfield's." Elaine spoke very quickly and avoided Allan's eye. She couldn't let herself think about personal issues; she had to focus on the task at hand. Noticing that he wasn't making any move to get her a cab, and not seeing any in the street, she moved quickly down towards Berkeley Square where there ought to be lots of vehicles. Perhaps she would jump onto a bus.

"You are going to let me take you, aren't you?" Allan shot

out an arm and flagged down a cab Elaine hadn't seen. She jumped into it and gave the order for Covent Garden, a bit disconcerted when Allan followed her in and sat beside her.

"I would really rather you didn't," she said. "The last time I saw you we didn't exactly part friends." When her eyes met Allan's he looked as embarrassed as she felt. "It's been a difficult morning, and you aren't making it easier, implying that I would cohabit with my cousin Rollo."

"I'm afraid I didn't realize he lived with his mother. But that shouldn't have mattered. I was mad to accuse you. And you're right. None of it is my affair."

A note of curiosity was evident in his voice. Elaine, still eager to talk over her grievances and somehow make sense of them, saw no reason to keep her new status a secret, especially as Allan had indirectly contributed to it. "I was thrown out of my room in the middle of the night. I came to my relations because they live closer to my office than my mother-in-law. Not that it matters, since I forgot to set my clock and promptly slept through most of the morning."

"Why were you thrown out?" He looked at her keenly, then turned away. "I'm sorry, that wasn't a fair question."

"Because of you," she said casually, looking at him sideways.

He turned back to face her and stared.

"I'm sorry." She smiled and gave a little shrug. "I couldn't resist shocking you. It's true, but only somewhat. My landlady's daughter spied me with a dreaded *man* when you and I were outside the house very late last Saturday night." She paused, trying to think how to explain Mrs. Beasley. "The woman has something against people who speak without an accent—"

"You mean earl's daughters."

"No, she had no way of knowing I have a title. I'm simply a type she hates. I've heard through the other women at the hostel that she's done this before. She picks someone, finds a reason to go after them, and then has the fun of a midnight eviction."

"I saw the lady the time I tried to bring flowers to you. She struck me as not being the most cordial person I'd ever met, but to be that cruel to an unprotected woman . . . Did she hold that against you? The flower incident?"

"She didn't mention it last night, but the flowers probably didn't do any good. I remember her saying something nasty at the time." Elaine smiled in reminiscence. "I was so silly, so afraid of offending that horrid woman, that I didn't take any of the flowers home from the office. I knew there'd be questions but I very much wanted to keep them with me. Instead I had to pretend I didn't care and let them wither on my desk."

"May I help you find some legal recourse? It doesn't sound at all the proper thing, to throw a defenseless woman out, unprovoked, into the night."

"I'm going to make sure I get my money back. She got rid of me before the month was out. Our family solicitor might write her a nasty letter. As for the rest, she's being punished enough simply by being who she is." Elaine sighed. "I do wish I could have helped her daughter, though."

"Her daughter?"

"A poor, shrinking, oppressed little thing who is overworked and under her mother's thumb . . . oh!" Tired though she was, she had actually thought of something. "I have it. Strike back at the mother by helping the daughter. Yes, I'll do it."

"What are you talking about?" Allan asked, sounding amused.

"My landlady's daughter is a downtrodden house slave with no prospects. I can suggest to Rollo's mother that she train the girl to be her longed-for live-in maid." This idea brought such comfort to Elaine, she nearly forgot her anxiety to be at her job. "Mrs. Beasley would have to hire a replacement to get the work done. Marvelous revenge!"

"I didn't know you had a wicked, vengeful side," said Allan in a thoughtful tone.

"Of course I do. I'll set the project in train this very evening. Rollo can take round a note; or I'll find some other way." Elaine turned a radiant smile on Allan.

"I can help as well as your cousins," he said, giving her a tender look. "Let me know. I'm glad to see you so happy about something." He took a deep breath. "Now, then, Elaine, I believe we have some talking to do—and not about your landlady's daughter."

Elaine noticed, through the window of the cab, that they were almost to Covent Garden. "I'm sorry, but now isn't the time. I'm about to jump out of this cab and rush for my life into Borderfield's." She definitely didn't want to have a sensitive talk in a cab in the middle of the street.

"But we mustn't leave it like this! Can we at least shake hands and resolve to talk at a later time?"

Elaine stared at the offered hand and drew back. Then, telling herself not to be a fool, she put her hand in his. They shook solemnly, distantly. The last time they had touched had been so different; but she couldn't dwell on that. "We don't seem to do very well at talking," she said with a helpless little shrug. "Let's resolve to be civil when we happen to meet."

"Civil isn't enough. When may I see you?" He was talking to her back as she sprang out of the cab.

He got out, too, having flung enough cash at the driver to make him tip his hat cheerily and drive away whistling.

"You're seeing me now," Elaine said. "Please, I really

can't stop. I'll have some fast talking to do once I get inside."

"Then I can reach you at Rollo's—at his mother's?"

"I really don't think you ought to contact me at all." Elaine looked at him in a mix of hope and dismay. He seemed to be able to take her hand without any physical consequences at all, while any more time in his company would reveal her desire—her need—to become much more than friends. Why should she give him a chance to draw back from her again?

Fumbling once more in her bag, she came up with a pair of spectacles, jammed these on her nose, and dashed in through the doors of Borderfield's.

Allan stood on the pavement looking after her. As an author of Borderfield's, he had every right to go in too. But he realized that if he did, she wouldn't forgive him. Perhaps he ought to do as she said and not contact her—for a while, at least. But that was surely impossible. These past days without a sight of her had been intolerable.

His passion was causing him to act irrationally. When Louis had received that telephone call this morning and casually mentioned that his sister had moved to Rollo's, and that Louis was supposed to go over to Mount Street for some reason, Allan hadn't hesitated. He ordered Louis to stay on the premises and assured the young earl that he would take care of any emergency at his cousin's.

He could still hear the vacuous, drawling tones of Rollo's mother floating his way from the landing. He must hope he wouldn't ever meet the lady socially. Her voice, proof though it was of Elaine's innocence, would forever make him cringe.

Hands in his pockets, he sighed and turned his back on Borderfield's, thinking.

Flowers? No, those hadn't worked out very well, though he

War Widow

knew now that she had at least liked his gift. A night on the town? She wouldn't go with him. A party to which he and she might both be invited? Now there was a thought. But he couldn't give such a party himself—that would tip her off—and he knew next to nobody in her social circle. Perhaps Oswald Van Vliet would invite her out again, and Allan could accidentally meet her as he had before. But though he had stood Van Vliet to drinks at the club a time or two, the American hadn't mentioned that he was keeping up his pursuit of Elaine. Not that a man would necessarily mention this to another man, but Van Vliet was so impressed by English titles that he probably would. Allan knew the American had taken Louis out to lunch, with the excuse of getting to know his landlord, but really to be kind to the youth—or perhaps to ingratiate himself with the brother of the girl he wanted? Yes, Lord Berry might be the best source of information.

Accordingly, when he arrived back at his rooms Allan flung himself onto the study sofa, took a hard look at Louis, who was settled at the desk busy with some papers, and said, "Is your sister going about much with Oswald Van Vliet?"

"I don't know, sir. She doesn't tell me about her goings-on with men."

"Tell me this, then, my lord. What would be the best way to your sister's heart?"

"What?" Louis peered through the plain glass spectacles he had picked up somewhere, which were supposed to make him look older, Allan knew. Was that why his sister had put on her own pair of spectacles before going in to Borderfield's?

"I'm expressing myself badly as usual," Allan said. "I ought to confine myself to photography, perhaps. I need to know how I can see your sister."

"Why, ask her to go someplace with you. The theater. She

likes the theater. And there's dancing and all that. Or a party."

"I'm afraid we're on awkward terms. I don't think she'd consent to an evening with me unless I could arrange for others to be there too." Allan thought of something. "How about you and Lady Miranda? Have you made plans for any more nights on the town?" Although he supposed that, if so, Louis would have been excited and told him.

Louis blushed. "She seems to have dropped me. Probably because I got sleepy on her last Saturday. It was two in the morning, and I'm not in training. The other fellows say you have to have practice at staying up all night, but it does come to you."

"I hope the other fellows also mention that sort of thing can get you into lots of trouble," Allan felt bound to say, since he was supposed to be guiding the steps of the boy. "Could you ring the lady up and suggest she come out with you and your sister—and me?"

Louis shook his head, looking down at the desk.

Allan didn't suppose he should insist that a sixteen-year-old boy, earl or not, pursue a fast young society flapper against said boy's will.

"I don't even want to go to her party," Louis mumbled. "Too embarrassing. Mr. Van Vliet about had to carry me out of the Purple Club."

"Party? She's invited you to a party?" Allan asked in a sharp voice.

Louis rummaged about on the desk in a space Allan had designated as his, and which was consequently filled with sports papers and other boyish paraphernalia. He came up with a note on heavy paper in a crested envelope, crossed the room and gave it to Allan.

The feminine scrawl was clear enough. Lady Miranda

invited Louis—and his sister—to join her and her friends at an address out in Chelsea on the following Saturday night, only two days away. She said something about making up for their having missed an event of the same kind when they had last been together.

"You have to take your sister," Allan said. "You must swallow your embarrassment—which is unwarranted—and make yourself do it, for Lady Elaine's sake. She's had a difficult time of it this week, and she should be taken about and entertained. As for Lady Miranda, she evidently hasn't given you up." He rose to his feet and deposited the invitation back in Louis' hands. "I advise you to accept this offer immediately. Meanwhile, I'll tackle Lady Miranda Winchapel. Where does she live?"

"You'll tackle her?" Louis said blankly. A small jealous fire appeared in the depths of his clear blue eyes.

"I mean I'll get myself an invitation to this gathering. To see your sister."

"Oh. Do you really like my sister?"

"Why wouldn't I?"

"She's, oh, I suppose Elaine is fine taken in small doses. She's rather a beast about some things, you know."

Brothers and sisters! Sometimes Allan was glad to have been an only child. "And Lady Miranda lives . . . ?"

"In Portland Place. You can't miss the Duke of Wincastle's house. Anyone could tell you. Here, I'll write it down."

Allan noted down the number and, with a final earnest appeal to Lord Berry to accept the invitation without stopping to ask his sister if she wanted to go, he went out again.

Since it was a good little jaunt to Portland Place, he went round to the mews and got out the car. If he had lived in Albany in the old days of the Regency bucks, he could have had his curricle or phaeton brought round, which would have seemed much more appropriate for calling on a duke's daughter.

Still, he found a perverse satisfaction in maneuvering the great, vehicle-jammed cultural desert of Regent Street, though he had to agree with most of his peers that motoring was really a sport more suited to the countryside. By the time he got to the Wincastle residence he had nearly settled on what he would say to her ladyship.

He was disappointed at the door, though, when a footman wearing the latest in antique livery informed him that Lady Miranda was not at home. "Went into Regent's Park," this worthy whispered when Allan, wondering whether "not at home" meant simply not receiving, or not on the premises, slipped a coin into the man's hand.

Perhaps he could happen to see her in the park, though it was a large target to hit. Would Lady Miranda be likely to visit the zoo? To walk her dog in the direction of Primrose Hill? Did she have a dog? Allan turned around to use up some more cash on the helpful footman, but the door had closed, and knocking a servant up again on purpose to bribe him seemed a bit much.

The sky was threatening rain, and the park wasn't crowded. After only a little strolling, Allan was beginning to wish he had a dog as a wholesome excuse for being where he was. Park idlers were usually men up to no good. Take that fashionable fellow swinging a walking stick, who was rather furtively tipping his hat to a lady—Lady Miranda!

Allan instinctively stepped off the path and behind a tree in new leaf, hoping no park wardens were about since he was only inches from a posted warning to keep off the grass he was standing upon. There was nothing to see, as it turned out. The two spent a moment in talk, then Lady Miranda parted from the fellow with a quick handshake, all with her back to Allan. Doubtless they were friends. He stepped from his inadequate hiding place and hurried after her.

"Lady Miranda!" When she turned and sent a puzzled look his way, he remembered that she, with her wide acquaintance, wouldn't necessarily remember having met him. He wasn't even sure they had formally met at all, though they had been included in the same gathering more than once. He approached her quickly, extending a hand. "You have no reason to recall me, but I'm Allan Marchmont. We met down at Berryhill not long ago."

"Oh. Yes. The photograph man." She gave him a speculative look from long, sultry eyes that wouldn't have been out of place on an odalisque. She had on sables against the chill spring weather, and a small, chic hat. "Are you going to stand me to a drink?" she asked, taking his arm. "Eventually I mean for every good-looking man in London to give me a drink. There's an amusing small pub right across the Euston Road."

Allan let himself be directed to a workingman's pub that Lady Miranda seemed to know quite well, judging by the familiarity with which the barman greeted her. Duke's daughters had changed, then, since prewar days.

"I'm glad you're letting me give you a drink," he said when they were ensconced at a little back table in the dark, wood-paneled place hung with dart boards, hunting prints, and notices of workers' meetings. "I have a favor to ask you, Lady Miranda."

"It must have to do with Elaine Westwood. And please call me Goggle."

He looked at her in amazement. "I don't know if I could. But why do you think this has to do with Lady Elaine?"

"You couldn't take your eyes off her the other night at Ciro's," Miranda said with a shrug. "Unless you've had the good sense to be suddenly smitten by my charms when you barely noticed me that night, I can't think of any other explanation for you approaching me. You probably think Elaine and I are close friends."

"You're not?"

Miranda smiled. "I'm not the type who has a lot of girlfriends. But Elaine and I are cordial enough. What is it? Shall I put a word in her ear about what a wonderful man you are? Are you a wonderful man, by the way?"

"Yes," he said with a grin. "At least, you're to say so should anyone ask. My lady, you're extremely astute. The favor does have to do with Elaine. I find that I want to be with her in a casual social setting. If I could wangle myself an invitation to the party you've invited her and her brother to out at Chelsea—"

"Oh, would you come? How jolly," Miranda interrupted him, looking delighted. "My dear friend from school lives out in Chelsea in a little house, and I'm to move in with her officially as soon as I can talk my mother round. Naturally, I've begun to entertain with her just to get my toe in. We can always use an extra man, and such a lion as you . . . yes, please come. Tell me, do you like to take photographs of people? In the nude, for example?"

"What?"

She shrugged. "It's merely that my friend will be sure to ask you that right off. She's always getting painters and sculptors to do her in the altogether. A sort of rebellious streak, I suppose, because her father's a bishop."

"Oh. I see I'm about to be inducted into the fast life. But do you think this will be a proper atmosphere for Louis—for Lord Berry?"

"Nobody actually takes off any clothes at these parties, or I wouldn't have invited Elaine. She's such a goody-goody." She paused. "But you'd know that. If you like her anyhow, I won't put my oar in."

"You're very kind to help me with what's been up to now a star-crossed romance. And I can keep an eye on his lordship if things get too fast for a lad of sixteen."

Miranda laughed, a sharp, tinkling sound. "He'll probably fall asleep before anything happens. If anything does, which is unlikely," she added quickly.

"Listen, pal," said a gruff voice with an American accent, behind Allan's chair, "this lady isn't interested in anything you've got for sale—"

"So!" Miranda glared into the space beyond Allan. "You *are* shadowing me. Do you think you're my nursemaid? Bugger off, as they say in some circles."

Allan felt himself hauled out of his chair, spun around and hit in the jaw. He went down in a crash of furniture, wondering why on earth his old friend Oswald Van Vliet was trying to do away with him.

Chapter Sixteen

Someone splashed cold water into his face. "I'm sorry, pal," Van Vliet said over the sharp throbbing in Allan's jaw. "Didn't know it was you. It's dark in these places, and, hey, so I don't wear my glasses all I should."

Allan opened his eyes. He was surrounded by splintered furniture, the apron-clad barman, two pub patrons in dark blue smocks and flat caps, and Lady Miranda Winchapel, who seemed to be kneeling beside him bathing his face in water from a basin. She dried him off with a bar towel as he blinked his eyes. Above him loomed the distraught face of his supposed friend from America.

Allan struggled to a sitting position and experimentally worked his jaw. His conclusion was that much worse had happened to him in the war: Specifically, in that little cafe near Rouen where he and his mates got into a brawl over a stolen tin of meat. He looked curiously at his assailant. "I've never in my life seen you in a pair of spectacles. Your aim is fine without them. What is this? A bizarre American form of greeting?"

"You should lie down," Miranda put in. "He's hurt you

very badly. Is there a sofa in the back?" she asked the surrounding onlookers. "Somewhere he could be carried?"

As the barman and another denizen of the place began to argue over this, Allan said, "I don't need to lie down, my lady. An explanation wouldn't come amiss, but I think I'll live to fight another day."

"Are you certain? You must have a jaw of iron. I'm sure you'll have a bruise." Miranda cooed over him and fussed, stroking his jaw with sinuous fingers, darting menacing glances at Van Vliet, who hung back looking guilty—as well he might. The other patrons, seeing that there was no serious injury and apparently no further fighting to be commented upon, went back to their own concerns in other dark nooks, and a young boy began to gather up the broken pieces of furniture. Out of the corner of his eye, Allan was aware of banknotes flashing between the hands of Van Vliet and the barman.

He went to sit at another table, Miranda supporting him as best she could, though he didn't feel unsteady on his feet. Van Vliet, looking very sheepish, joined them in a few minutes. The barman brought a round of drinks.

"I think I heard you say that you believed I was someone else," Allan said, giving his friend a stern look.

"Yeah. Someone has been trying to get too close to Lady Miranda, and I thought I had the big stiff. You look like anyone else from the back, you know."

"I'll take that as flattery, old man."

"You don't have my permission to hit anyone I know," Miranda said to Van Vliet in a sort of well-bred snarl.

"Some people you know need hitting," Van Vliet retorted.

Allan was surprised. He hadn't known these two were well enough acquainted to quarrel, or to hit each other's friends, for that matter. On reflection it seemed entirely natural. He could imagine that Miranda, reputedly eager for any new experience, would be happy to be on some footing of intimacy with an American of no particular social status but abundant fortune. Van Vliet was extremely impressed by titles. It needed nothing more.

"No hard feelings, I hope?" Van Vliet said with an appealing look at Allan. "If you want, you can take a swing at me."

"That won't be necessary." Allan rubbed his jaw. "I don't believe you did any harm. I remember your reputation. You must have only given me a love tap."

"Well, my fist was halfway to connecting when I realized it wasn't getting the guy I thought I had. Glad you're not the type to hold a grudge, Marchmont."

"It's one of my finer qualities," Allan said dryly.

"You said it." Van Vliet slapped him on the back, causing Allan's jaw to reverberate.

"I ought to be going," Allan said when he had finished his drink, which happened to be a steaming mug of tea: Unusual tavern fair, but comforting in the circumstances. "My car isn't far away. May I drop you anywhere, Lady Miranda?"

"Yes, as a matter of fact," the young woman said with a sidelong glance at Van Vliet.

"Do you want me to take you instead, Lady Miranda?" Van Vliet asked. "Glad to."

Miranda gave Van Vliet an incredulous look but said nothing. She didn't even say good-bye to the American as Allan escorted her out of the little pub; in fact, she gave Van Vliet a haughty stare such as one of her ancestors might have flung toward a peasant who had intruded himself upon her notice.

"You're such a dear not to ask a lot of awkward questions," Miranda said to Allan when they had crossed Euston Road. She squeezed his arm. "Mr. Van Vliet is an odd creature. I know a lot of Americans, and they don't all nose their way into one's affairs."

War Widow 191

"From what I know of Oswald Van Vliet, his inborn chivalry has come into play. He thinks he's protecting you from this ordinary-looking person he thinks has been bothering you, or trying to encroach, or . . ."

"I'm sure he didn't mean to suggest you were ordinary-looking, Mr. Marchmont." Miranda slid into his car as though she had no bones at all, pointedly ignoring Allan's reference to the person Van Vliet had really been trying to injure.

Since she had already complimented him for not asking too many questions, Allan resigned himself to his curiosity on this point remaining unsatisfied. "I'm not complaining. One finds it useful now and again to blend into the crowd."

"You could never do that, Mr. Marchmont. May I call you Allan?"

Allan recognized this as standard flirtation, perhaps meant to make him forget about any questions he might have regarding Miranda's associates. He responded with good humor. He was not averse to having beautiful young women flatter him. "You may definitely call me Allan. I think you asked me earlier to call you something? Gigi, was it?"

"Goggle. My name from school. Dreadful, isn't it, but everyone calls me that. I hated it for the first two weeks, but it's become what I answer to. Even to myself."

He doubted his ability to address a lady by one of those stupid boarding school names; but if it would please her, he'd try. "All right, then, Lady—Goggle. How is that?"

"Without the 'lady,' please," she said with a low laugh. "One doesn't always like to be reminded one's a lady." She paused as he eased the car out into traffic. "If one is," she then added in a musing tone. Her hand strayed to his knee, and she must have noticed the slight stiffening, for she patted it in a friendly way and withdrew her hand to her side of the car. "Oh, that's right. Elaine."

"You're a very understanding young woman, er, Goggle. I'll get used to it by and by! And I do thank you for letting me crash your party in order to see Elaine. You're a brick. Now where shall I take you? Home?" The back of Allan's head throbbed intensely, which confused him. Yes, he must have fallen on it, for nobody had tried to pound him there. He would have thought his jaw would hurt the worse of the two. He knew that he would be better off on the sofa at home, he and a bag of ice and a bottle of aspirins.

"No, thanks." She named a street in Kensington. "If it's not too far out of your way?"

"I live to serve the fair," Allan said cheerfully, seeing his sofa and ice bag receding into the distance. He maneuvered into the traffic, hoping for a clear road.

"What a nice old-fashioned thing to say. What did you do before the war? Did you take pictures then, too, or only play croquet and boat along the Thames?"

"I'm afraid I took pictures when I wasn't mucking about at my cousin's factory." He wondered why he and Elaine hadn't had a chance to sit and chat as he and Miranda were doing now. He and Elaine had scarcely ever had a quiet moment alone together. He continued his tale, wishing Elaine was the one with him. "As a matter of fact, I was in Africa taking pictures when the war started. Thinking of a book, but I hadn't made a name for myself, I was merely taking advantage of my father's indulgence instead of buckling down to honest work after university. The paper mill didn't thrill me. Still doesn't."

"Lucky you. And then came the war, and you got to fly."

"Because I'd done that before the war too. Handy way to get around in some parts of the Dark Continent."

"Will you go back to Africa, or did you photograph all the animals you wanted?"

"I have a thought of going to Central America to see the

Mayan ruins and the native wildlife—another book of photographs, of course—and then an old friend has invited me to take pictures of his archeological dig in the Hindu Kush. *He* wants to write a book."

"How glamorous it all sounds. Will you be leaving soon?"

Allan smiled ruefully, noticing how his head pounded harder when he thought of Elaine. "I have some things to sort out in England first."

Miranda managed to look as though she knew precisely what he was talking about.

After her inquiries about his past, Allan felt honor-bound to ask Miranda about herself. He wondered how to phrase such queries. It didn't seem the thing to ask her if she'd always been a frivolous gadabout. "Were you too young to take any part in the war-work?" he asked as a way to get the conversational ball rolling.

"Heavens, no. I insisted on doing my part, and Dad agreed, though my mother thought it was silly. I was seventeen when it all started, and I trained for dispensary work at once instead of coming out. It was rather bad form right then to come out in society, so I really never have. I worked in St. Anne's Hospital right through the war."

"Good for you."

"Then peace broke out and life got boring again. I try to keep myself amused, but perhaps Elaine Westwood has the right idea with her real job." Miranda sighed deeply.

A silence fell as Allan headed around Hyde Park Corner and into Knightsbridge, then up the Kensington High Street and around into one of the quieter byways. He pulled up in front of a respectable looking door, and Miranda let herself out. "Will you come in and meet my friends?"

"No, thanks, I'm off to rest my jaw."

"No need to remind me how bad I've been to keep you up when you should be reclining somewhere. I am sorry that

Mr. Van Vliet hit you because he thought he was helping me. The colossal nerve of the man!"

"Don't give it another thought."

He left her waving at him from the pavement and made his way back to Piccadilly feeling that there was more to Lady Miranda Winchapel than most people thought.

His head didn't get worse, but his jaw began to ache persistently, putting him off his driving. After a close call or two, he considered himself lucky to arrive back in his rooms. Louis wasn't in, but Allan's valet made him comfortable on the sofa quite as Allan had been dreaming about, even thinking to supplement the longed-for ice with a slab of raw beef.

Elaine's first impulse was to panic.

After she parted from Allan out on the pavement, she concentrated all her energies on getting into Borderfield's with the minimum of fuss. In this she was luckier than she could have imagined. The switchboard girl winked at her, and many sets of eyebrows flew up as she passed by people's desks on her way to her own typing table, but nobody said anything. Katherine ducked her head in the annoyingly respectful greeting she had been affecting since finding out Elaine had a title.

Elaine hunkered down in front of her machine for a while, dreading to draw attention to her presence, yet aware that the very silence of her typewriter spoke volumes. She was deathly afraid of being called to account by Miss Tarrant; but after a full ten minutes passed with nothing of the sort happening, she heaved a deep sigh and reached for the work in her box, wondering why she, a grown woman, had just been acting like a frightened child. The business world was run by adults, after all, and she would simply work through

War Widow 195

her lunch to make up for the time she'd missed. Nothing else was going to happen.

Only when her fingers reached out to pick up a piece of typing paper did she remember the volume of Uncle Montague's diary that she had been hiding under her coat. A frenzied search of her coat, handbag, and the floor around her followed; then a supposedly casual retracing of her steps as far as the office door. As a last resort, she went out onto the steps and desperately scanned the pavement outside: Nothing. Had she dropped the book on Aunt Pen's stairway; and what would Aunt Pen say when she found it? Though this would be very awkward, Elaine devoutly hoped that something of the sort had happened. Otherwise, she would be in dreadful trouble—her own honesty would cause her to resign.

Elaine rolled the paper back and forth in her machine, wondering what she would do without her job. Could people get new jobs after having lost the ones they had through carelessness? She had never thought about it before, but losing a position through a ghastly error of one's own would surely be as bad as being a domestic turned off "without a character." Still, she knew she must confess what she had done.

On reflection, she didn't think she would make this confession on the spot. She still had to search Aunt Pen's flat. And she could call the taxi office and ask if the book had been found in the cab she and Allan had taken this morning. As long as there was hope of finding the manuscript, she wouldn't upset people unnecessarily. It would be cruel to put a man of young Mr. Borderfield's years into a dither without cause.

She briskly opened Volume One of the reminiscences—the schoolboy diary that had not held her interest the day before—and continued where she had left off. After an unpromising beginning, the adolescent scratchings formed a plot of sorts and the work began to focus Elaine's attention. Perhaps Uncle Montague would turn out to be a better writer than she had thought at first. She continued to type away as the other workers left for lunch, telling herself not to use what mental power she had free to think about the volume she had lost—and as a result thinking of nothing else.

In the noon hour Borderfield's took on the hush of a church, tomb, or other still, vault-like space. Elaine's typewriter echoed in the high-ceilinged room but other sounds stood out, they were so infrequent. The noise made by a pair of high heels tapping smartly roused Elaine from her communion with her machine.

She looked up into the expertly made-up face of Lady Miranda Winchapel. "Goggle! Whatever are you doing here?"

"May I sit down?"

Elaine indicated Katherine's desk chair not far from her own, and Goggle sank into it with a sigh, kicking off her shoes. "I've just walked all the way from Kensington," she said.

Elaine now noted that the younger woman did look a bit windblown, most unusual for her. "Why would you do such a thing?" Miranda's travel about town wouldn't be limited by any financial considerations. She had her own car as well as an ample allowance for cabs. "Are you in some sort of trouble—that is, why have you really come to me?"

"I'll be honest with you. I scarcely know any people."

At this Elaine laughed. Miranda Winchapel was one of the most well-known young women about town. She must have hundreds of friends.

"No, I'm being straight with you." Goggle looked a bit hurt by Elaine's reaction. "I'm one of those who has a thousand friends and no intimates. I don't complain of it, in general. I suspect I'm not overly fond of people as a rule. But the difficulty is that I can think of no one better than you to do me a favor. And since we've scarcely been close, I hate to ask it."

Elaine was silent a moment. "At least you're honest," she finally said.

"Also, you know the man involved."

Elaine's thoughts immediately jumped to Allan Marchmont, the one man on her mind.

"I needed time to think. I walked across the parks and halfway to the City before I even knew I was coming to you," Goggle said reflectively. "Even then, I had to go into a bookshop and find a copy of Allan Marchmont's book to see who had published it—I knew you worked for the people—and then ask a couple of bobbies to direct me here."

"You went to a lot of trouble."

"Yes. Now, then." Goggle dug into her smart handbag and came out with a small, wrapped box, about the size of a match-case. She handed it to Elaine.

Elaine made no comment as she held the little box in her palm.

"Could you promise me very faithfully not to look inside this? To turn it over to another person without so much as peeking?"

"Yes, I could." And indeed, remembering the many distasteful tasks that had been asked of her during her hospital years, Elaine didn't think she would have any trouble in simply not opening a small box that was wrapped in paper. "Whom am I to give it to?"

"To Mr. Oswald Van Vliet. That's all." Goggle flushed a deeper tone than her artfully applied rouge.

"I'd be glad to, but I don't know if I'll be seeing Mr. Van Vliet anytime soon." Elaine had the feeling that, despite the pleasant way they had got along together on Saturday night, she and Van Vliet hadn't "hit it off." There was also the problem of her change of address, though she supposed that if he wanted to see her again, he could find her through her mother.

"He lives at the Ritz. Go to tea at the Ritz tomorrow," Goggle suggested. She looked over Elaine's costume. "I won't say today. I know you'd want to fix up a bit."

Elaine bit back a sarcastic retort. She could sense that this mission was something important. Had Van Vliet and Miranda become entangled so quickly since last Saturday night? Today was only Thursday. Perhaps the box contained a jewel the rich American had offered to tempt the duke's daughter into indiscretion, and Goggle was returning it in maidenly scorn. No, that didn't sound right. Or did it? There was no telling with Goggle, as everyone in society was fond of saying; and Van Vliet was certainly an unknown quantity.

"I can't afford tea at the Ritz. Perhaps I could wait in the lobby."

"No, go in to tea. He can buy it."

"Evidently you're speaking to him. If you can tell him to give me tea, why not just hand him this yourself? Or send it through the mails?"

"My trained-on discretion. I can trust no one—but you. Mr. Van Vliet's been disappointed in me. Some of my so-called friends have been tempting me to do something he really disapproves. I even disapprove, and I thought it would be even more exciting to go against myself. Do you understand?"

"Not altogether." Elaine knew that fast young Londoners were up to almost anything, but she really had no idea what in particular Goggle was talking about.

"When he found out about this he interfered. I can't stand being interfered with. But now I've changed my mind—I simply can't admit to his face he was right—if you can give this box to him for me, it could make all the difference."

War Widow 199

"For you and Mr. Van Vliet." Elaine held back her other questions with difficulty.

"And you'll promise not to open it?"

"Yes, I'll promise whatever you like." As she spoke the jaunty words, Elaine searched the younger woman's face. Under the skillful makeup, Goggle looked tired. She had dark shadows under her eyes and rather a hunted, hectic look in those eyes.

She broke into a smile, though, when Elaine promised to do as she asked. "Be at the Ritz tomorrow at five," she said, fishing about on the floor with her feet to find her shoes.

"I'll try very hard." Elaine wondered how, after coming in late one day, she could justify disappearing earlier than six the next. She shouldn't have made the promise. But something about Miranda was unexpectedly endearing today. It was as though she might sincerely need help only Elaine could give. Such an attitude was a sure way to Elaine's heart.

"You're an angel," said Goggle, and to Elaine's total amazement, she reached out and gave her a hug.

Chapter Seventeen

On Friday morning Miss Tarrant treated Elaine to an interview which left her in no doubt about any future irregularities in attendance. "You won't talk Mr. Parkington around into helping you next time," the elder secretary finished darkly, mystifying Elaine until she remembered Mr. Parkington had seen to it that she could take that day out a week ago, to go with Mr. Van Vliet down to Berryhill. Had it really been only a week ago? And had Mr. Parkington also put in a good word for her about her late arrival of the day before?

She would have a chance to explain matters to Goggle the next evening, for Louis had told her he had promised both of them would go to one of Goggle's fast-set parties.

Elaine was relieved that, if Louis did mean to venture into such waters, he would not hesitate to take his sister. Considering what Louis thought of her, he was practically stating up front that he had no intention of having any fun.

She sighed as she typed up yet another page of Great Uncle Montague's journal, or, as she supposed she ought to think of it, the manuscript of that soon-to-be bestseller, *The Racing Saxonbury*. There had been no sign of the missing volume at the flat in Mount Street; no furtive or accusing looks from Aunt Pen or Rollo when Elaine asked if anything had been found by the servants. She must have dropped the thing in the cab or in the street, and she would likely never see it again. The taxi office denied all knowledge of the journal, but it could have been left in the cab and picked up by the driver's next fare.

She had already put an advertisement for its return in the newspaper. The next step would be that confession which would put her out of a job—but she wouldn't have to think about that until she was certain no one would answer the advertisement.

Just when she was at the messiest stage of changing her typewriter ribbon she found Allan Marchmont standing beside her chair. He looked down at her with a friendly smile. "I didn't stop to torment you or embarrass you. I'm here on business, but I thought it would be rude to come into Borderfield's without saying a word to you."

"I'm glad to see you," she faltered, knowing she mustn't start a conversation. She couldn't say anything of a personal nature with all the people within hearing distance paying close, if subtle, attention to every word that might pass.

"Good. Well, I'm sure I'm late for that appointment, considering that I was already late when I walked into the building. Until later, Lady Elaine—Mrs. Westwood." Allan held out his hand and she shook it, still with that sense of unreality, not aided at all by the shock of his fingers on hers. Their eyes met, and Elaine supposed it was written all over her face that she wanted nothing more than to be somewhere alone with him where they could do more than shake hands. She seemed to read something similar in his eyes.

"He's a handsome one," Katherine leaned over to whisper when he had passed down the room and out the door at the end. Evidently admiration for the man had broken through

Katherine's newly deferential manners; Elaine was grateful to Allan for that. "Does he have a title?"

"No." Elaine shook her head and smiled. "You may find this hard to believe, but I've never even liked anyone with a title. My husband didn't have one."

"Oh." Looking disappointed and not at all believing, Katherine bent over her work.

Elaine was glad she had "fixed up," as Goggle had tactlessly put it the day before, and was wearing her best office clothes. She had even borrowed one of Aunt Pen's furs when she still had some faint hope of tea at the Ritz. Allan hadn't seen her in the glory of the fur, but he had at least seen her best court shoes, silk stockings, and nicest blouse. He had also seen her hands covered with ink from the typewriter ribbon, she realized, holding them out before her as she started off to the ladies' room. Remembering they had shaken hands, she wondered if Allan was also now covered with ink.

A messenger boy popped round the corner and nearly ran into her. "Mrs. Westwood, you're wanted in Old Beaky's office. Now, they said."

"I?" Elaine exchanged a terrified look with Katherine.

"I don't suppose because you were late yesterday they're going to sack you, and they have to have young Mr. Borderfield do it because you're a lady," Katherine said in a bemused tone. None of the typewriter girls in their memory had ever been summoned to the office of the head of the firm.

Elaine laughed, rather shrilly. "There's a comforting thought, but after Miss Tarrant chewed me out right and proper this morning I thought I was safe. I'll come at once, as soon as I've washed," she added to young Jem. Once again she was glad she happened to be looking well today. Clothes would give her confidence in whatever trials lay ahead.

The walk down the corridor to Mr. Borderfield's office

seemed absurdly short, and entering Mr. Borderfield's suite of offices was one of the most difficult things Elaine had ever done. The outer room was the sanctum of the very grand Miss Rothwell, a lady of formidable demeanor who had been young Mr. Borderfield's secretary for years. What Elaine and her title now were to Katherine Marsh, Miss Rothwell was to Elaine. Word had it the elder lady had started behind a typewriter in the common offices and worked her way up to her present awe-inspiring perch. Everyone knew that, considering Mr. Borderfield's age and state of health, Miss Rothwell really ran the company.

The lady looked up now from behind an imposing mahogany desk. "Mrs. Westwood. Haven't you brought it?"

"It?" Elaine stood in the middle of the room at a complete loss.

"That boy is impossible. I suppose he forgot to tell you to bring along the manuscript of that racing memoir, the one you were just set to typing a day or two ago."

"I'm afraid he said nothing about it. I can run back . . ."

"Never mind. Is it on your desk? I'll send Jem right back there." Miss Rothwell pressed a button on her desk. "Meanwhile, my dear, you must go in," she added not unkindly, indicating the door. "Mr. Borderfield is most impatient."

Elaine nodded. Was she to be accused of having taken the missing volume, or was this going to turn out to be her opportunity to confess that she had lost it? She tapped shakily upon the door, received some barked acknowledgment from inside, and with one last encouraging glance from Miss Rothwell, went in.

"Oh," she said blankly.

Young Mr. Borderfield rose from a leather chair by his fireside. "My dear young woman, I little knew what a jewel

I had in my crown," he said in a creaky voice befitting his fragile physique and head of white hair. He clasped Elaine's hands and beamed at her.

He was much of a piece with the old-fashioned, richly appointed office, no different from the study in any great house except that the books on the shelves had all been published by Borderfield's, and the portrait above the mantelpiece was of Mr. Borderfield's father, the solid Victorian founder of the firm, rather than of some Georgian ancestor. Elaine's eyes registered her surroundings and Mr. Borderfield's frail presence in a flash, because the real object of fascination for her was a lady seated in a chair opposite the publisher's.

"My child, you're surprised to see me." Lady Berry rose and took Elaine in a motherly embrace as soon as Mr. Borderfield loosened his grip on her hands. "I'm sorry the dark secret of your identity is out due to your meddling mother, but I couldn't resist having you sent for. Dear Cavendish—I mean Mr. Borderfield—was so surprised to find out he had my daughter working for him."

"What are you doing in London, Mother?"

"What should she be doing but paying a call on her greatest admirer," Mr. Borderfield said with his canine laugh. "Now, my dear, your mother and I are going to steal you away from your labors, and you can tell us the whole story of how you came to work for my company because your mother had told you so much about me. Lady Berry has consented to take tea with me at Brown's Hotel, and we need you for a chaperone."

"Oh. How very kind of you, sir." Elaine held back a smile. So Mother had been embroidering on things, as usual. Elaine hadn't applied to this publishing firm because of her mother, but Mr. Borderfield didn't need to know that. "But I shouldn't leave my desk. I'll send you and Mother off without me. If you won't find a tete-a-tete too shocking?"

"Nonsense, my girl. Lady Berry's daughter is a privileged figure around here. Only don't say that to the other young women." Mr. Borderfield gave her a bawdy wink from behind his thick spectacles and wagged a finger at her.

Elaine had a bold idea. She was in a strange dream world now, talking on terms of intimacy with the head of the firm while her mother looked on approvingly; sleeping in a comfortable bed in Mount Street rather than on her dreadful sagging mattress near Euston Station. She might wake up at any time. Since it seemed that for the moment she could do no wrong, she ventured a suggestion. "Could we possibly go to the Ritz for tea?"

"Ah, Brown's is too sedate for you young people," Mr. Borderfield said with a chuckle, not even asking for her reason. Lady Berry looked rather amazed at Elaine's nerve, but she made no comment. "The Ritz it is, if it meets with your approval, my lady?" He turned with a courtly bow to the countess.

"Dear Elaine must have her reasons for upsetting your plans," Lady Berry said with a smile. "Don't you, dear?"

"I do have to meet someone there, and I was wondering how I'd manage."

"Oho, a someone! We can't let her miss the someone, my lady."

"Thank you so much. I must go and get my outdoor things." Elaine found herself bobbing something like a curtsy before leaving the room. She paused just outside the door to collect her thoughts. Things were changing so fast. Was her job at Borderfield's even hers anymore? As Mr. Borderfield's pet she would make all the other women justifiably jealous. She wished that her mother hadn't come in. Why on earth had she done it?

She nodded to Miss Rothwell, who now had the journals of Uncle Montague piled on her own desk. "Did Mr. Borderfield wish to discuss the manuscript with me?" she asked.

"No, my dear, he wanted you in to meet your mother. As for the manuscript, I needed to catalogue it before it went to be typed, and it somehow slipped past me the other day," Miss Rothwell said, writing something in a ledger.

Elaine shuddered quietly and made her escape to the corridor. Knowing Allan to be in the building, she couldn't help looking all around as she went back to her place, but there was no sign of him or of anyone besides the office staff. When she arrived at her desk, she noticed she was breathing hard and sighed deeply in an effort to calm herself.

"Well?" Katherine leaned forward, curiosity lighting her eyes with almost the old intimacy. "Did you get sacked?"

"No, but I have to leave for the day." Elaine kept taking calming breaths, wondering at her own agitation. Well, seeing her mother had been a shock.

"Something's wrong," was Katherine's diagnosis, as she eyed Elaine keenly. "Could I help you? Finish your work or anything?"

"No, thanks. Jem came and took my project off to be catalogued, didn't he?"

"Yes, and a fine talking to I gave him for mucking about on your desk before I found out it was under orders from the Rothwell herself."

"Then there's nothing anyone can help me with until I get the manuscript back." Elaine tidied up her desk, which did show signs of boyish rummaging, and got out her hat, handbag, and the fur.

"Ooh, don't you look nice. Going to tea at the Ritz?"

Elaine stared at her incredulously. At the same time Katherine realized she had guessed right, and she flushed deeply.

"Must be nice to be a lady," she muttered. "And here I really believed you were worried over your job just because you were late."

Elaine said rashly, "Tell you what. You and I will go to tea at the Ritz before the month is out." Heaven only knew where she would get the money to fulfill that promise. Toast and a poached egg at the ABC was more within her means.

Katherine gave her a lopsided grin. "Right-o, your *ladyship*."

"And don't call me that," Elaine added with a laugh, winding the fur piece around her neck and putting on her gloves.

She met the others out front, and off they went to the Ritz in Mr. Borderfield's large Rolls. Elaine hadn't been out to tea in some time, and she was pleased, as they were shown to their table in the Palm Court, to be dressed so well and to bow to some friends of hers and her mother's whom she usually didn't encounter in town. She gave the waiter a folded message to be carried to Oswald Van Vliet.

Snooty-looking servitors vied to present the obviously important old man and his two ladies with tea and accouterments. "Well, young lady," Mr. Borderfield said from the depths of his Louis XVI chair, as a waiter hung over him, "where is this 'someone' of yours?"

"I hope he'll come down shortly. I sent him a note. It's our new tenant, Mother. Mr. Van Vliet."

"My word! I didn't know you and he—"

"We're merely friends, and I'm doing another friend of his a favor." Elaine had the discomfort of seeing her mother and Mr. Borderfield exchange knowing glances but there was no way of changing their minds except by showing them, as she hoped to do shortly, that she and Van Vliet didn't behave at all like sweethearts. She began to cast hopeful looks around the room, not knowing which direction he was likely to come from.

"She's looking out for him," said Mr. Borderfield with a chuckle, accepting a cup of tea from Lady Berry's hand.

"He's a very nice young man, and of course wealthy, but an American of whom we really know nothing," the countess worried aloud. "And that name. Dutch, do you think?"

Elaine stared at her mother in indignation. "Friends," she repeated. Then her face broke into a smile as she saw Van Vliet enter the room. She waved to him, and he approached around the gilded fountain.

He began to speak to her with only a nod to her companions. "Lady Elaine! I'm glad you could meet me after all. Now what's this all about? Lady Miranda said it was important. She's not trying to get you and me together, now, is she?"

"Lady Miranda hasn't ever been known for matchmaking," Elaine assured him with a friendly nod. "Do join us. Lady Berry, my mother, you know of course. Mr. Borderfield, may I present Mr. Van Vliet of New York? Mr. Borderfield is my employer."

"And the gallant knight of these ladies," Mr. Borderfield added, half rising to shake Van Vliet's hand. "See you don't get out of line, young man."

"So you're a knight, sir?" Van Vliet's eyes lit up.

Some moments were passed in explaining that he wasn't meeting another titled person, and then Van Vliet sat down near Elaine, accepted a large plate of tea cakes and sandwiches as well as the requisite beverage, and gave Elaine a questioning look.

"I hope they know I'm not your boyfriend," he said in a low voice, under cover of one of Lady Berry's society tales.

"We must convince them of it," Elaine replied, fishing in her handbag. "Here." Without further ado, under cover of the table cloth, she pressed the box from Goggle into Van Vliet's hand.

"What's this?"

Mr. Borderfield was still engrossed in Lady Berry, who had mercifully turned away, or Elaine wouldn't have grasped Van Vliet's hand to close his fingers round the little box. "I don't know. It's from Goggle—from Lady Miranda. She made me promise not to open it, and naturally I haven't. She said you'd understand, but if you don't wish to have to explain to a circle of interested onlookers why I'm passing you things, you'd better get it out of sight."

"Good advice," he muttered, pocketing the box with a mystified look. Then all of a sudden Van Vliet's expression lost its puzzlement and broke out in relief or even happiness. "Why, this is great news. It changes everything."

"Goggle said it would," Elaine remembered.

"You've been a sport about this." He leaned closer. "I was afraid some of the wrong crowd might be influencing her too much, if you know what I mean. She laughed off my warning, said I should mind my own business. But her giving me this!" He patted his pocket. "It means she's changed her mind."

Elaine felt he was being a bit too subtle; she didn't understand at all. "Changed her mind about what?"

Van Vliet was very expressive with his eyebrows, or tried to be, but Elaine continued to be mystified. Finally he mouthed a certain word.

Drugs! Elaine felt a wave of shock, then relief at Goggle's having turned away from easing her boredom in such a ruinous way. "I'll keep this a dark secret. How kind of you to take an interest."

"Nothing to do with kind," Van Vliet said gruffly. "I intend to marry that girl."

By a strong effort of will, Elaine didn't fall out of her chair. "You mean, if she hadn't taken your advice, you wouldn't have . . ."

"It would have taken a bit longer to bring her round to my way of thinking, that's all," he said serenely. "I'll marry her no matter what. But she doesn't know yet."

"Ah! She won't hear it from me. Are you going to her party tomorrow night?"

"As a matter of fact . . ."

But whether or not he was going to the party in Chelsea remained as great a mystery as the box had once been, for at that moment, Mr. Parkington from the office stopped by their table. He had another man in tow, a man who hung back deferentially. Allan.

"Howja do?" Parkington spoke in a hearty manner that Elaine was sure was meant to cover his embarrassment. "Room for two more?"

Everyone, especially the nearby waiters, looked at him as though he was mad. Elaine sensed from the expression on Mr. Borderfield's craggy face that the young editor had never taken such a liberty before and was unlikely to do so in the future. She had to feel sorry for her mother's swain. To tolerate Elaine as so-called chaperone to his interlude with Lady Berry was one thing, but to accommodate crowds of young blockheads was quite another.

Lady Berry seemed to sense this and said, "Elaine, why don't you take all these gentlemen off to another spot? Mr. Borderfield and I haven't had a proper chance to talk, and you can keep an eye on us from that table over there." She paused and gave her elderly admirer a mischievous glance. "In case he goes beyond the line."

Elaine obligingly gathered her handbag and her assorted men and moved across the way while the older couple exchanged coy looks. She wondered again if her mother had some reason for meeting the publisher that Elaine wasn't privy to. Surely it couldn't be merely that Lady Berry hoped to make her daughter's path at work easier? If so, she had done the opposite. Elaine was by now nearly certain that after such a display as going out to tea with the head of the firm, her job would be unbearable from now on.

"Well, then," Mr. Parkington began. He settled into his chair with a mischievous look once they had all been served with tea. "Go to it, captain. No time like the present."

He seemed to be addressing Allan, who made his first contribution to the conversation. "Parkington, I'm going to flay you alive."

"Sounds active, at least. You're getting nowhere on your own; you told me so only today. Here a fellow's only trying to help out . . ."

"What is going on, please?" Elaine asked from her place behind the silver tea service. "Mr. Parkington, whatever are you doing here? I don't think Mr. Borderfield was any too happy to be interrupted."

"He's a cousin," said Parkington. "When all's said and done, I'm a hard one to sack. So I thought it best to follow all of you here and look after your interests."

Elaine exchanged a glance with Van Vliet, who was sitting back looking amused.

"What interests?" she asked coldly.

"You and Marchmont, here."

"Mr. Parkington, how could you?" Elaine felt her cheeks reddening.

"It's the war. Makes us dare anything, even the wrath of an old comrade-at-arms," Parkington said with a wink.

"You let him bring you here." Elaine turned on Allan. "Did you ever—I can't imagine how either of you gentlemen thought I would be pleased to be interrupted at my tea engagement in such a public way."

"Lady Elaine, I had no idea until we walked in and I saw you that I was doing anything more than accompanying my old friend. I admit I thought it odd that he chose the Ritz at tea time rather than his club for drinks."

"That was only after the porter at Borderfield's told me where they'd nipped off to," Parkington said. "It was a spur of the moment idea, what? And now here you are, together." He addressed Van Vliet. "Shall we leave the lovebirds alone? Don't believe we've been introduced. I say, old man, I hope you're not a deadly rival of old Marchmont's."

"Mr. Parkington, this is taking on the trappings of a nightmare," Elaine said. By now her face must be scarlet—she could feel it—and Allan looked murderous. She was gratified that he really didn't seem to have been in on this harebrained plan. "Mr. Van Vliet is not to be run out of here when he and I are having tea together. I *invited* him."

"I have an idea," Parkington spoke up. He addressed Van Vliet. "What say you and I, sir, slide on over to the bar if you've had enough tea?"

"What do you say to that, Lady Elaine?" Van Vliet asked, looking at her keenly.

"Well, I—this is very irregular. I have nothing private to say to Mr. Marchmont." Not the truth, but the only polite thing to say under the circumstances.

"Of course you don't, but you don't want spectators by while you say it, all the same," Parkington said in a soothing tone. "See you later, Marchmont."

With no further ado Parkington rose to his feet with the

aid of his walking stick, made a motion with his head to Van Vliet, and the American followed him tamely down the steps of the Palm Court in the direction of the bar.

"Elaine, I hope you know that I had nothing whatever—blast, this *is* a nightmare."

"I'd like to shake Mr. Parkington. What is the matter with the man? I thought only old ladies threw people together against their will."

"I believe that's usually the case. He was so infernally clumsy at it one can tell he doesn't make a habit of this sort of thing." Allan was glancing across the way, and Elaine, following his gaze, noticed that her mother and Mr. Borderfield were observing them closely. First the whispered, intimate-looking conversation with Van Vliet, and now this. She gave them a little wave to indicate that all was as it should be, and both older people studiously looked away.

"But is it against your will, Elaine?"

"What?" She looked into his eyes and felt the warmth that had been receding from her cheeks return with a vengeance.

"Michael is a clumsy ass, but I admit that I've wanted nothing more than a chance like this, a chance to talk things over with you."

"Things? What things?"

"Whatever things you'd like. The weather, what dances you like best, the state of the world. We seem to have arrived at a certain intimacy without having had a chance to talk."

"How could you mention that?" she said in a low voice. "I mean for both of us to forget that unfortunate occasion in your car." Kissing in his car. Feeling overwhelmed by a new and welcome passion in his car. Then having him stop . . . "No gentleman would refer to it," she added, as embarrassed as she had ever been.

"I don't seem to be a gentleman when I'm with you. I

make gaffe after gaffe, or I'm tongue-tied. I thought if we started our acquaintance over, we might make a better job of it. Let's pretend we've just met." His gray eyes had such an appealing, pleading look.

She was charmed by his words and fell back on a joke to ease the moment. "Then don't I have to step on your foot?"

"I mean for us to meet in some other way than in the corridor at your office. At a ball or an opera. I'm to be dressed as a hussar, and you're in a ball gown designed by—who?"

"Poiret," Elaine suggested, warming to the game. "I've always wanted one. But what if I'd like to pretend that I'm really a typewriter girl, and you did succeed in getting me to come out with you? What do you talk about to the lowly typewriter?"

Allan gave an uneasy but relieved smile. "I expect I compliment her on her beauty. Ask her where she comes from. What she likes to do, and why she took up typing as a profession rather than work at something else."

"And could she ask you all those things in return? I know much less about you than you know about me since we've spent our entire acquaintance surrounded by my family."

"And that's not about to end," Allan murmured with a smile over his tea cup. He raised the cup to her in what she recognized as a mock salute of farewell.

Elaine looked up to see her mother standing over the table. "Mr. Marchmont!" Lady Berry looked radiant. "I thought that was you. So did Mr. Borderfield, though he says his eyes aren't what they used to be. He would like most particularly to tell you about how a poetess tried to trap him into doing something or other with your book. I dislike to interrupt your conversation, but I want to keep Mr. Borderfield happy. I have a favor to ask of him, and before that happens I must cater to all his whims."

"What favor is that, Mother?" Though annoyed at the

interruption, Elaine was still eager to know why Lady Berry had sought out her superannuated admirer.

"Oh, nothing you would care to hear about, dear. I'll tell Mr. Borderfield you'll move to our table, shall I?" Lady Berry bustled away, gesturing to a passing waiter.

"Tell me," Allan said with half a smile, "if I took you off with me right now to the tea dance at the Savoy, would we come upon uncles and cousins of yours?"

She sighed. "No. But Mother and Mr. Borderfield would post after us. Thanks for the thought. It sounds marvelous."

"And for the future, Elaine?" He spoke hurriedly. A helpful waiter was bearing down on them, obviously intent upon moving them across the way.

"We shall have to see."

"Soon, I hope. We'll have our chance soon." He leaned forward, almost as if he was about to kiss her. She found herself swaying towards him.

The waiter cleared his throat.

Elaine and Allan exchanged identical exasperated looks before he rose to help her out of her chair. The Palm Court was not going to be the solution to their longstanding problem, no matter what Michael Parkington might have thought.

Chapter Eighteen

"When I say it's time to leave, we leave."

Elaine spoke in her sternest and most forbidding tone. Louis, handsome in evening dress, nodded meekly. She took a deep breath, added, "I suppose there's nothing for it," and rang the bell of the Chelsea residence of Miranda Winchapel's friend.

The door wasn't opened by a servant but by a young man in evening clothes whose long eyes were kohl-rimmed, or so Elaine imagined. "Come along, I'll take you to Goggle," he said without asking who they were.

Elaine and her brother passed through a tiny entrance hall and then into an amazingly crowded room, following the young man. Within one second, they lost sight of him in the throng of gaily dressed people. Elaine took an elbow to the rib cage when a highly made-up woman turned round, laughing at something another was saying.

"Sorry, love. Oh, my!" The woman had spun out of Elaine's range right onto Louis' chest. "Heavens, I haven't seen you before."

Louis smiled. Elaine gritted her teeth and smiled, too; and

then she steered her brother across the room to where she thought she glimpsed Goggle's dark bobbed head. She knew how stern duennas of yesteryear must have felt in places like Vauxhall.

"I've about had my fill of this party already," she murmured, more to herself than to her brother. The dark head proved to belong to someone else, not Goggle. Brother and sister kept on struggling through the crowd, trying not to get drinks or cigarette ash spilled on them. Then, quite by accident, Elaine and Louis sort of popped through an archway and into another room, a chamber that was much less crowded than the first parlor.

"I say." Louis' blue eyes were wide open, and he mopped his forehead expressively.

Elaine merely stood near a vacant stretch of wall and took deep breaths until her heart stopped beating quite so fast. She had never liked crowds.

"Darlings, there you are!"

Elaine never would have thought of Goggle as her savior but she nearly threw herself into the other girl's arms. She tried to think of something flattering, but true, to say. "Your party is quite a success, my dear, if this crowd is any indication."

"Oh, I suppose it is." Goggle, semi-draped in white satin, with a bandeau round her head from which several feathers drooped in a careless way that was the last word in fashion, gave a little shrug. "I'm so glad to see you two. Come, I'll put drinks in your hands and you can meet some people. Do you want to leave your wrap in the bedroom, Elaine?"

"If I can get to it."

"You're in it, actually." Goggle made a motion of her elegant head toward a corner, and Elaine could glimpse through a screen of people a richly draped Turkish-style bed in one corner of the room. It was piled with furs and other outdoor things. Elaine crossed to this, leaving Louis with Goggle, and dropped her bead-trimmed scarf on top of some other wraps, wondering if she would ever see it again. Though there were mirrors in the room, she couldn't really primp, so she merely straightened her low-cut frock and hoped it was all right in the back, where she had fastened a paste-diamond clip at the v of the neckline. She had thought the clip an original idea when dressing in Mount Street, but among the fantastic costumes here, her little flight of fancy was anything but daring.

"Elaine, you're looking lovely. Black is a stunning choice for blonds," Goggle said. "We ought to pose for a picture together, don't you think? Night and day. Perhaps your photographer man could do it. Now for those drinks, and then the dancing is about to begin."

"Dancing? Here?"

"There's some space in the back garden out by the studio, and Phyllis and I have rigged up a sort of dance floor as long as it doesn't rain. You can hear the musicians through the window. You must meet Phyllis. It's her house, though I hope to be sharing it with her before long. All these pictures are of Phyllis." Chattering hard, Goggle led the way down some stairs—past some startling nude artwork, presumably of Phyllis—and into a kitchen, where a beleaguered person in a maid's uniform was pouring out drinks from a punch bowl.

Elaine started to say something, but Goggle, with swift, economical movements, grabbed a couple of punch glasses and filled them from a bottle labeled ginger beer. She presented them to Elaine and Louis with a wink.

Louis drained his cup and held it out for more; Goggle obliged.

Elaine sipped at her drink, looking gratefully at her hostess. There was something different about Goggle tonight—

not in looks, for her carefully made-up face was as exotically beautiful as ever and her gown was causing Louis' eyes to pop. She had dropped her usual languid pose and was talking very hard, but Goggle had the reputation in society for sometimes racing her words when she wasn't acting half-dead from boredom. No, it was almost a sort of sheepishness. As though, for whatever reason, she was anxious for Elaine and perhaps Louis to approve of her and her friends and knew they wouldn't.

"What should we do first?" Elaine asked brightly, suddenly sorry for Goggle and her showy, empty life.

"I imagine you'd enjoy watching the dancing," Goggle decided after a thoughtful moment. "Let's go outside. Here, we can use the back door. And I do hope we can run across Phyllis."

Off they went, threading around the house toward the back garden, Goggle stopping to introduce them to the occasional person. Most of these seemed to be artistic folk, for they had to do with making films, or sculpting, or painting, or writing for little journals, from Goggle's caption biography of each partygoer. "Evelyn Frobisher . . . has a showing now at the Barrow Gallery . . . you must know Miss Lamartine by sight, she's on the films . . ." To each of these people Elaine and Louis were identified, not by remarks on their careers, but simply as Lady Elaine and Lord Berry. The titles seemed to startle the partygoers as much as the exotic occupations impressed Elaine.

She hoped Louis was not bored. Everyone was much older than he, and he had met enough artistic people over the years at his mother's parties that he would probably not think the bohemian set anything special.

As they reached a crowded, grassy stretch hung with Japanese lanterns, a series of screams rang out. Goggle and Elaine, trailed by Louis, ran forward to where a crowd was forming around something or someone. Goggle, with the authority of a hostess, pushed her way through, and Elaine took the opportunity to follow her. Stretched out on the grass was a beautiful auburn-haired girl in a green silk dress that hugged her perfect form. Over her a man in evening clothes was crouching, chafing her limp wrists.

"This," said Goggle with a disgusted gesture, "is Phyllis."

"Well, we had better get her off the ground," Elaine said. "Unless"—thoughts of a thriller she had borrowed from Griselda crossed her mind—"she's all right, isn't she?"

"No shots rang out," said the man on the grass, getting to his feet. Elaine was not too surprised to see that it was Allan, nor that, considering it was Allan, he seemed to have read her mind. He hoisted the limp Phyllis into his arms. "Make way, everyone. Lady Miranda, have you somewhere quiet where she could rest?"

"And you'd better have a doctor," said another male voice, an American one. Oswald Van Vliet pushed his way through the fascinated partygoers. "In case."

"Miles can go—can't you?—the next house but one, up the street, there's a funny little man there who's a doctor." Goggle gestured to a young man on the sidelines. He gave her a mock salute and headed off. Elaine noticed that Goggle was staring very oddly at Van Vliet. Perhaps she hadn't expected him to come to her party; perhaps he'd refused. But now things would be different . . . "In here," Goggle said. She directed Allan to follow her and they moved on into the house, Elaine coming after because she had nursed through the war and thought she might be useful. Van Vliet and Louis stayed behind in the garden. Elaine noticed that, rather horribly, the jazz musicians had never stopped playing.

The only unused corner in the little house was apparently a small maid's room in the upper reaches. There were other upstairs rooms, but people had crowded into all of them with their smoke and noise. Allan eventually laid the prostrate Phyllis on a narrow iron bed where she continued motionless, looking very beautiful and absolutely unconscious.

"Gassed," said Goggle, shaking her head. "It's much too early in the evening for this kind of stunt. I suppose it's just as well to have the doctor, but Mr. Van Vliet is wrong. There's no 'in case,' for Phyllis doesn't approve of drugs."

"Alcohol can be quite as serious, my lady," Allan said.

Elaine was busy feeling Phyllis' clammy forehead and loosening her garters. There didn't seem to be much in the way of other undergarments to be loosened, so she didn't tell Allan to leave. "What happened?" she asked, shoving a pillow under Phyllis' head and covering her with a shabby quilt that had been folded up on a chair. She then grabbed the girl's wrist and felt the pulse. It seemed steady enough.

Allan said, "Miss O'Brien and I were merely discussing my photography, and then she suggested we dance so as to get the others started. Suddenly she pitched over backward." He frowned as though trying to recall the details. "I believe she'd had a quick drink of something. The glass flew out of her hand."

"She knows she shouldn't drink," Goggle muttered. She was leaning against the door frame, looking unconcerned. "Was she asking if you would take her picture in the altogether?" She laughed. "I mean, of course, with *her* in the altogether."

"Ah! I wondered if she asked all the boys." Allan spoke in a light tone, but Elaine noticed he looked embarrassed.

Elaine wondered what answer he had made to his lovely hostess. Those portrayals of Phyllis already on the walls that weren't cubist showed a magnificent figure that the thin silk of her gown was doing little to conceal. Surely for any artist—any man—it would have been a hard invitation to resist. She wished she knew if he had.

"Elaine, can you stay with Phyllis? I must fly; the other guests might need herding," Goggle said. "The doctor should be here any minute and you can escape. Are you coming, Mr. Marchmont?"

"Certainly." Allan glanced at Elaine, and she glanced back.

She supposed there was no real way to hold him in this room. It was already improper that he had been by while she loosened Phyllis' stockings, and the doctor would probably want to do more. Phyllis needed a woman with her for the coming examination, and Goggle, though probably being selfish, was also perfectly right that the remaining hostess should go down and keep an eye on the party.

"I'll wait for you outside the door, Lady Elaine," said Allan.

"There's no need for that. I can find my way down the stairs. Would you mind very much seeing how my brother is getting on?" Elaine turned to include Goggle in the smile she really meant just for Allan. "It was so kind of you, by the way, Goggle, to give us both ginger beer without raising a fuss. I appreciate it."

"But Lord Berry might find something stronger if we don't keep him in hand," Goggle said. She grabbed Allan's arm. "Come along, you've a job to do."

Elaine wasn't left alone for more than a few minutes before voices were heard ascending the narrow staircase, and a scholarly, grey-bearded man with a monocle entered. The young man who had apparently escorted him peeked in at the door, nodded at Elaine, and disappeared.

The bearded man was wearing evening dress, minus the

War Widow 223

tie, and house slippers. He carried a black bag. "How do you do? I'm Dr. Mandrake."

"Elaine Westwood." She extended her hand.

He assessed the patient while Elaine stood by, answering what questions she could. "Well, young woman." Finally the doctor gave Elaine a searching look. "There's not much time to lose. I think you said you nursed in the war? Any experience of the stomach pump?"

Elaine came weakly down the stairs a while later. She was very thirsty, she realized, but for the moment she didn't want to see food ever again. Phyllis would come along nicely now, the doctor told Elaine in between mutterings about flappers and their stunts. Being a doctor in wayward Chelsea, he was often called out upon this sort of mission.

Elaine, who had nothing in her purse, was forced to tell him he would have to apply to Miss O'Brien later for his fee, at which he scoffed and muttered something further about neighbors. That said neighbors were irresponsible flibbertigibbets didn't alter his chivalry. He would see himself out. Elaine must find a maid who could stay with Miss O'Brien.

Not knowing which of the several uniformed young persons belonged to the house—if any did—Elaine tried to find Goggle again. Phyllis was peacefully sleeping but she was better not left alone, and Elaine would have to go back up herself if she couldn't find anyone suitable. The party had been unusual enough for her already. There were reasons why she hadn't stayed in nursing after the war, and she had just been reminded of them.

Goggle was impossible to find, she didn't see Allan either, or Louis for that matter, and after a period of hopelessness Elaine simply began to inquire of people in maids' uniform if they worked in the house all the time. The second query worked, and Elaine sent the girl up to what was probably her own room to see to her mistress. She had grabbed the maid's tray of canapes to free her, and people continued to take things. When one fellow asked her to find him more anchovy toast in the kitchen, she thought her career in service had gone far enough and slapped the tray down on the nearest surface—which happened to be the floor.

"You've been working too hard," someone said, close to her ear. "Let's dance."

Elaine turned around to see who was grabbing her arm. "Oh! Mr. Sanguinetti. How do you do." She was glad she remembered the man's name from their brief meeting.

The large American gave her an ingratiating smile. "How about that dance?"

Elaine smiled back, though uneasily. She could hardly tell this nice but intimidating man she wished he was someone else. She seemed to remember that, of the three friends of Oswald Van Vliet's whom she had met last Saturday night, this man was the one who could dance. "Why not? I'm looking for my brother, but you could help me while we dance."

"Whatever you say." And steering her by her arm, which he had never ceased to grasp, he moved with her through the crowded room and out through a pair of French windows Elaine hadn't noticed before. A couple of shallow steps led onto a minuscule area paved with flagstones which would have been the dance floor had it been big enough. As it was, the lantern-trimmed grassy bit serving as the real dance floor was close by the stones of the little terrace. Mr. Sanguinetti pulled Elaine close to his hard-muscled body, sort of butted their joint way into the dancers past a press of bodies, and initiated an intimate two-step.

Elaine pulled back, continuing to dance. "I know it's close

in here . . ." she began in what she hoped was a playful tone.

"Right," Sanguinetti's pleasant baritone rumbled. "You're a lady. Capital L." He loosened his grip a little.

Elaine laughed and began to enjoy what was her first recreation of the evening. She did wish she could see Allan in the crowd; and she knew she ought to be looking for Louis. Once she relaxed a bit she noticed all the admiring glances her large dancing partner was getting from the ladies. If only she knew one of these women so she could introduce him, thus giving pleasure and shedding herself of him at the same time.

A familiar face on the sidelines caught her eye. Mr. Sanguinetti was forceful at leading; there was no way Elaine could urge him in any direction. Luckily, the music stopped.

"Come over here, and I'll make you known to a charming partner," she said, enjoying her own antique words as she grasped the American by his arm. He had no choice but to follow her, since they weren't dancing, over to that poetess creature who liked Allan.

Elaine had recalled the lady's name. "Miss Averil, meet Mr. Sanguinetti, who dances like a dream." She sort of thrust them at each other and quickly excused herself, leaving the unlikely pair together, both with blank looks. She remembered Van Vliet's other two American friends, Messrs. Brown and Porter, and kept an eye out in case they, too, were at the party. She had no fond memories of their talents on the dance floor.

"I say, this is a treat, Lady Elaine." Mr. St. Marle of the Panic Press was advancing on her. He had two drinks in his hand, one of which he pressed on her. She took the glass but didn't drink; she needed a tumbler of very cold water. "I didn't know you frequented the bohemian set. I come because so many of my authors do. Dance?"

"I just did, thanks, and I'm rather tired," Elaine said,

trying to back away. "Thank you for the champagne. I hope the lady you were bringing it to won't be disappointed."

"It was merely for our hostess, Lady Miranda. Co-hostess, I should say. She's thinking of doing me a tell-all memoir of society at play. I can't have enough of those."

"Do they really sell? A memoir by a young woman in her twenties would be so short."

"Ever since that Russian female's diary was published years ago, the younger the woman, the better. Makes her reminiscences more naive, more to the point."

"I see." Elaine and St. Marle had been moving to the side of the garden, near a low wall that overlooked the neighbor's dust bins. They were by no means alone, for which Elaine was grateful. She could tell by his good-natured leer that Mr. St. Marle was attracted to her, and since her mother approved of him she would have to be careful not to offend him. It was much easier to achieve this when surrounded by other people.

"Aren't you afraid of lawsuits if you print something too sensitive?" Elaine asked, thinking of Uncle Montague's diary. Her advertisement for the missing volume's return would be in tomorrow's paper. If only she could get it back!

"A legal brouhaha can only lead to sales," St. Marle answered with a wink. "Are you thinking of doing me a memoir yourself, Lady Elaine? I must say I could use a *roman à clef* rather more at the moment. Everyone in town is doing me a memoir."

"I don't think so. I don't spend enough time watching society at play. Aside from my mother's, this is my first party in years."

"Oh. Well. If you do think anything up, one of our staff writers could help you over the rough patches, you know. You wouldn't have to labor on it."

"I'll come to you if I do any such thing." Elaine felt perfectly safe in promising this much. She stood on tiptoe, trying to see over a group of three people in front of her and the publisher. "May I ask you, sir, do you see my young brother anywhere? I must keep an eye on him, and I'm not doing very well."

"Slippery fellow, is he?" St. Marle said with a chuckle. "We can probably see him better from the dance floor." He took her glass and set it on the wall along with his own, then held out his arm.

Elaine shook her head. "I really don't mean to dance any more. I only want to collect Louis and take him home. These are late hours for a schoolboy."

"It can't be that late," protested St. Marle. He was probably doing his best to look satyr-like and inviting.

Elaine felt in her bones how late it was. An eternity had passed since she knocked on Phyllis O'Brien's front door. Fishing in her evening bag, she drew out Bingo's watch. "There! It's nearly one in the morning."

She became aware of someone other than St. Marle staring at her. Looking up, she saw Allan. His eyes were fixed on the watch in her hand.

"You fool," Elaine whispered to her image inside the watch. Then she shoved it away and extended her hand to Allan. "Mr. Marchmont! I hope you've been enjoying the party."

He had no choice but to approach her, but she thought he looked reluctant. "Lady Elaine, I'm glad to see you again. Good evening, sir." This to St. Marle, who bowed. "I've kept my eye on the young earl, by the way, and just now sent him off home with a chap he said was your cousin. I hope the name Jeremy Porthault means something to you."

"Why, yes. Our first cousin, Mother's nephew. What could

Jeremy have been doing here, I wonder? He's more one for cricket matches and hunting parties, but Louis should be safe enough in his company. Was he exhausted, poor boy?"

Allan smiled. "More like getting his second wind. I exchanged a fatherly glance with your cousin Porthault and suggested he take Louis back to the Albany. I told them to go in and have my man give them supper, and they seemed to go away in good enough spirits."

"Yes. Since Jeremy is engaged, and I haven't seen his betrothed here tonight, he had better leave well enough alone and forget this party."

"As you say."

"I'm most grateful."

"Devilish kind of you, Marchmont, old fellow," St. Marle said, putting his arm around Elaine's waist. "We'll be off to dance now."

"But I've told you I'm too tired for any more dancing," Elaine said, removing the arm. "I do appreciate the thought, and you'll be the first to know if I write a book."

It was an obvious dismissal. With a snort and a suspicious look back at them over his shoulder, St. Marle finally moved away.

Elaine sighed in relief.

"I quite see you had no choice, but now we can't dance, can we?" Allan looked at her keenly, his gaze seeming to stray to the little bag on her wrist.

Drat that watch! She knew he would be thinking she carried it as a memory of Bingo, and what if she did? It was the only timepiece she had, and Bingo had been her husband as well as her longtime friend, whom she was surely allowed to remember. Elaine resolved not to mention the watch.

"No, we can't dance. It would be so very rude to Mr. St. Marle. But you and I seem to quarrel when we dance, so perhaps standing here and talking would be better."

"I agree. What do you think of our friend Van Vliet and Lady Miranda?"

"Why, I don't know." Elaine didn't feel she should reveal the American's plans to marry Goggle.

Allan gestured over his shoulder, and Elaine could see that Goggle and Van Vliet were indeed talking, heads close together, not far down the garden wall. Goggle's white satin headgear shone clearly in the moonlight. "They've had a dance or two. They seem to know each other pretty well."

"Interesting, as they only met last week." Elaine shrugged. "I find Mr. Van Vliet to be a perfect gentleman. Goggle is surprising me on better acquaintance too. They ought to be safe with one another."

"How boring that sounds." Allan came closer. "Have I had a chance to tell you how lovely you look this evening? Black suits you somehow; one would think you'd be too fragile to carry it off. I hope the choice of black isn't . . ." His voice trailed off.

Elaine knew well enough what he meant. "No, it isn't meant as mourning, it's meant as one of my only good dresses. Thanks for saying it suits me."

"Then again, I've never seen you wear anything that didn't suit you perfectly." The expression in his eyes had grown warmer, Elaine thought, with her assurance that her black costume didn't indicate mourning.

"Isn't this the most dreadful party?" she burst out.

He laughed. "At last we agree on something. I made Lady Miranda invite me, all with the thought of seeing you here, and what with your nursing duties and your popularity with the other men, I haven't spent any time with you. If it makes you feel any better, I've spent the whole time with your brother."

"Which you do every day anyhow, since you were kind

enough to give the boy a job. How can I thank you for keeping him under your eye tonight and sending him home as you did? Now I only have to worry about getting myself home."

"Mount Street now, isn't it? I'll take you there whenever you want to go."

"I wasn't angling for a ride." She paused, embarrassed. "I don't really think—it's too soon after the other time for me to ride in a car with you."

He looked startled, then conscious. "Then I'll put you into a cab. Everything as you wish. Shall we wander about and see if we can enjoy this party?"

"Let's simply stay here and talk. Tell me all about your photography. I feel I barely know you. Goggle told me you used to photograph big game before the war. How should she know that, and not I? And Louis tells me you're actually a businessman with some sort of a mill in the country."

"Paper mill. Hampshire," Allan said with a little smile.

Elaine shrugged. "I don't mean to complain. But it seems that everyone knows you better than I, when you and I have . . ."

"Have what? This? Not since last week." Without any warning Allan drew her back into the shadows of the garden and kissed her, molding his body to hers. He kissed her deeply, seeming to reach out to her very soul. "The longest week of my life," he murmured into her ear.

"We shouldn't," Elaine whispered. Then, in direct contradiction, her mouth found his again and she was lost, not caring whether they were alone in the dark or on some West End stage surrounded by lights and spectators.

A stricken little cry told her they were not at all alone. Elaine dragged herself from Allan's arms to investigate the sound.

She might have known someone would see them. For a

wonder, most of the other partygoers were turned away. It was only Ann Averil who stood alone, a small book clutched in her hand, gaping at them in evident horror.

"Mr. Marchmont," the poet whispered, "I was coming to read you my poems. How could you?"

Chapter Nineteen

"Why on earth be interested in the Agony column?" Aunt Pen asked as Elaine, bleary-eyed, pored over the newspaper late on Sunday morning in the breakfast parlor of the Mount Street flat. "You aren't looking for someone to say, 'All is forgiven,' are you, dear? Nor wishing to invest any capital in a diamond mine?" When this attempt at wit went begging, Aunt Pen sighed and returned to her toast.

"Sorry, I wasn't attending." Elaine rattled the paper, folding it down. There it was! Her advertisement said there would be a reward for a small green-covered journal and gave a box to write to. She scanned the rest of the column quickly as she had every day since the loss of the book, hoping against hope that today, by some glorious chance . . . "Oh, my goodness," she suddenly exclaimed, jumping up.

"What is it, dear?"

"Oh . . . nothing." Elaine sat back down, knowing her relation must never suspect that there, in the Agony column of the paper, was not only Elaine's "lost" advertisement but one which said, *Found journal. Covent Garden. Write with details to reclaim your property.* Elaine thought quickly of

232

something to appease Aunt Pen. "I was simply surprised that Sylvia Carr has found someone else to marry." Luckily she had seen the photograph earlier, inside the paper.

"Let me see." Aunt Pen reached out for the paper, which Elaine folded back to the proper page. The conversation turned to weddings, with glancing thrusts at Elaine's future with Rollo on Aunt Pen's part, and good-natured parrying on Elaine's, until the two ladies finished their breakfast. Elaine wasn't even annoyed over the hints about Rollo; she would have stood far more if it meant Pen wouldn't suspect the real story.

As soon as she could excuse herself she wrote a note to the box number, describing the journal as well as she knew how and begging its owner to meet her for its return at the ABC nearest Covent Garden after working hours on Tuesday. She would wear her small hat with the red feather to identify herself. Keeping safety in mind, she gave no name and no address but the newspaper box number. This being Sunday, she would need tomorrow for her note to be delivered, for the person to collect it and then to make plans to meet her.

Still thanking a benevolent providence, she went into the drawing room when her task was finished to be proper company for Aunt Pen. She had yet to broach the subject of Albertina Beasley as a trainable servant. A grateful, gushing note from the girl had come in answer to her proposal—the answer written on the back of Elaine's original, indicating that the poor child didn't even have access to paper of her own. The next step was to secure Aunt Pen's goodwill on the project.

But the elder lady wasn't to be seen. Elaine sank down into a chair and stared at the fire. A tiny Pekinese jumped into her lap, and she stroked him absently.

As usual, any leisure of mind led to thoughts of Allan.

What was to be done? After Miss Averil's interruption the night before, Elaine and Allan had broken apart like guilty lovers and not gone near each other again. Due to her own fatigue and the sudden change of mood, the rest of the time at Goggle's party was a blur to Elaine. She thought she remembered Miss Averil making an accusing comment to her, or bursting into tears, or both. As formal as a stranger, Allan had put Elaine into a cab and shaken her hand in farewell. Startled and embarrassed by Miss Averil's behavior, Elaine had been quite as stilted.

She scooped up the Pekinese and gave it a longing kiss on its little flat nose. "Oh, Allan," she said aloud.

"His name is Nanki-poo, dear," Aunt Pen said, coming into the room with her needlework basket and a sheaf of papers. "I've got a lot of addresses from friends, of possible places for Daphne and you to live. Would you care to look them over?"

On Monday, Elaine was relieved to notice at work no change in her status after the way she had left on Friday with her mother and Mr. Borderfield. Perhaps Elaine's concerns were not at the top of everyone's list.

Now that she knew there was a good, almost certain chance of getting back the missing journal, she could scarcely wait. Even her uncertainty about Allan and whether they would ever in life be given the opportunity to know each other properly went by the board as she planned on the Victorian diary's triumphant return to her possession. She could easily explain to Miss Rothwell that the volume had slid behind the desk, and that was why it hadn't been catalogued before.

On Monday, Allan sent her a letter asking her to join him and a pair of his cousins for the theater on Friday night. The offer cheered her as nothing else would have, and she returned a formal acceptance to him at the Albany, amused by the thought that Louis, as Allan's secretary, would doubtless see her note.

Elaine began at once to overhaul her wardrobe and found next to nothing. She was mortally weary of appearing all the time in the same frocks. Lady Berry happened to be coming into town on Wednesday to look at flats, so Elaine made a trunk call to ask her mother to bring a couple of old evening dresses from her debutante years.

Tuesday dawned rainy and unseasonably cold, but Elaine ignored this as an omen. She stuffed her feathered hat into a bag to bring to the office and got into her all-weather macintosh, though under it she wore her best office clothes. The work day simply crawled by as she typed her way through Uncle Montague's school years, but at last she was free. Heart full of hope, she flew through the rainy streets, bumping umbrellas with most of the people in the world, or so she imagined.

The ABC was not crowded when she shook herself and her umbrella off in the vestibule, but there were enough customers and staff to make her feel secure meeting a stranger in the barren atmosphere. She ordered a pot of tea and sat down at a centrally located table, then, trying for nonchalance, took off the battered felt she wore on rainy days, smoothed her hair, and brought out the little hat with the red feather, all the while watching the door for mysterious strangers carrying parcels.

She was almost finished with her tea when the door opened and Allan walked in. He came straight to her after a startled look at her hat. "Elaine! Are you box forty-seven?" He clasped her hands, warming them between his own, although, since he was the one who had just come from outdoors, it ought to have been the other way around. She noticed the raindrops from his coat and hat were falling on her; she was happy for the intimacy. But why did he look so worried?

"Then you're the one who has the journal?" she asked in delight. "I can't believe the luck." It had to be in his pocket.

Allan sat down across from her and released her hands, which caused her a pang. "I'm the one who *had* the journal," he said, looking grim. "I came to tell you—I came to tell the person who wrote—that I gave the journal yesterday to its owner. There must have been two such items. I'm sorry."

"Who took it?" Elaine whispered. Something like terror rose up in her; a stupid overreaction, she chided herself, about a mere book . . . a mere job . . . a mere family scandal.

"As it happens, you know him. St. Marle of the Panic Press. He is to publish it."

"The Panic Press?" Elaine stared off into the distance. "No, I don't think anything could be worse." She focused her attention back on Allan. "Don't say anything. Simply let me describe the book to you. A journal with entries dated in the 1870s. Its cover was a sort of military green, with gold edging wearing off. The front leaf was nearly torn off, but not quite. Most of the ink was black and had turned brown, except for the blue, which had turned a sickly sea-green. The handwriting was nearly illegible and the spelling had no rhyme nor reason. Am I close?"

"It sounds like the same book. But, my dear, how could this happen? And what have you to do with it? Are you here on an errand for your publisher?"

"Yes and no. Borderfield's knows nothing. It's more on my own account. I'm the one who lost the journal."

Allan sighed. "And I'm the one who found it in front of Borderfield's, mere seconds after you'd gone in at the door that morning I went with you in a taxi. It never occurred to me you would have dropped it. That is, I did think of you, but having looked inside the journal, I couldn't imagine it was connected with you."

"Oh, that dreadful morning." Elaine looked woefully into Allan's face. "The Panic Press! How did Mr. St. Marle ever identify the journal? He never bought it. It wasn't his!"

"His story was plausible," Allan said, looking bewildered. "I couldn't imagine a better one. He said it would be a journal of the life of a racing man from Victorian times, and so it was."

"Yes," Elaine answered sadly, "my great-uncle. And now I'm in greater trouble than I thought possible with my family. I would bet any amount that Mr. St. Marle is the publisher who spoke to Aunt Pen in the first place. She sent him off in injured dignity, refusing to sell him the journals, but Rollo heard the encounter and got the idea of making some easy money. He must have thought publishers were all the same, for he ended up at Borderfield's—for which I was grateful enough."

"I should say. At least you might control the situation at your own house."

Elaine smiled at the image of herself as a controlling force at Borderfield's.

Allan appeared to be thinking hard. "How would St. Marle have opened the subject to your relations in the first place? I know he mixes with your mother's set and with Lady Miranda's—the infernal man seems to be everywhere I don't need him to be. Does he simply go to aristocratic families hoping for risqué material?"

Elaine remembered her conversation with Mr. St. Marle at Goggle's party, when he had mentioned Goggle was "doing a memoir" for him and when he had suggested that Elaine herself write a *roman à clef*. "You know, I believe he does a certain amount of just that. But in the case of Great-uncle Montague, rumors of the diary have been circulating for years. Anyone who cared to know did know that Rollo's grandfather was supposed to have written down every scandalous thing he or his friends ever did."

"And so St. Marle naturally approached your cousins."

"Yes, I'm sure that's what happened. Mr. St. Marle would hardly have been too shy. And if he's looking around for lurid things to publish, he probably has his staff seek out material in all the ordinary places—such as the agony columns in the papers." She sighed. "Consider yourself lucky if there are no Marchmonts with literary ambitions! I can almost tell, even though I'm only typing the first volume, that Uncle Montague had his eye on publication even in his schoolboy days."

"And he had quite a lot of writings, more than St. Marle made off with?"

Elaine sighed. "It's a multi-volume diary, covering most of Uncle Montague's misspent life, written in school copybooks and leather journals. But if the Panic Press has its hands on that one volume, there will be the end of any hope of discretion for my family. They'll publish it verbatim, and it names names, Allan. Important names in society, most of whose descendants are our most intimate friends today. Tells who cheated on what races and slept with whose wife. I read that volume. I took it home because I thought the middle of his life would be more interesting than the schoolboy volume, and was it ever!"

"I'm sorry to hear all that, for your family's sake, but I still think we might retrieve this situation. I'll have to think how it might be done." Allan looked upset and guilty. "This is my fault, for passing the thing into his hands. Can you ever forgive me?"

"Oh, Allan, you couldn't know." Elaine was unwilling to take the comfort of handing the blame off to someone else. "He sounded as though he owned the diary. Heavens, he described its contents. Should I go to him and beg him not to publish?"

"If, as you say, St. Marle is ruthless, it wouldn't do any good and might put you into an uncomfortable position. Remember he's quite attracted to you; you wouldn't like to give the wrong impression. Let me think what I might do."

"I suppose you're right, but I must help somehow." Elaine squared her shoulders in resolution. "The first thing is to go in tomorrow and make my confession to Mr. Borderfield. My absolute stupidity, the incredible carelessness, has been weighing on my mind for so many days that it will almost be a relief to lose my job over it."

"But perhaps that won't be necessary. Let me try to get the journal back from St. Marle first."

"After you gave it over into his very hand, I don't think you'll succeed."

"Still, I must try."

Elaine gave him a grateful though hopeless look. "If you insist."

"You may be sure I do. And don't blame yourself. If I remember correctly, you were going through a rough patch on the day you lost it. Ejected from your boardinghouse, and then to have me rant around accusing you once you got to Rollo's house."

She had to smile at him. "Confession is good for the soul, though," she said thoughtfully. "I ought at least to point out that I'm related to the writer of the manuscript."

"If it makes you feel easier, certainly do that. They'll think they're lucky to have such a conscientious employee."

Elaine said, puzzled, "You don't seem at all like the insufferable man I danced with once. The one who didn't think I ought to have this sort of job."

"I was merely letting my old attitudes pop out when they should have stayed buried. I went through the war as well as anyone; I saw what women are capable of in all fields. You must do the work you want." He paused. "Am I forgiven?"

She nodded, too pleased to speak.

"Now, let's see if we can't cheer you up. I know a little French restaurant in Soho."

"Oh, I would love that." Elaine sighed with obvious regret. "But I'm expected back in Mount Street for dinner, and Aunt Pen is all alone, what with Rollo gone off to Kent to a house party. I mustn't seem ungrateful for all she's doing for me."

"You take on too much for your family. But if you insist, I'll wait till Friday. Then I mean to show you the town, although we will be with my cousins."

"Yes." Elaine thought serenely of the coming respectable engagement. "Well, I can't go to dinner with you, but I have an hour. Why don't you order a pot of tea and get me another? Tell me all about what you do with yourself all day. The photography, whatever you'd like. Did Phyllis O'Brien really ask you to take a portrait of her in the nude?"

"That's what you want to know? It's pretty common knowledge she asks every artist of whatever stamp to portray her in the altogether." Allan hesitated, then gave her a slow smile. "If you're interested, I told her I wasn't doing that sort of portrait at this time."

"'At this time.' You're leaving yourself open," Elaine said in a teasing tone.

"I never say never."

Elaine gave him what she hoped was a look full of meaning. "Neither do I." Let him take that as he would.

He smiled at her even more warmly. "Let me order that pot of tea."

Allan squired Elaine to her relations' door in Mount Street and walked down the street afterward towards Piccadilly in the gathering darkness with a heart mostly light. He had spent an hour with her; an hour untroubled by outside interests, other people, or physical contact. He would never have thought of an ABC as the place for romance to blossom; but simply because he couldn't kiss her in front of a lot of onlookers, they had finally had to talk. Elaine had all sorts of questions for him, and he had as many for her, though, as circumstances had fallen out, he really knew a lot more about her than she knew about him.

Then that walk to Mount Street; a long walk, but she had sensible shoes, as she assured him, and walking even in the rain was so much more pleasant than being shut up inside any kind of vehicle. Not to mention that the rain let up to a slow drizzle which only seemed to make the early evening smell sweetly of springtime rather than the usual soot.

As they took that enchanted walk, Allan was near to asking Elaine to be his forever and risking a rain-soaked public embrace, but he held stoically to his plan to court her slowly, to introduce her to his family, to do all the proper things. He was silently congratulating himself on his self-control. Then Elaine, rather than simply asking Allan what time it was, hauled out Bingo's watch and stifled Allan's prideful thoughts of a heart nearly won. She looked stricken when she saw him eyeing the watch.

On his return to the Albany Allan dressed for the evening, made Lord Berry do the same, and carted the boy off to his club, where he thought he had seen St. Marle appear from time to time. He hoped now that the fellow was a member. At least someone at the club might know where St. Marle was to be found out of office hours.

"I say, sir, this is top hole, giving me dinner out on a Tuesday. Want me to put in a good word with Elaine?" Louis sighed in contentment over the roast beef; not that he couldn't get as good food at the Albany, cooked by Allan's excellent manservant, but being admitted to a gentleman's club virtually as an equal with older and wiser souls still evidently intoxicated him.

Allan took pleasure in the spectacle of Louis enjoying himself much more than he appreciated the rather ordinary food. He had let half the evening go by without touching on the important business on his mind; now was the time to take care of it. "Actually, I wanted to get us out into the world in the hopes of encountering a fellow named St. Marle. Publisher of the Panic Press. He was at Berryhill that weekend. Do you know him?"

"Can't say I remember. The Panic Press, you say! They're all over town with that dirty book about the music-hall lady."

"Er, yes, the very same. Well, the footman out in the lobby, that sharp-nosed one, will surely know about Mr. St. Marle. He knows everything I've ever asked him."

"Shall I go and ask him, sir?"

"Exactly what I had in mind, my lord, but you don't have to interrupt your dinner—well, go ahead, then. Thanks."

Louis, eager as ever to prove himself in the role of secretary, sped off on his errand while Allan stared into the distance, wondering what the most useful approach would be should he manage his goal of coming upon St. Marle as if by accident.

Louis was back in a flash. "The footman says he's not a member here, but he's a great friend of a Mr. What's-his-name, who is, and they come in most evenings after the theater to play cards."

"Ah. Well, that's a long time from now. Keep eating, and I'll send you home after coffee." Allan supposed he himself could lurk about in the hope that St. Marle would wander in, but it would be slow going. He cheered himself by the thought that he was doing it all for Elaine; and he hadn't read all the day's newspapers, after all.

After dinner Lord Berry went cheerfully enough back to the Albany, and Allan settled in where he could see the door to the card room. He had read all the news the club subscribed to, and was down to lists of wedding presents in the society columns when the after-theater crowd finally started to appear, discernible by the arguments over whether the respective show had been bearable, not up to pre-war standards, or merely trivial. He had almost given up when at long last St. Marle, with the manners of one who did not belong to the club, strode heavily to the card room door in the company of another middle-aged fellow: Mr. What's-his-name, no doubt.

Allan stood. "A word with you, sir?"

"Marchmont! It's my old friend Marchmont. Bevis, you hardly know what a favor this chap has done me. Thanks to him I'll have the racing world and all of Mayfair society on its ear before long."

St. Marle performed quick introductions, and Mr. Bevis, sensing the seriousness of Allan's purpose or merely eager to get to his game, excused himself. Allan led the way to a couple of out-of-the-traffic armchairs and indicated that St. Marle should sit down.

He saw no use to beat about the bush. He had thought of many different ways of beating about it while he waited for the other, actually, but none seemed likely to serve. "I'll put it to you straight, old boy," he said, trying for an air of intimacy. "That diary I gave to you was someone else's property. I'd consider it a rare favor if you'd give it back."

St. Marle laughed as though this was the best joke he'd heard all night. "That's rich," he finally said. "No, my lad, what's done is done. Sorry if it puts you in difficulties."

"It does rather. Let me put it another way. How much?"

The other cocked an eyebrow. "I ought to be insulted, but I'll put it down to your inexperience in the publishing world,

Marchmont. You couldn't possibly make the loss of that volume worth my while. Not for any amount."

"And that's your final word?"

"Rather. Now, do you care for cards? We could use a fourth in there. I'll gladly take your money that way."

Allan admired the swift change of subject. He, too, saw the wisdom of keeping on a friendly footing. "Another time. Good night, St. Marle." Quite calmly, he collected his things and left the club. He had muffed it for sure. He wouldn't tell Elaine quite yet. There might be something else to be done.

Elaine's mother came to town the next day, bringing a couple of the requested "deb gowns" in a valise, and spent the hours from luncheon until tea looking at flats in the company of Aunt Pen. When Elaine got back to Mount Street after work, she wasn't surprised to see Lady Berry, but she was a bit taken aback to find that her mother had commandeered her own bedroom and was arraying herself in devastating evening attire.

"Mother! Obviously you're going out tonight. Will you be staying over? I can camp in Rollo's room."

"That was our idea, dear. What do you think? With or without the paste diamonds?" Lady Berry held up a chain which much resembled a certain real one that had been one of the first casualties of the Saxonbury fortunes.

"Oh, with." Elaine surveyed her mother's low-cut ensemble of flame-color. "Once you've gone that far, subtlety is useless. New dress?"

"Don't you recognize it? I ordered it for my weekend party and never wore it, but I thought I showed it to you." Lady Berry's eyes had the usual evasiveness when admitting extravagance to her daughter.

"Well, never mind. Who is the target of your seductive

appearance? I didn't know you were after a man," said Elaine, trying for a mischievous tone.

"It's not quite like that. If you must know—and I think you must, considering—Mr. Borderfield is taking me to an intimate supper club."

Elaine stared. "What will you be eating, gruel? And should he be out that late?"

"Don't laugh. That man holds the key to all our hopes of the family dignity."

"Oh." Elaine sat down on the bed, right on one of the "deb gowns" her mother had laid out for her inspection. "Uncle Montague's diaries. Somehow, you heard."

"Of course I heard that dear, innocent Rollo, not knowing what he was doing, Elaine, so you mustn't blame him . . ." Even in the midst of family troubles, Lady Berry seemed not to want to discount Rollo as a matrimonial proposition.

"Rollo is a sort of law unto himself," Elaine said with a shrug. "So it's all over town that he's sold the diaries to Borderfield's?"

"Not precisely all over town. Certain people seem to be in the know, though for a wonder it's been kept from Pen." Lady Berry had always claimed to have a network of social spies, and apparently she really did. "I came up the other day to find out if it was true. That's why I had tea with the dear old gentleman. But he was evasive and did nothing but hint for this supper engagement; so I suppose he wants me on his arm for an evening, and then, as a sort of payment, he'll admit he has the diary. You know about it, do you?"

"I'm typing it."

"Good heavens. Well, never you fear, darling. I'm going to appeal to Mr. Borderfield's sense of chivalry. I'm prepared to do anything up to but not including marrying the man."

"At least there's that," Elaine said, relieved. "You mustn't sacrifice all for the family honor. Though one must admit it wouldn't be a long marriage."

"And I could keep my title if I wanted," her mother said with a wink. "But I'm sure things won't have to go that far. The dear, sweet man will do anything I ask him. Everyone says so, after all."

Elaine had no doubt of the countess' powers. Chivalry would win the day, and the diary would be pulled from possible publication. She had a sick feeling, though, thinking of the lost volume in the hands of the Panic Press. She didn't think her mother's feminine wiles would get anywhere with Mr. St. Marle—and Elaine wasn't even going to try out her own, fearing that those might.

"Mother, you are the limit. Are you sure you know what you're doing?"

"Eminently. I can save my family as well as any martyr of old. Now, what do you think of these old dresses of yours?"

Lady Berry had lots of practice in changing the subject when talking to her daughter; and Elaine had no reason to argue with her any further. She would be perfectly safe and enjoy a night of display in her shocking new gown. Mr. Borderfield could hardly overcome the countess and attack her no matter how she put on the charm; Lady Berry was much the more robust of the two.

"If you weren't already wearing that dress, I'd ask to borrow it," said Elaine.

"This is miles too big for you, darling, but you might indeed take up the front of the skirt of that one you're sitting on. That was a very elegant gown in its time. With the front shorter in the latest style, it could still almost trail behind. Cooper could manage it."

"But you didn't bring Cooper, I suppose." Elaine longed for the efficiency and ingenuity of an accomplished seamstress.

"Alas, no. If you must know, I couldn't afford her train fare."

"I'm amazed you could afford your own, unless some money from Mr. Van Vliet is already in the coffers."

Lady Berry was fastening some large not-quite-diamonds into her ears at the glass. "No, not yet. I'm merely speculating with all this flat-shopping, and you'll notice I didn't even suggest you buy a new frock if you wish to look nice on Friday. I know you'd never do it unless we were rolling in cash. Which young man is it, then? Pen wasn't sure."

"Mr. Marchmont," Elaine said, feeling as shy as a schoolgirl.

She was surprised when Lady Berry, looking as absolutely serious as a middle-aged woman in a flame-colored evening dress could do, drew her down to a little couch near the bedroom fire and looked deeply into her eyes. "Elaine, I need to know, as your mother with your happiness at heart, if you're really over Bingo. Can you think of someone else? I'm always trying to get you to do so, but if you're not ready, then the subject is closed."

"I don't need to get over Bingo." Elaine stared at nothing at all. Then she finally looked at her mother. "I need to add to him, not erase him, if that makes any sense."

The countess seemed satisfied. "Then I can keep throwing possible males at you? I'm astonished Mr. Van Vliet hasn't won your heart. You could keep living at home, since he'll be leasing it. And he's rather an entrancing man, in his way."

"He is." Elaine smiled, thinking of the last time she had seen the American. "But do you know, I think he's winning the heart of someone else. Is Mr. Van Vliet really your favorite? What have you against Mr. Marchmont?"

"Against? Why, nothing at all, my dear." Lady Berry

leaned down to adjust her diamanté-trimmed shoe strap. "I merely want your happiness."

"So do I," Elaine murmured, closing her eyes as she lay back on the bed, heedless of the evening gowns around her. She could scarcely wait until Friday.

Chapter Twenty

Elaine was perfectly confident of her mother's powers. She had no doubt that, aided by the flame-colored gown, Lady Berry could and would bring young Mr. Borderfield around her thumb if given half an hour alone with him. What Elaine hadn't counted on was the fact that Mr. Borderfield, though not possessed of equally dashing apparel, might also have wiles.

"It's perfectly simple, and it will be all for the best," Lady Berry told her daughter the next morning, as she took her early tea in bed before Elaine left for the office. "You see, dear old Cavendish explained to me that a publication of this sort can be very dignified. A duty to the nation, even, to preserve the history of those times. We discussed ways to protect the family, and though I swear he had thought them up beforehand, he made them sound like all my own. A clever man," Lady Berry said in some surprise. "I should have known he was clever. He has the good taste to be in love with me."

"What are these ways to protect the family?" Elaine, sitting on the bed, poked at her mother's knees under the counterpane. "I can't believe you didn't succeed in your mission, Mother. I expected you to return with his promise never to publish the journal at all. Now, tell all, and quickly, for I have to be leaving in just a few minutes."

"For one thing, Mr. Borderfield will agree to be discreet about the names. He says he always intended merely to say 'Lord L.' and 'a certain lady' and so forth. He said he doesn't need to sink to the level of the Panic Press." Lady Berry sipped at her tea in a dreamy fashion. "Really the most extraordinary man."

"You aren't succumbing, are you, Mother?"

"I don't need anything but very good friends at my time of life, darling, though I will always leave an opening for a grand passion. Your father would be extremely hard to replace, you know." She stretched luxuriously under the covers. "I'm afraid I can't see Cavendish in the light of a grand passion."

"I'm glad to hear it. Mr. Borderfield seems a bit frail for husband material. So he's going to leave out the names. Anything else?"

"Now this idea I believe was my own, at least half my own, and you must tell me what you think. You know Rollo could use something to occupy his time."

Elaine was more than aware of that. "A job might do him the world of good. Give him something to concentrate on."

"Precisely. Editing and writing a narrative to tie together these journals would be quite a job, and the diarist's grandson is really the only proper person to do it."

At this Elaine's imagination failed her. "You mean for *Rollo* to do a job of writing? Are we talking about the same Rollo?"

"The boy is perfectly capable. He went to Oxford. And an editor at the house could help him, you know."

"Oh. In that case..." Elaine could see that such an assignment would be a boon for Rollo, who badly needed something to do, as long as a true professional looked at the result of Rollo's labors. Mr. Parkington, perhaps. "But how will we break the news to Aunt Pen?"

"Leave it to me to reconcile her to the situation. She's a sensible woman." Lady Berry paused. "Besides, by the time this book is done I mean to see it is a charming thing, with old illustrations of races at Newmarket and portraits of Uncle Montague at all ages. It will be a thing to be proud of, and Pen's own son will have something to his credit out of it."

The only flaw in this plan of perfect felicity was the missing volume which the Panic Press would no doubt bring out before the sedate tome from Borderfield's, if not at the very same time, for effect. Elaine shut her eyes, feeling a headache start as she tried to imagine how Allan would ever wrest the missing journal from the vice-like grip of Mr. St. Marle. If anyone could do it, Allan could, though Elaine had an unsettling, fleeting vision of herself, dressed in her mother's flame-colored gown, slinking her way to Mr. St. Marle's flat and demanding the journal. No. She wouldn't.

"Is something wrong, dear?"

"No, but I must be going. I should just have time to make the dash to work."

"And that's another point I brought up with Mr. Borderfield," Lady Berry said with a disgusted look. "Your office work is obviously too much for you. He agrees with me that you should come in at luncheon time, if you like, and stay the afternoon, but this losing your beauty sleep must stop if you're to attach a man."

"Mother!" Elaine simply gave up and fled.

* * *

Allan stood talking to Miss Gabell at the Victoire Gallery, wondering if he had been wise to ask Oswald Van Vliet to meet him here. But he had noticed, on his many visits to the gallery, that the place was usually crowded enough to make a meeting unobtrusive. And drier than the street itself on this rainy day. Van Vliet had not wished to be seen at the Albany or to have Allan go to him at the Ritz on this occasion.

Miss Gabell flung gossipy tidbits at him but he barely noticed as his gaze swept the room, looking at the offerings. His photographs were still hanging, and a clutch of small and large cubist paintings by a new man. Also recently added were a quantity of life-size marble statues in a Greek revival style, though none with missing limbs. Allan wondered if the voluptuous figure nearest him, the one posed holding her abundant hair above her head, was really of Miss Phyllis O'Brien, or whether the resemblance was coincidental.

"Those things must cost the earth," he remarked to Miss Gabell. "I didn't know there was that much marble in the world."

"He imports it," Miss Gabell said. "Signore Fascetti has been old-fashioned for years, but he's finally catching on as a reaction to the other schools. As for cost, if you have to ask, young man, you can't afford it."

He grinned. "I wish you luck with them. Excuse me! Here's the man I'm meeting."

Miss Gabell let him go with good humor and gravitated towards a gentleman who looked wealthy and in a buying mood.

Van Vliet was at the entrance, digging in his pocket for the requisite shilling. A gallery assistant thrust a catalogue at him, and he absently stuffed it into a pocket. His eye met Allan's and they moved to a wall not far from a photograph of a blasted tree in the Ardennes.

"No trouble at all," were Van Vliet's first words. "A snap,

the guys said. St. Marle cracked as soon as Porter got out the brass knuckles."

"You must thank them for me. And remember that price is no object."

Van Vliet chuckled. "It's a favor to you and to the lady. A little persuasion—it goes on all the time nowadays in the, er, business world. I only wish I could've been there to see it happen."

Allan had an idea of the kind of business Van Vliet and his friends engaged in. He was best off not knowing the details. "I can't tell you how grateful I am."

"Don't mention it." With no further ado, Van Vliet took a paper-wrapped package from his pocket and passed it to Allan, who took it reverently. "Besides, I owe you for finding me Berryhill."

Allan cleared his throat. "You haven't mentioned that to Elaine, have you?"

"No, but you should. Might cut you some ice with the lady."

"I'll tell her later, in my own good time." After he had made her love him. He had no wish for gratitude to be mixed in with the feelings he hoped to inspire.

"Whatever you say, pal." Van Vliet found the gallery catalogue in his pocket and rattled it. "What do you think? Do I have to buy something to excuse my being here?"

Allan laughed. "Not at all. But what would you choose, if you did buy?"

"Not one of your pictures, no disrespect meant. Too gloomy. But the marble broads are swell, some of them." Van Vliet leered good-humoredly at the Phyllis O'Brien look-alike statue. "Say! That one's familiar."

"London is a world unto itself. A small world."

"Let me ask how much they want for that one with the big—" Seeing a party of ladies nearby, he merely gestured to describe a bosom. Allan would have been interested in the American slang term. "It'd look swell down at Berryhill in the garden. Sort of a house gift for the Berry family when I leave too."

Allan was sure that at least Louis would appreciate the statue, and the others would appreciate the thought. He chuckled as Van Vliet went off to confer with the assistant. Seeing his friend was in good hands, he headed for the door and nearly ran against Lady Miranda Winchapel going in. She looked bright and expectant, as though she might be planning on meeting someone.

"My lady," he said with a formal bow that had enough humor in it to elicit a laugh from Goggle.

"You're in a mood," she said. "Rushing off? Pity."

"Yes, I know. But go I must."

He went quickly on his way, out of the genteel maze of Shepherd's Market and into the busier thoroughfares. Covent Garden was his object.

Elaine was at her desk worrying over the lost manuscript journal. Though Allan had told her he was taking care of the problem, she couldn't be certain, for the tenacity of Mr. St. Marle was a factor that couldn't be predicted. A couple of days had passed with no word on the diary, for good or ill.

She rolled in a new page and continued her struggle with Uncle Montague's scribbles, from his Oxford years now, for she had finished the earliest volume and put it aside.

"Do you know," said Katherine, craning her neck over her own machine, "your cousin is coming in today to talk about him working on the book. That book there."

"Rollo is coming here? Oh, that's nice." Elaine noticed that Katherine had a new bunch of composition cherries on her jacket. "And he's taking you to lunch after, is he?"

Her friend blushed. "He don't seem to mind being seen

with me. It's nothing serious, you understand. I know my limits."

"That's nonsense. Grab him if you can. He needs to find a girl who will understand him. A girl who understands about the war."

"And what would your family think of in-laws from Putney?" Katherine asked, sticking out her chin.

"Let them think whatever they want. I believe you're just the girl for him, and it's Rollo's happiness that counts."

"Truly?" Katherine's sunny smile made Elaine's heart go out to her; then she watched the smile grow more blinding than ever. A glance over her shoulder told Elaine that Rollo was coming jauntily down the row of desks. Imagine Rollo Saxonbury causing that look of pure delight on any face! Katherine must have him if he was to be had. Elaine made a mental note to let the young couple take care of it themselves. The encouragement she had just given Katherine was more than enough meddling.

"Greetings, ladies." Rollo came to a stop between the two girls. "What do you say, Elaine? Your mother called me back from Kent on this mission. Says I'm to be an author."

"You are indeed. You're to uphold the family dignity by giving the coming publication your seal of approval. Write an introduction about how it's been in the family and you decided reluctantly to bring it to light for the good of posterity. You know."

"Right-o," Rollo said, though his eyes popped at Elaine's estimation of his duties.

"And then sort of tie the diary parts together with narrative about your grandfather's life," Katherine added, looking at him shyly.

"My word, you're johnny on the spot. Does everybody here know what Rollo is supposed to do?" Elaine asked, fascinated.

"No, only them who's interested," Katherine muttered into her typewriter.

Elaine wished she had bitten her tongue. "Oh, my dear, I didn't mean you shouldn't know! I was merely surprised to find you as well informed as my own mother, who concocted the plan just the other day. I thought she'd told only me."

"Oh." Katherine didn't quite sniff, but she had definitely retreated back behind her "other class" barricade.

"I say, are you two scrapping?" asked Rollo. His eyes lit. "Hello, is it over me?"

"Rollo, don't you have an appointment with someone? Hurry so it won't run into Katherine's lunch time."

"Right you are." Rollo ambled down the corridor, and Elaine shook her head at his retreating back.

"You oughtn't to be that mean to him."

Elaine met the other girl's eyes. "Don't you like it?"

"I don't. So there!"

"My dear, let's not quarrel. I wish you the best of luck with Rollo, and I hope before long you know all his private concerns. I was merely surprised that news is out in the office about the memoirs and Rollo lending his hand."

Katherine was still defensive. "Well, why shouldn't it be?" She paused. "Well, it isn't. I snooped."

Elaine was just as glad the whole affair wasn't common knowledge. "Bless you for admitting that. Now, let's plan our tea at the Ritz for next Wednesday. As a sort of welcome to the family."

"Go on." Katherine's eyes danced. "But you're not taking me anywhere. I know you're hard-up as ever I am. Rollo told me."

"We'll fight it out another time," Elaine said quickly, for she had just seen Allan turning the corner into their area.

Katherine glanced over her shoulder and saw too. "Oho. Want me to leave?"

Elaine shook her head. "Kind of you to offer, but we still wouldn't be alone." There were many other desks within hearing distance of Elaine's, and the other office workers were looking quite interested already, their attention caught by Rollo's interchange with the two young women. "But thank you for the thought."

So it was in front of the eyes of Katherine and anyone else with a view that Allan stopped in front of Elaine's desk and caught her hand to his lips in an old-fashioned gesture.

"Oh," groaned somebody. Elaine, turning, saw that the elderly Miss Plumb had her eyes fixed on Allan in apparent ecstasy.

She turned back to Allan. "Good day, Mr. Marchmont," she said demurely, as the Victorian Miss Plumb would no doubt approve.

"Mrs. Westwood, your servant." He smiled down into her eyes. "I have something for you." Reaching into his pocket, he pulled out a package wrapped in brown paper—a package of just the right size and shape.

Elaine took it carefully into her hands. "You did it. You're wonderful." She tore off the paper to reveal the familiar, tattered green cover of Uncle Montague's journal. "Thank you, Allan. I have no words to express . . . thank you."

"It was nothing. But I have to warn you, Elaine, that it was in St. Marle's hands for several days. He might have taken photographs of it, or he might have set someone to copying it. You might still wake up someday to find the Panic Press bringing out its tell-all version of this volume." The other ladies nearby had ostentatiously returned to their work, but Allan still spoke in a low voice, since the subject was so private.

"I thought of that. But you know, we've done all we can do." Elaine, speaking quite as softly, turned to a page within the diary: The faded ink, the hard-to decipher scrawl gave her a measure of safety. "If it's a case of photographs, I can hardly think they would come out. And if he's found a copyist, well, all I can say is that I'm an efficient typewriter, and I worked extremely hard to transcribe a volume in a longer time than Mr. St. Marle had the journal for. Whatever happens, thank you for good and all." She picked up the volume and hugged it to her chest, then put it away in a drawer. "I'll take it to join its fellows this afternoon. They're all in Miss Rothwell's private office. I've been going there to change them, and I've been leaving them all locked up there at night. My own thought."

"And a good one. Is there a chance we could have some time to ourselves, speaking of private offices?" Allan was still speaking low; the neighboring typists were still pretending very discreetly not to try to hear. Katherine let out a snicker.

Elaine felt her cheeks heat. "You might take me out at lunchtime."

"That's too long to wait. There's an hour or more to go before then. You wait here." Allan's dark eyes took on a devilish sparkle. "I'll go over to old Parkington's office and demand he clear out."

"You can't do that." Elaine was shocked at the mere idea.

"Watch me."

Allan strode down the corridor, feeling every inch the masterful man of action. He had slaughtered the dragon for his lady fair and would pick off anything else that came in his way. When he came to Michael's office, he turned in without hesitation. "Parkington in, Miss Tarrant?" he asked crisply of the startled lady behind the secretary's desk. Luckily her name was on a plate, otherwise he wouldn't have known what to call her after meeting the colorless woman a mere once or twice.

"He's left orders not to be disturbed, sir." The lady's scandalized voice trailed after Allan as he opened the door to Michael's sanctum without knocking.

Michael had his feet up on the desk and his eyes closed. He came to life with a snort. "What the devil, Allan? Is it lunch already? I don't remember a lunch with you."

"With good reason. We aren't going to have one. Well, old boy. You're always hinting that I should follow your example and settle down with a nice girl. Now's your chance to help. Clear out of here and leave me your office for a little while."

"How little? I'm expecting an author to telephone."

"Nothing easier than to stop by the switchboard on your way out and tell the girl to connect your calls to the cloakroom, or the boardroom, or wherever you're going to be. There's a good fellow. Now, out."

Parkington, still fuzzy from sleep, blinked behind his pince-nez. Either obliging or mesmerized by Allan's air of command, he gathered his coat from the chair and put it on, frowning. "You're using my office to meet a woman? I say, there are gardens and river walks and many better places than this, Allan."

"Do you remember your ham-handed visit to the Ritz with me in pursuit of Mrs. Westwood? If you help me now, you can call yourself a matchmaker—and a best man."

"Oh." Light dawned in the sleepy eyes, and Parkington was off.

Allan followed, but only because he was not imperious enough to order Miss Tarrant to fetch the lady of his desires. He went back as far as Elaine's desk, grabbed for her hand, and pulled her to her feet. "Come on. I've got us a corner where we can talk."

She followed along, too tamely for Elaine, but he supposed she was too surprised to put up much of a fight. She did gasp when he propelled her before him into Michael Parkington's outer office, past an astonished Miss Tarrant, and then guided her into the inner room. He shut the door behind them with a click and turned the key.

"Now, my girl. Let's have it out at once. First off, tell me what time you have."

"None. I should be at my desk this minute," Elaine said, sounding dazed.

"I don't mean that kind of time. What's the hour?"

"Isn't your wristwatch working?" Elaine pulled Bingo's watch out of a pocket in her skirt. "It's a quarter past eleven."

Allan closed her hand over the watch, then covered it with his own. "Why do you always carry this with you, Elaine? Is it because you can't forget? Is all this hope on my part merely wishful thinking? Is it too soon?"

Elaine stared at him. She put her other hand over Allan's. "This is the only timepiece I happen to have. My old one broke a couple of years ago, when I knocked it against a stile down in the country. And of course Bingo's memory is dear to me. I wouldn't be much of a person if it wasn't. But if you want the truth, I suspect I carry the watch now because I know you carried it for so long. It brings me close to both of you, you see."

"Elaine! That's a grand thing to say." Allan stared at her, drinking in what he seemed to see in her eyes.

"It's the truth." Her voice was not quite steady.

"I've come to my senses about what made me draw away from you," he said before he could lose his courage. "It's that I don't deserve you. That is, I don't really deserve to be alive instead of your husband. I'd thought of you with longing even when you were his. And to have you for my own—to be happy with you—it seems so hard on Bingo, somehow."

War Widow 261

Elaine took a deep breath. "Yes, it's hard on him. I'm still angry that he died. But you know, we can honor his memory best by going on living. That's really all we can do."

Allan's fantasies of the past several years were perilously close to coming true. He knew he must tread carefully; that the next few sentences he uttered would mean his life one way or another. His brain seemed to grind to a halt and he simply blurted, "Elaine, we've had remarkably little time for being straight with each other. Answer me now, please: Will you marry me?"

"Yes," she said, almost as though she was surprised he had to ask the question.

He picked her up around the waist and spun her around. "This is amazing. This is simply too good. All I had to do was ask?"

"That's how most marriages happen," said Elaine, putting her arms around his neck as he set her down. "And Allan. You have my whole heart."

He gazed at her as though she were the angel whose photograph he had loved for years; as she was, but so much more. He hadn't looked for this kind of reassurance yet. He had hoped to grow in her heart, of course. He had even hoped to overshadow Bingo someday, but he had assumed it couldn't happen all at once.

"I loved Bingo, yes. He died a long time ago. And now I love you, and I'm so terribly grateful that you're in the world for me to love," Elaine said, looking almost shy. "Is there anything you'd like to tell me?" She dropped her arms demurely and stood back.

"Tell you?" He was dazed with happiness, but she must see that; he wouldn't have to mention it . . . mercifully, all at once he knew what she was getting at. "I didn't say it, did I? I merely asked you to be my wife. I didn't mention I love you with all my heart and soul. But I won't forget again. I'll write it in the sky every day, if you like."

"Only if I can go up with you in the plane to write it," Elaine said, touching his cheek. "Now, since you've gone to all the trouble to get us this private moment, I suggest we make use of it."

"Right you are, my darling." And Allan closed his arms around her at last.